LOST KING

KINGS OF RETRIBUTION MC MONTANA

SANDY ALVAREZ
CRYSTAL DANIELS

TWO PENS-

CRYSTAL *Daniels*

Sandy ALVAREZ

-ONE STORY

DEDICATION

For all the adventurous souls with hopelessly romantic hearts and dirty minds.

1

QUINN

Music playing from my phone wakes me from sleep. Reaching over, I swipe my thumb across the screen, silencing the alarm. It's early—just before sunrise. Stretching my arms wide, I lay in my bed for a few minutes and stare at the ceiling. Currently, I live here at the clubhouse. Not because I can't afford my own place, but because I choose to. When the time comes, I'll settle down in a nice home. For now, until I get what I want—until I get *who* I want to share my life with, I am perfectly content where I am. My lips lift in a smile, thinking about her—thinking about my Sunshine always puts a smile on my face. Emerson Evans. The beautiful, intelligent, headstrong woman I've been on the hunt for it seems my whole damn life. I can't explain it. The feeling I get when I'm around her; there are no words I can think of that would accurately describe the energy I feel when I'm near her. I've become a junkie. I'm addicted to Emerson, and I haven't even tasted her yet.

Closing my eyes for a moment, my mind drifts back to the first day I laid eyes on Emerson. Younger than other doctors I had seen before, that pint-sized, dark-haired woman took charge of the entire ER room when Bella was brought in nearly lifeless over two years ago. Her hair is a different color these days. Platinum blonde, to be exact. She has the perfect athletic body, and the slight flare of her hips does crazy things to my overactive imagination. Feeling my cock swell, I throw the sheet from my naked body and come to sit on the edge of the bed. It's not her looks though that I find most attractive about her. No. It's her heart. She cares for people—deeply. You see it when she works, and I've seen her in action many times. Every time she has ever been there to care for one of my own, I stood back and watched in awe at her calm demeanor. In a quiet and reserved manner, Emerson is a force of nature. To say I was intrigued right away, even amid the chaos, is putting it mildly. The first time her eyes connected with mine; *Fuck.* Those light, smoke grey eyes captivated me.

Absently, my hand begins to rub my bare chest. It felt as if she reached into the depths of my soul. She sealed my fate that day, and I've been on the hunt ever since. My dad always told me not to worry, that one day a woman would come along and I would know she was the other half of my life. She would consume me, and I would move mountains to have her and give her the moon if that's what she wanted. I never questioned it either. That's the kind of love he has for my mom.

Needing to rub one out before starting my day, I walk my ass to the bathroom. Twisting the knob, I start the shower and let the water get nice and hot before stepping in. I hadn't jerked off this much since my early teens when I got my hands on my first nudie magazine, but ever since Emerson moved to town, I have no interest in anyone else. Reaching down, I stroke the length of my rock-hard cock. Letting my head fall back, I close my eyes, and images of Emerson in her tiny as fuck bikini come to mind before they quickly turn to much more. Placing my left palm against the shower wall, I hang my head as I close in on my release. "Fuck," I moan. Feeling some relief, I finish my shower.

Dressed in dark washed jeans, a white shirt, boots, and my cut, I pull my hair back with a hair tie and head downstairs to find some food. When I enter the kitchen, I see Austin and Blake sitting at the table and Ember standing at the stove with a spatula in her hand, flipping pancakes.

"Pancakes." I rub my hands together and inhale the smell of bacon. "Mind doing up some extra for me?" I ask Ember as I pull a chair from the table, taking a seat next to Blake, whose eyes are on her. Leaning close to him, I lower my voice so only he can hear what I say, "When are you gonna give in and go for it?"

Lifting his fork, Blake mumbles, "I'm not good enough for her, brother," before shoving a bite of pancake dripping with syrup into his mouth.

I shake my head. Blake is a good guy. Been through some shit, but a good guy. His entire family was murdered in a robbery gone wrong when he was a kid. Blake was the only one to survive. He spent years jumping from one foster family to the next and getting mixed up with the wrong crowds. "You've been clean for over five years now, and you've always been good enough, brother. Don't sell yourself short in life because of fear. Grab it by the balls. We only have one life, man. Don't waste it," I tell him.

I've never wasted one minute of my life not going after anything I ever wanted. From day one, my parents taught me to go after everything life has to offer. I'm aware I was given a second chance when my birth parents decided they were too young to care for me, leading to my adoption and the life I have today.

Ember turns to bring a plate full of food to the table, causing Blake to quickly drop his gaze back to his meal. She smiles as she sets breakfast down, her warm, chocolate brown eyes peeking through her dark lashes as she steals a brief glance in Blake's direction then frowns when she takes in his avoidance of her. She likes him. It hasn't been too hard to see that since she joined the club. "Thanks for getting up early and making us breakfast, sugar," I say to her, earning a small smile.

"No problem, Quinn," she replies softly before glancing in Blake's direction one more time, then heading toward the sink and cleaning.

"So, you guys ready for today?" Blake pushes from the table, taking his plate to the sink, rinsing it, and placing it into the dishwasher.

Stabbing some pancakes with my fork, I pile four of them onto my plate along with some bacon. "Fuck yeah, I'm ready," I boast, popping a bite into my mouth. "Have you seen the new tools and equipment at the garage? That shit is going to make workin' so much easier and a hell of a lot faster."

The door to the kitchen swings open and Doc walks in with Lisa, looking pretty damn chipper. I wave at him. "Hey, Doc. What's got you happier than a fly on shit this early in the mornin'?"

Clasping his hand over my left shoulder, he says, "Besides waking up next to my woman, we finally get to see the shop reopen. After Jake lost what his dad built years ago, I'm fucking happy as hell for him and this club."

"Heard the mayor was attending the ribbon cutting as well. The city council wants to make a media thing out of it," Blake chimes in on the conversation.

"I think it's fantastic that the community is showing support for Jake and the club. His garage has been a part of this town for decades. And we all know how much The Kings give back. Jake deserves it," Lisa energetically gives her opinion on today's happenings.

Nodding my head in agreement, I continue to eat. It's been a couple of months, but our brand-new garage opens today, and I, for one, will be damn happy to see the place open for business again. Prez rented a small building not long after the dust settled after the fire, so we could continue pulling in some income. Pretty much everything was a total loss. All but some of his old man's tools and a few bike parts. Thank fuck for insurance because a couple of our customers lost their bikes in the blaze that day.

Glancing at the clock above the stove, I take notice of the time. Prez wants everyone to be at the garage at least thirty minutes before the ribbon-cutting, which gives me close to two hours to head to my parent's house then get to the garage. My dad needs me to swing by and take a look at an old Ford Galaxy he has been working on in his spare time. With the last of my food eaten, I stand and walk to the sink to rinse and load my plate.

"Your parents gonna be able to make it today, Quinn?" Doc looks over his shoulder as he goes to pour himself a cup of coffee.

"They wouldn't miss it. My dad is having a hard time starting his car, so I'm about to head out." I chuckle at how excited and proud my dad is that he found the exact car he took Mom on their very first date. He had been searching for more than a year, and just before last Thanksgiving, he received a call from a guy stating he had what he was looking for sitting in an old junkyard he acquired back in California. He's been trying to restore it ever since. "Catch ya later." I wave as I disappear through the door and make my way outside to my bike. With the morning sun rising, I pull my shades over my eyes and mount my bike. A moment later, I'm cruising down the open road.

As the wind whips at my face, my thoughts drift back to the day I rode my first Harley. I was sixteen and had saved up all my part-time job money to buy a fixer-upper from a guy Prez knew. Any spare time I had was used fixing my baby up, and I'm still riding her today. I tighten my hand on her throttle and race down the highway. My parents moved us from California to Polson when I was fifteen. I hated leaving my old friends and starting over in a new town. Starting a new school was the toughest adjustment. It was my second week at the new school when the trouble I had been having with a bully escalated. That's when I met Logan and Reid. Hell, if it weren't for them, I'd have continued to have gotten my ass beat by bullies at school. I was the new kid and a skinny little fucker too. Those two things alone made me an easy target. They walked in on someone giving me a hard time in the boy's bathroom one day and took care of business. They never asked me to tag along and follow them everywhere they went, I just invited myself. From that day on, no one messed with me.

As I come within view of my parents' two-story home with a large front porch, I shake my thoughts off for another day and pull alongside my mom's car, put the kickstand down, and turn my bike off. Before I take my helmet off, my kid sister rushes through the gate that leads toward the backyard with Remi, Jake and Grace's daughter, right beside her.

"Quinn!" She throws herself in my arms and hugs me tight. Chuckling, I squeeze her back.

"How's it going, KitKat? Hi, Remi. What are you ladies getting into today?" I ask them. Releasing her hold, Kat backs up so I can get off my bike.

"Since we didn't have to go to school today, Remi and I have been hanging out in the treehouse."

"Dad in the garage?" I ask her.

"Yep," she says, emphasizing the P.

Grabbing Remi's hand, she smiles at me and says, "See you later. Love you," then Remi shouts, "Later!" I watch them walk off in the direction of the backyard before I turn my back on them and head toward the detached garage on the opposite side of the driveway and enter through the side door. My dad is sitting in the driver's seat of his car with the door open, scratching the dark whiskers on his face.

"Hey, Dad."

I hear him sigh heavily when I walk up beside him. "Hey, son.

Thanks for coming by. She's spinning over, but I can't get her to fire up. Can you take a look at it for me?"

"Spin her over so I can have a listen," I tell him as I walk around and lean over the engine. "One more time, Dad." After listening to it the second time, I'm pretty sure I know what's wrong. "I think the timing is off," I inform him.

He climbs out of the car. "Damn. Well, we don't have time to fool with it today. I need to go inside to get ready for the grand reopening. Your mother is looking forward to having a little visit with Grace today," he tells me as he cleans his hands with a shop rag. Grace and my mom have become good friends since she's been back home.

"How about we work on it together this weekend?" I offer, knowing my dad loves this kind of one-on-one time with me.

"Sounds like a good idea to me." He smiles and pats me on the back. "I know you can't stay long, but be sure to say hi to your mom before you leave, will ya?" Closing the hood of the car, my dad starts to put his tools away.

"I'll see you later, Dad, Love ya."

"Love ya too, son."

My mom is in the kitchen, typing away on her computer when I walk inside. Leaning down, I kiss the top of her head. "Working?" Spotting some cookies on the counter she must have baked for the girls, I walk over and grab a couple and pop a whole one into my mouth.

"Save some for your sister and Remi," she says, eyeing me over the bridge of her glasses.

"I can't stay long, Mom. Prez needs us at the shop before the camera crews start showing up," I tell her while snagging one more cookie for the road. "Love, ya." Shaking her head but wearing a smile, she tells me she loves me too then I head out the door and back on the road.

I pull into the already crowded parking lot in front of the shop twenty minutes later and back my bike up alongside where my brothers' bikes are parked. It looks like I'm the last to arrive. I take my time before walking into the storefront. I whistle. "Damn." Someone put some finishing touches on the walls. From the sleek black countertops and the vast collection of Harley art on the walls, it feels like I've stepped onto a showroom floor.

The door to the garage swings open. "It's something, isn't it?" Logan's voice carries across the room. "My dad's idea of a reopening present."

"I like his style." I continue walking around and admiring everything. The layout of the building is still set up almost identical to the original building. The one modification was making Jake's office a little more substantial. Prez comes striding out of his office with Ellie Kate in his arms and Grace by his side. It makes me happy seeing a good man like Jake get his forever-person. I've watched all my brothers find good women over the years; Logan being the first one to fall. No sooner do I have these thoughts, when the shop door opens, and the sun floods in just before Emerson—my Sunshine walks in with Bella and her and Logan's kids in tow. Emerson's eyes lock in on mine, and I feel my heart tug against the inside of my chest. It's the same pull I feel every time I lay eyes on her, and I smile. Her flushed skin betrays her every time she gets near me. I know she feels the electricity between us too.

"Showtime," Prez announces.

Breaking eye contact with Emerson, I follow Prez outside. The bay doors slide open, and the rest of the club members come to stand out front. Logan and I join them. Kissing Grace and leaving her with Bella, Alba, Mila, Emerson, and his mom, Jake, along with his dad, walk together to join Ben Ainsworth, our mayor. I watch them talk amongst themselves for a few minutes before walking over and standing in front of us men. Scanning the crowd, I find my parents watching alongside the women and children.

The fact that they support everything in my life fills me with pride. Not once have they judged who I am, what I do, or the friends I keep. They know the club members and their families are good people because they got to know them before judging them. Are they aware there has been less than stellar activities going on throughout the years? I suspect that they do. At the end of the day, what's important to them is my happiness and wellbeing. They know I'm happy, and they know my brothers have my back.

A couple of camera operators from the local news stations wait for their cues. Ben gives a short speech. Prez says his thank-yous of appreciation, then his dad cuts the celebratory ribbon. Our friends and family cheer. The entire thing lasts all of ten minutes. It doesn't take long for the media and the Mayor to load up and leave. It is what it is. It's the start of a new day, and they have a job to get to like the rest of us.

"I need to get over to the job site, brother. Nikolai is holding things down for now, but we have the owner of the place we're building coming by before lunch," Reid mentions. He stops briefly to shake Prez and his dad's hands before walking toward his pregnant wife and daughter, kissing them goodbye, then mounts his bike and leaves. One by one, everyone takes off. I steal a glance Emerson's way as she walks off toward her car on her way to work herself.

Gabriel and Logan help their woman load the kids into their vehicles and watch them leave before Gabriel and Blake walk across the street to the tattoo shop. Now the parking lot is empty aside from me, Austin, and Logan.

Prez claps his hands together, catching our attention as the crowd has dissipated. "Alright, men. We are an hour behind opening time. Let's get to work. We have a full day ahead of us. We can celebrate at the end of the day at the clubhouse with a few beers."

2

EMERSON

"See you tomorrow, Dr. Evans," Tracy, one of the nurses who works the night shift, says as she heads across the hospital parking lot to her car.

"Bye, Tracy, drive safe." I've been working the graveyard shift for the past two weeks. Thank god last night was my last shift before I start back on days. Using the key fob in my hand, I unlock my Jeep. Opening the door, I toss my bag over to the passenger seat, climb in, shut the door, and lean my head back on the headrest. My body is tired, but my brain takes longer to catch up. I'm always wired after my shift ends. A few months ago, I took up Muay Thai at the kickboxing studio. Lucky for me, Rhett opens every day at five o'clock in the morning. The studio has been a lifesaver. When working the day shift, I could go to the gym and work off the day's stress, but before Rhett's studio opened, I didn't have a place to go this early in the morning. Polson's local gym hours do not cater to my work schedule.

My cell phone ringing grabs my attention, and I turn my head in the direction of my bag. I let out a deep sigh because I know who's calling. Only one person would call me this early in the morning—my mother. The ringing stops when I don't make a move to answer, only for it to start again seconds later. She is relentless, and I know she will keep on until I pick up. Answering the phone, I greet my mother, "Hi, Mom."

"What took you so long, Emerson?"

Sighing, I roll my eyes. "I just got off shift, Mom."

"Well, I'm calling because your father and I would like for you to come home this weekend. It's been months, Emerson," she scolds.

"That's because every time I come out to Seattle, you and Dad try fixing me up with someone."

"Oh, please. Patrick was lovely and a perfect match. You didn't even try to get to know him, Emerson."

"He's almost thirty years older than me, Mom!" I practically shout into my phone. "I'm not interested in someone old enough to be my dad. And the fact that he's dad's friend makes it creepier."

"What about that other gentleman, Harris?" she asks.

"Harris talked about bowel obstruction all through dinner. He was a hard pass."

"That's your problem, Emerson. You're too picky. You'll never find a suitable man being like that."

At my mother's statement, I don't bother to respond. We've had this same conversation a hundred times. To her, a suitable man is one who works in the medical field and someone of her choosing, but when I think of what I want, only one man comes to mind. He's my complete opposite in every way. *Quinn.* My parents would never approve.

"Look, Mom; I have to go," I say, wanting to cut the conversation short.

"So, I'll see you this weekend?"

"Yeah, Mom. I'll come home Friday after my shift."

I don't give her a chance to say anything else before ending the call. Do you want to know what my one weakness is? It's this—my parents, and disappointing them. I've never been able to stand up to them. Not like my twin brother Easton. He has always been able to say, *Fuck you!* And does so with a big smile on his face. He's not afraid to go after his dreams. Easton dropped out of medical school to pursue his love of music. Now he and his band East of Addiction have made it big, and they are currently on tour. My parents love Easton but still refuse to acknowledge his music as a real career. I thought my father was going to drop dead of a heart attack the day my brother announced he was dropping out of school. I, for one, was and am very proud of Easton and a little envious. I want to be more like him. Don't get me wrong, I love being a doctor, even though it's what my parents chose for me. Being a doctor is my dream. For as long as I can remember, all I wanted to do was help people just like my parents. Only my goal is to have my own practice. Something small. I'd love to have my own clinic right here in Polson. I hate the hustle and bustle of the ER, it's not for me, but my parents believe in climbing the ranks just as they have.

Both of my parents attended Johns Hopkins University. That's where they met. Once they finished medical school and were established in their careers, they had Easton and me. As far back as I could remember, they had planned mine and my brother's paths in life. We excelled in school, both graduating high school a year ahead of our peers. Then we were both accepted into Johns Hopkins. The day I received my acceptance letter in the mail, I was ecstatic. My brother—not so much. He always knew the medical field was not for him, and so did I. My parents will never understand how someone as smart as Easton would turn down Johns Hopkins. Thinking about my brother brings a smile to my face. We were thick as thieves growing up. Easton is my best friend. And even though he's away on tour, he still texts and calls me every day. I have never gone one day of my life without talking to my brother.

Pulling up in front of Rhett's studio, I park. Looking around, I take in my surroundings before climbing out of my Jeep. Hanging around The Kings the past few years, I have learned to be more aware. Not that I need to be. It appears a particular biker knows my schedule because anytime I work nights, I am hyperaware of the sound of his motorcycle followingo me from the hospital to the boxing studio. And as I step out of my Jeep, I hear the rumble of a bike. Looking to my left, I see Quinn ride by. His eyes lock on mine as he drives past. My stomach does a little flip-flop knowing that he's always watching.

I remember the first time I met Quinn. Bella had been brought into the emergency room at a hospital I worked at in Seattle. I had just informed Logan and everyone else about her condition. I remember being nervous and intimidated by all the men. Then there was Quinn. Intimidating in his own right but not like the rest. He carries himself differently. More easy-going and approachable. Quinn stands at six-foot-two and has shaggy blond hair that has grown longer over the past couple years, and he now wears it in a ponytail. His body is strong and lean, with just the right amount of muscle. Quinn's skin is a light golden color, and he keeps his beard cut close to his face, just enough to where I can see his full lips every time he smirks at me. And if that's not enough, my breath catches every time he looks at me with those knowing blue eyes. I swear he can see right through me. The first time he spoke to me, he called me Dr. Pretty and asked for some coffee. I blushed the whole time he tried to carry on a conversation. *"Your blush is the most beautiful thing I've ever seen, Sunshine."* A couple of hours later, I saw him outside Bella's hospital room, and he was flirting with a nurse. He was leaning in real close, whispering into her ear as she giggled at whatever he was saying. I learned right then Quinn was a flirt and all the sweet things he had told me; he was speaking to every other woman that would give him the time of day. I'm young and don't have tons of experience when it comes to men, only one casual boyfriend in college to whom I lost my virginity to, and a fellow doctor I worked with in Seattle. We weren't serious, just used each other from time to time. We had a mutual understanding. I have zero tolerance for bullshit. If I'm with a man, whether serious or hooking up, I won't stand for him sleeping with another woman. And everything about Quinn screams player. I will admit his persistence over the past year has me second guessing his intentions. He makes it sound like he and I are a done deal. Like I'm already his. I would be lying if I said I didn't secretly love the thought. The thing is, I like Quinn, but I'm not willing to risk my heart, but that's me, always playing it safe.

"You coming in or what?" a deep voice asks me from the open door of the studio, and I see Rhett looking at me expectantly.

"Yeah, I'm coming."

Sliding in past Rhett as he holds the door open for me, he asks, "Everything okay? You were standing out there next to your car like you were lost in thought."

"I'm fine." I smile. "It's been a long day. I was trying to collect my thoughts."

"You know, anytime you're having a bad day or just want to talk, I'm here, and I'd love to take you out sometime." As flattered as I am by Rhett asking me out, I can't accept. Something about it feels wrong. Don't ask me why. He's a great guy and sexy as hell, but he's just not *him. God, this is ridiculous.* Here I have a good looking and kind man asking me out, and I can't stop thinking about Quinn long enough to accept. Deciding not to rule Rhett out completely, I answer, "I think I might like that sometime. I'll let you know." The words taste bitter in my mouth, and I instantly know it's a lie. I have no intention of going out with Rhett.

Two hours later, I'm back in my Jeep, driving down Wicker Street on the way to my apartment. When I pass Grace's bakery, I see her about to step inside, so I honk my horn and give her a wave as I continue to drive by. When I first moved to Polson a few years ago, I never dreamed I'd find such good friends. Learning Bella lived here was a shock. When I treated her in Seattle, I vaguely remember her saying she lived in Montana but didn't know it was Polson.

I heard about an opening at Polson's local ER from a colleague of mine. Leaving Seattle and taking a job in a small town was the only time I had done something for myself and not my parents. Moving to Polson has been the best decision of my life. I love my parents, but the friends—the family I have here are the best. Bella, over time, claimed me like family and therefore so did The Kings. When the club decides you mean something to them, you are considered family. They don't care where you come from or what kind of past you have. Once you are a part of The Kings of Retribution family, it's for life. And you won't find a more loyal family than them. Jake once told me after I saved Bella's life and helped Sofia that I became someone they would forever be indebted to. He said that if I was willing to stick my neck out and risk my career for Sofia, then I was worthy of their loyalty. And that's exactly what Jake told me the day Bella was discharged from the hospital in Seattle, along with giving me his number. He made me promise to call if I ever needed him or the club.

My parents are the only people who I keep my involvement with the local motorcycle club a secret. If they knew how often I risked my license and job for them, they would lose their shit. Easton knows all about my life here. We tell each other everything. He's the one person who keeps pressing me to make a go of things with Quinn. My brother also knows I can't do hookups with someone I have feelings for either, so he understands why I'm hesitant.

Walking in the door to my apartment, I set my bag down on the kitchen counter, grab a bottle of orange juice from the refrigerator then make my way to my sofa picking up my laptop from the dining table along the way. Sitting down, I tuck my legs and set my computer in my lap. I need to book my flight home for Friday evening. Once my flight is taken care of, I pull up a group text on my phone. I was supposed to have lunch with the girls on Saturday. Now I have to tell them I need to cancel. I hate it because it's not often I get a weekend off and I was looking forward to seeing the girls.

Me: Hey girls, can't make lunch Saturday. Flying home to see my parents. It's been months. Couldn't get out of it.

Bella: Damn, that sucks. But I understand.

Alba: Booo!!

Mila: What they said.

Grace: That's okay. We'll plan for another lunch. Or maybe dinner. You back on days again?

Me: Yep. Back on days.

Alba: Yes! Let's make dinner plans!

Mila: I'm game.

Grace: Me too!

Me: Okay. Let's do dinner next week.

Bella: Wait! What about the patch-in party for Grey Sunday night? Are you still coming to that?

Alba: Party girl! We all have babysitters. Please say you're coming.

Me: Yep. I have a return flight home Sunday morning. I'll be back in time for the party.

Mila: Hell yeah!

Grace: Can't wait to see you.

Bella: See you Sunday.

Me: See ya girls Sunday.

Once all the ladies had said their goodbyes, I toss my phone to the cushion beside me then use the palms of my hands to rub my tired eyes. I don't know how much more of the ER I can take. Today a teenage girl was brought in. She had been in a car accident, and she was not wearing her seatbelt. She made it but is in a coma. Seeing the kinds of trauma I see, day in and day out is starting to take its toll. Car accidents, drugged-out women in labor, men who beat their wives, and gunshot wounds. I don't want any more of that. I want sore throats, earaches, and sprained ankles. I also know the only person who can change my situation is me. I have to quit being a chicken shit and stand up to my parents. Maybe when I see them this weekend, I can finally do it. I can finally take my life and my future in my own hands. I need to let my fear of disappointing them go.

3

QUINN

Another day, another dollar. Right now, I'm changing the oil in Mila's vehicle that Reid dropped off about forty-five minutes ago. Work in the newly built shop has been smooth sailin' since we opened a couple of days ago. Having more space and better equipment makes the job and the day go much faster.

"You comin' with us out to Charley's tonight, Quinn?" Logan peers over the rear fender of the bike he's working on.

Charley mentioned about a week ago he had a couple of guys come in nosin' around and askin' the local barflies questions about our little town and the people in it. The good thing about Charley's is all the regulars know us and don't say too much. The last thing we need is any more asswipes comin' around our town tryin' to stir up shit.

From what we know, they haven't been back, so Charley thinks they were a couple of nosey fuckers passing through. It's been a while since any of us have hung out at his place, so we figured it was high time we pay a visit and make our presence known. Just in case. "Naw, brother, not tonight. It's the second Friday of the month, man." Opening another quart of oil, I pour it into the funnel. "Plus, I told my dad I would help him on his car this evenin', but if you run into any problems, I'm there," I tell him.

"Thanks, brother." Logan nods.

"Damn, something is smellin' good," I remark, screwing the oil cap back on.

Logan tosses a wrench into the toolbox beside him and stands. "Bella came by to cook lunch for everyone today. She and the kids are back there in the break room."

My stomach rumbles. "That's what I'm talkin' about. Feels like forever since she has treated us to some lunch."

"She's had her hands full with Bree and Jake. I'll go see if the food is done." Turning, Logan walks toward the back where Bella is. It doesn't take me long to put my tools away and wash up. As soon as I walk through the break room door, I see Logan has Bella up on the counter, his hand under the front of her shirt and his lips on her neck.

"If I eat all my food, will I get dessert too?" I waggle my eyebrows the moment Bella's eyes open and look in my direction.

"I don't share, brother," Logan rumbles, helping Bella down. I do my usual mock pout before Bella walks over, hugging me.

"How ya doin', sweetheart?" I ask her.

"Tired. Two little ones keep me busy." She peers over toward her kids, both fast asleep in a playpen; the smile she wears on her face saying it's all worth it. It causes my chest to ache because I want the same for myself one day.

"I had lunch with your beautiful mom the other day." Bella sits a bowl of potato salad on the table along with a platter loaded with pulled pork sandwiches.

Scooping food onto my plate, I ask her, "She helps put your mind at ease about Bree?" *What if she feels like she doesn't belong? What if she wants to find any of her biological family when she's older?* These were just a few questions that were weighing on Bella about the baby she and Logan recently adopted. Knowing my mom probably went through the same emotions and had the same questions, I suggested she talk to her. I mean, I gave her my perspective on things, but for her to bond with someone else—another mother who has gone on a similar journey in life would put things in a much better perspective than I ever could. "My mom is the best," I wholeheartedly express.

Within the next moments, Gabriel and Austin stroll in, sit down, and start eating. Checking on the kids, Bella kisses her man. "I'm going to take Jake some food. The man has been working nonstop. He needs to eat."

Logan pulls her closer and leans in for another kiss. "I'll eat with you when you get back, Angel."

As soon as she walks out of the room, I ask Gabriel, "You ever order that new barbell for me?"

"Came in yesterday," he tells me.

"Sweet." I rub my hands together, and Gabriel shakes his head. "I'm considering another piercing," I take another bite of food. Gabriel stares at me. He reluctantly did my first one because I didn't trust anyone else. That and he's the only shop in town who does them.

"Not touchin' your dick again," he grumbles.

Austin chimes in with a surprised expression. "You have your dick pierced? Do women like that shit?"

"Hell yeah. I never met one who didn't. You considering one?" I look at him. Austin has gauges in both ears, tattoos slowly covering both arms and small barbell piercings below a knuckle on his right hand, so for him to show interest in a cock piercing doesn't surprise me.

"Thought about it." He nods. "This chick I'm seeing has her hood pierced. Fuckin' hot if you ask me," he says.

Before he can finish the rest of his description of his woman's artwork, Bella reappears at the same time her children begin to wake from their naps. Logan grabs their son while Bella reaches for their daughter, and the two of them sit down. After finishing our meal, we thank Bella for lunch, then Gabriel, Austin and I get back to work, leaving her and Logan to enjoy their lunch together.

I knocked off work an hour early today to head toward the youth center. The center is about a block from where my mom runs her practice. At least twice a month for the past five years now, I have been volunteering my time. I like hanging out with some of the local young men who come here for various reasons. Sometimes, they need extra help with school work, and others may have to do community service, some just need someone to talk to. All of it helps to keep them off the street and out of trouble.

Reid's old man helped start the program, which teaches any kid, male or female, a trade skill. Reid has continued what his father started years ago by providing hands-on training with the addition of getting the kids involved with charity builds. I do what I can by teaching them mechanical skills, and along the way, it becomes therapeutic for them. The kids learn something and get to talk about what may be going on in their lives in an environment they feel relaxed in. I fell into the role relatively quickly. For whatever reason, people find it easy to open up and talk to me about things. It's been that way my whole life. When my brothers would need someone to listen—I was there. When these kids need someone not to judge them—I'm there.

The club gives back to the community in many ways, but just about all of us do a little extra on our own, and this right here is mine. I'm passionate about helping the youth in the community. Am I the best role model they could have in their lives? Not by most societies' standards. Do I give a damn what others think? Fuck no. I care about those kids, and I want to be there for them, and in the end, that's what matters. Reality is, life can fuckin' suck sometimes, but it's how you choose to handle it; it's the path you decide to make for yourself that will help determine the outcome. They don't need someone to teach them to sit around and wait for change. They don't need a handout; they need a hand up. We all have the power to control our own destiny—our own future. You want it, make it happen. That's what I teach them.

I walk around the back of the building where a small shed big enough to house a beater car happens to be located. Unlocking the padlock, I swing the door open and walk inside. Along the back wall is a collection of second-hand toolboxes that have been donated to the center over the years. My phone chimes. Reaching into my cut, I take it out and swipe my thumb across the screen to read a text from my dad.

Dad: *You staying for dinner tonight?*

As I type out my answer, I grin. I love my mom's cookin'. Since she knows I'm comin' over, maybe she'll make my favorite meal; meatloaf.

Me: *Does a bear shit in the woods?*

I'm always trying to come up with a joke to reference his job in forestry. About half a minute goes by before he replies.

Dad: 😄

I laugh as I stare at the smiley face on my phone screen. Dad loves technology, but when it comes to texting, he doesn't get it. If he wants to have a conversation with you, he calls. That was until KitKat decided he needed to get with the times, so he does it for her. Don't even get me started on the time he sent me a text meant for my mom. Knowing where my dad wanted to put his eggplant was more than I needed to know, but fuckin' with him about it every chance I get is priceless.

The sound of shoes hitting the pavement outside the shed grabs my attention. I shove my phone back in my pocket as Liam and Aiden come into view.

"How's it going, Quinn?" Liam, the older of the two, greets me with a firm handshake. Liam is a senior in high school. Skippin' classes and fallin' in with a couple of older guys he wasn't aware were small-time drug pushers landed him in some trouble. He's been coming to the center for over a year now. Tough kid. Built like a linebacker, with a broad chest and broad shoulders. He was court-ordered to be here, so he didn't come willingly—at first.

"Can't complain, man," I respond, then turn my head and look at Aiden. Aiden is fourteen. He comes here after school for a place to hang out while his mom works. Aiden has had a hard time fitting in and making friends since moving to Polson six months ago. I can relate. I was once that kid. "What's up?" I ask, lifting my chin.

Aiden rubs the back of his neck. "Not much." He casts his eyes to the ground and scrubs the toe of his shoe across a dark spot on the grease-stained floor.

The kid looks like something's bothering him. "Want to talk about it?" I ask. Liam walks to the back of the shed and starts to dig in a toolbox, purposely giving me time with Aiden to find out what's goin' on. "Someone been fuckin' with you at school?"

"No. It's nothin'."

I lift the hood of the car, and Aiden walks up beside me. "Well, you see, there's this girl—" he draws out the last word, hesitating to say more. Immediately, I get a shit-eating grin. Aiden is a good looking kid, but his confidence level is zero, and he's shy as hell. "You thinkin' on asking this girl out?" I question him.

The kids gather the necessary tools they need to start disconnecting parts from the motor. As I guide them along, the conversation begins to flow.

"I see her sitting alone sometimes when my mom and I pass that ballet studio over on Baker Street on my way to my piano lessons."

The kid is a fuckin' musical genius.

"She looks sad. Something in me doesn't like that," he more willingly tells us.

"There's nothing to it. Just walk up to her and ask," Liam grunts and puts more torque on the bolt he's trying to loosen.

"I can't do that," Aiden answers with a sigh.

"What are you so afraid of?" Liam asks.

Liam doesn't have an issue with the ladies. I would even venture to say he's a little bit of a player. "The worst she can do is say no. Go for it," I do my best to encourage him.

Aiden never says any more about the subject as we steadily work and talk about other issues, but I can tell he's thinking heavily about it. Before I know it, an hour has passed, and it's time to go.

"Alright, guys." I wipe the excess grease from my hands with a shop rag. "I got to run. Liam, let me know if you're still interested in that bike you were lookin' at. I'll ride with you to take a look at it and make sure the guy is givin' you a fair deal."

"You got it." He waits for Aiden and me to step out before closing the shed doors and locking the padlock.

"Aiden." I clasp my hand over his shoulder, giving it a firm squeeze. "Ask her," I say before letting him go.

With a confident grin, he lets me know, "I'm gonna do it."

"That's what I'm talkin' about, kid."

I'VE BEEN under the hood of my dad's car all of ten minutes after telling him about my day when I feel his eyes burnin' a hole through the side of my head. "There somethin' you wantin' to ask me, Dad?"

"With all the good, solid advice you give these kids, you can't take the same advice you're dishing out? If I remember right, you've been pining after a particular doctor for a while now. When are you going to do something about it?"

He had to call me out. I tighten the bolt one more turn. "I'm not pining."

He grunts in response.

"Okay, maybe I'm pining a little." Standing from being bent

over the backside of the motor, I snatch my beer that's sitting on the front bumper of the car and take a huge gulp. "She's not making it easy, ya know," I confess.

My dad laughs and drinks down the last of the beer he was holding in his hand. "The right woman won't make it easy for you to catch her, son. I knew the moment I saw your mom; she was the one. I've been stupid crazy in love with her since the day she sat next to me in chemistry class years ago. She didn't make it easy either; let me tell you. I was a slacker surfer boy. I lived and breathed the beach—the waves and chasing girls. Your mom was popular, smart, and had her shit together and wanted nothing to do with me and my reputation."

I've heard all about my dad's high school days, so my mom had every reason to worry if she would be just another notch on his bedpost.

"I had to prove to her I wanted her and only her," he finishes.

"Took him over a year to convince me to go on that first date."

Startled by the sweet sound of my mom's voice, my dad and I look over at the garage door to find my mom leaning against the doorframe with one hand on the door's handle. My dad walks over, grabs her waist, pulling her close, and admiringly looks at her. "It was worth the wait. I'd do it all over again to be able to relive the first time my lips touched yours." He kisses her.

They are the example of what I want.

My mom offers her opinion on the Emerson matter, which means she had been standing there listening longer than we realized. "I see the way she looks at you when you aren't looking, sweetie. I don't know her well enough to know what she's battling, but I assure you, Emerson wants you too."

My mom is right. I catch her stare often.

I feel the energy in it.

It's high time I make my intention very clear to Emerson.

4

EMERSON

I'm sitting at a stoplight on my way to the airport when I hear the rumble of a motorcycle. I smile, thinking of Quinn. But when I turn my head to the right and look out the passenger window of my Jeep, the smile I had moments ago falls. The person on the motorcycle next to me is not Quinn. In fact, he's not even a King. The man is wearing a cut like The Kings, but he is sporting different colors. When he turns and looks at me, I instantly feel the hairs on my arms stand, and a shiver runs through my body. We both sit there at the light holding each other's stare until a car behind me honks their horn. A second later, the biker drives off before I even get a good look at the name on his cut. I make a mental note to say something to one of the guys when I get back in town. I'll see them on Sunday at the patch-in party. I don't like to involve myself in anyone's business, especially the club's, but something tells me I need to say something.

Parking at the airport, I grab my overnight carry-on bag from the seat beside me, lock my door and make my way inside to catch my flight to Seattle. I dread this trip home. I wish I could have a regular visit with my parents, one that involves hugs and catching up on life, but I know that won't be the case. My mother, no doubt, has something up her sleeve. Probably another blind date. She means well, and I know she wants to see me settled down and happy. I just wish she would ask me what would make me happy —what I want. With a heavy sigh, I store my bag in the compartment over my seat before sitting down. Once the plane has taken off, I take my phone from my purse, put my earbuds in, and turn my playlist on. The flight to Seattle from Polson is a short one, and I need to relax before getting there. Lord knows I'm going to need all the patience I can muster.

"You going to get out, lady?" The driver of the taxi I am currently sitting in asks, knocking me out of my daze. I didn't realize we'd arrived at my parent's house. "Yes. I'm sorry," I tell the guy as I gather my things and get out of the car.

"Alright, Emerson. Let's get this over with. It's only one day," I say, giving myself a pep talk. Using my key, I let myself into my parent's house—the same house I grew up in. They bought it a year before Easton and I were born. It's a two-story house in the suburbs of Redmond, which is about twenty minutes from Seattle. My mother is the attending physician at the Seattle Children's Hospital, and my father holds the same position at Northwest.

"Hello!" I call out and shut the door behind me.

"Hey, sweetheart," my dad greets me as he walks down the stairs. "You should have called me to come to pick you up," he chastises, kissing me on my cheek.

"I took a taxi. It was no bother. Where's Mom?"

"She's in the kitchen finishing up dinner. She insisted on cooking."

"Okay, I'm going to say hi."

"Tell your mom I'll be in my office. I need to make a few calls before dinner."

"Will do," I say over my shoulder as I make my way to the kitchen. I can already smell the roast cooking before I even enter the room. I love my mom's cooking. No matter how busy she and Dad were, she always made time to cook for Easton, and I home-cooked meals at least four days a week. "Hey Mom, something smells good," I sing-song, pushing my way through the double doors of the kitchen and see my mom pulling a large pan from the oven.

"Emerson, how long have you been here? Why didn't you call your father to come to pick you up?"

"I only just got here, and like I told Dad, I took a taxi. It was no biggie." My mom huffs and gives me a look, but doesn't say anymore. "You want me to help with anything?"

"No, I have dinner covered. Why don't you go upstairs and get cleaned up? Dinner will be ready in an hour."

"Okay," I say as my mom walks around the island and gives me a warm hug.

"I'm glad you decided to come home for the weekend."

"Me too, Mom. I'll be back down after I freshen up." On the way up to my room, I breathe a sigh of relief. Maybe this visit will be different. Perhaps I can visit my parents without my mother trying to shove another date down my throat or her telling me I need to leave Polson and come back home to Seattle. Once I make it into my old room, I decide to take a shower since I didn't have time to take one after my last shift. After I've finished, I change into a pair of black jeans and a red long sleeve silk blouse. I made sure to choose an outfit that covers my tattoos since my parents have never seen them. I decided to keep them covered, so I don't have to add my ink to the already long list of things they don't approve of. I got my first tattoo while in college. My tattoo covers my entire hip and runs up my side. I chose a peacock because a peacock is a possessor of some of the most admired human characteristics and is a symbol of integrity and the beauty we can achieve when we choose to show our true colors. That is what I aspire to do one day. I want to be brave enough to show my true colors. I also started a sleeve on my left arm, hence the reason for a long sleeve shirt.

As I'm about to walk out of my bedroom door, I get a text. Opening my phone, I see it's from my brother.

East: What's up?

Me: Hold. Sending pic.

Holding my cell out in front of me, I snap a picture of myself with my childhood bed behind me and press send.

East: Good luck with that.

Me: Thanks. I'll need it. Where are you?

East: Miami. It's hot as balls here. Houston tomorrow. I found out from my manager today we'll be in Missoula in a couple of weeks.

I squeal and do a tiny dance of joy at the news. Missoula is a little more than an hour from Polson. I haven't seen my brother in months.

Me: This is the best news! I can't wait to see you.

East: Our next show won't be for three days after the one in Missoula. I can stay for a day before heading out. I have to go. I'll call later with the details. Love you.

Me: Can't wait! Love you too.

My brother's news comes at the perfect time. I needed a pick-me-up and my Easton fix. This is the longest we have ever gone without seeing each other, and the facetimes are few and far between. This tour has been something he and his band worked so hard to get, and they deserve it. Hearing the doorbell chime brings me out of my thoughts, and I instantly feel irritation and dread settle in the pit of my stomach. I should have known this visit would not be any different. Squaring my shoulders, I walk out of my room and downstairs to see who my parents have invited to dinner. When I descend the last step, my insides fill with rage when I look at who is standing just inside the front door of my parent's home. My mother is the first to notice my presence.

"Emerson, sweetheart. You remember Phillip and Beth Stewart and their son Parker. Didn't you two go to prom together?" my mother asks.

Not taking my heated disgusted stare off Parker, I answer, "We did."

The whole time Parker smiles at me as if I have forgotten *that* night.

"You look good, Emerson," he says with a fake smile still plastered on his face.

"I know," is my only response. I can tell by the irritated look on my mother's face, she is not pleased by my behavior. I can't bring myself to give a shit.

"Why don't we all go sit in the dining room? We don't want our dinner to get cold," my mother suggests, trying to diffuse the current tense and awkward moment.

I take my seat at the large dining room table, and Parker sits down directly across from me with his parents sitting to his right. We all serve ourselves, and conversation flows between my parents and the Stewarts'. With my appetite suddenly gone, I block out the voices around me and absently push my food around my plate. I can feel Parker's beady gaze on me. He makes my skin crawl, and I hate him.

Prom night was one of the worst nights of my life. After the dance, Parker drove us to Nash Curtis' house. Nash was the star baseball player at our school and was hosting the after-prom party. Parker was the perfect gentleman all through the dance, but once we got to the after party—gone was the doting date. I asked him to show me where the restroom was, only he didn't. Parker led me upstairs to an empty bedroom, where he proceeded to force himself on me. Thank god he'd had a few drinks. His drunkenness worked in my favor, and I was able to fight him off. I will never forget my victory and his cries of pain when I grabbed a handful of his balls and twisted. I would be surprised if he'd be able to reproduce after that.

Afterward, I ran down the stairs and out of the house. I ran four blocks all the way back to my house. Both my parents were working that night and didn't see me when I came home at two o'clock in the morning with a ripped dress and a tear-streaked face. But Easton was. My brother didn't go to prom, and he was lying on his bed with his door open when I came up the stairs. He rushed up to me and took my face in his hands. I saw the rage in his eyes when he took in my appearance. Easton didn't even ask me what happened. He knew. In fact, he had warned and begged me not to go out with Parker. I was blinded by my crush on him, though. Easton kissed me on my cheek, walked back into his room, grabbed his car keys, and walked out of the house without a word. I knew what he was going to do. My suspicions proved right when I returned to school the following Monday and saw Parker's left arm in a cast, and he had a black eye along with a busted lip. We never spoke of the incident, nor did we tell our parents.

"How is Easton these days?" Mr. Stewart asks. Lifting my eyes from my plate, I look to my father to see how he responds to the question.

"Easton is still toying around with that little band of his."

"It's not just some little band. East of Addiction just signed to a major record label and is currently on tour. They happen to be amazing. You would know that if you bothered to go see them."

"Emerson, did you know Parker recently made partner at his father's firm?" my mom asks, drawing the conversation on to a different subject when she sees my father squirming in his seat.

Looking at Parker, I decide to play along as I plaster a fake smile on my face. "Good for you, Parker. What kind of law do you practice?"

"Criminal law," he responds.

"Oh. That's right up your alley. You know, defending rapists and all." I honestly cannot believe I just said that, and by my mother's gasp, she can't either.

"Emerson!" she snaps. "What has gotten into you today?"

"What's gotten into me is every time I come home to see you and Dad, you pull shit like this," I say, pointing at our guest across the table. "Now if you will excuse me, I've lost my appetite." Standing, I toss my napkin on the table and ignore the stunned look on everyone's face, and for once, I am proud of myself. As I make my way out of the dining room and up the stairs, I pull my phone from my back pocket to call an Uber. I'm going home—tonight. No sooner do I make it to my room. I get another text from my brother. I know he's checking up on me.

East: Well?

Me: Dinner was a nightmare. Mom invited the Stewarts'.

I'm not surprised when my phone rings two seconds after I press send.

"Hey," I answer my brother.

"Was the motherfucker there?"

Sitting down on the edge of my bed, I sigh, "Yes."

"Son of a bitch! I guess that pussy needs another reminder about staying away from you. I think I'll break both arms this time," Easton grinds out.

"You don't need to do anything. I'm a big girl now. I can handle pricks like Parker."

"I know you are, Em, but you're my baby sister. I always got your back."

"Yeah, I know you do, East. And you're older by only two minutes." I chuckle, trying to lighten the mood.

"Doesn't matter. Older is older," he says, and I know he's grinning behind the phone. Seeing headlights shine through the window, I look out and see my Uber is here. "Look East; my ride just pulled up. I'm going back home tonight. I'll text you when I get there, okay?"

"Alright, Em. I love you."

"Love you too."

Disconnecting the phone, I grab my overnight bag from the dresser and do a quick work at gathering my stuff from the bathroom. Walking down the stairs, I can hear the murmurs of my parents and their guests still talking in the dining room. I don't bother going back in there to say goodbye. At this point, all I want is to get back to Polson, where I belong.

5

QUINN

Liam called last night, and as promised, I got myself up this morning and made a run to the other side of town to check out the bike for sale he was thinking about buying. The kid has good taste. A Dyna Super Glide is an excellent choice for a guy his size. It will make riding more comfortable. Needs work, but the kid is willin' to put in the hours to have somethin' to call his, and you gotta respect that. Nothing like knowing you put the time in to make your ride custom. After helping him load it onto the trailer he borrowed to haul it home, I congratulated him on his new ride and jumped on my own to head back toward the clubhouse. I love mornings like today. The air is crisp with the changing of seasons, and the Montana sky is the perfect shade of indigo blue, making the mountains and the sea of green pastures look like a painted canvas as I cruise down the road.

I'm fuckin' stoked because later today, the club is throwing a patch-in party for Grey. I think we all knew the moment he started prospecting for us, he would make the cut. Once Logan told me that Bella mentioned Emerson would be coming to the party, it made the celebration that much sweeter because tonight I'm going to end all this dancin' around. It's time to stop avoiding what we both want.

The unmistakable sound of a Harley revving its engine from behind me as I hit the industrial area of town has me shifting my attention to my side mirror to catch a glimpse of who it might be. Just about the time I slow my speed to try and get a good look, the fucker guns it, speeding past me so close and so fast it causes the standing water on the edge of the road from last night's rain to kick up, soaking me in the process. I don't recognize the bike and waste no time taking off after the dickhead, but before I can catch up to the ballsy son of a bitch, he swerves around a delivery truck stopped at a flashing railroad crossing. The train whistle blows on its approach as the guy effortlessly dodges the guard rails a mere minute from becoming bug guts on the front end of the locomotive. *Damn it.* I slow to a stop. Keeping a close eye on my surroundings, I wait for the train to pass. *Who the fuck could this guy be?* Maybe he's a young punk out joyriding and decided to be a complete bonehead. I think back to the reason a few of the brothers went to hang out at Charley's the other night. From what they reported, it was a pretty uneventful night. Either way, maybe I should say something to Prez.

When I make it to the clubhouse, I notice the only bike outside belongs to Grey, so I back my bike up alongside his. Besides Rain and Ember, Grey, Austin, and Blake are the only members who also live here. For now, the place is quiet, so walking inside, I decide to head upstairs and take a quick shower.

"What happened to you?" Grey says, emerging from his room upstairs as I head down the hall to my room, one half my body wet with muddy water.

"Some asshat sped past me on my way here," I acknowledge him, pushing my hair from my face.

"Damn, brother, he must have come pretty close to soak you like that."

"Too fuckin' close," I tell him. "I'll catch you downstairs, man. Gonna clean my ass up."

Grey nods his head and heads downstairs. I open my bedroom door, walk into my room, and strip out of my wet clothes before I walk my naked ass to the bathroom and start the shower. Not wasting time, I wash the grime off, step out of the shower and wrap a towel around my waist as I look at my reflection in the fogged-up mirror. Running my fingers through my hair, I pull it back, securing it with a hair tie. Rubbing my palm over my beard, I debate whether or not to trim it or go for a completely clean shave, but I decide to keep it and opt to shape it up a bit before retrieving a pair of jeans from my dresser drawer and get myself dressed.

Once downstairs, I run into Logan and Reid sitting at the bar, both drinking a cold beer. After walking behind the bar and grabbing a cold one for myself, I plant my ass on the barstool to the right of Reid. In the process, I catch the time on the clock on the wall. *Hell, already noon. Things should start picking up soon.* "How's it going?" I lift my beer toward my brothers.

"Can't complain. Heard some dickhead got too close for comfort on your way here earlier?" Logan questions. They probably came in lookin' for me, and Grey filled them in. "Some fucker decided to go all Evil Knievel on their bike down near the old metal fabrication factory on the other side of town. Came this close," I gesture, holding two fingers an inch apart, "to being minced meat by a fuckin' train in the process."

Logan and Reid give me their full attention, and Reid asks, "You get a look at the guy?"

I shake my head, "Naw, I heard him first, though. He revved his bike before gunning it. Almost like he wanted me to hear him first. He was making himself known. He sped past me, and with a face full of muddy water, I didn't get a good enough look at the rider before taking off after him."

"You thinkin' it's just some punk ass kid?" Reid leans against the back of his barstool.

Shrugging my shoulders, I take a swig of my beer, "Not sure. It could have been. The guy was reckless."

"I have a gut feelin' we shouldn't pass it off as some dick tryin' to showboat. He was behind you and would have seen your cut." Logan's brows furrow. "So, I'm not convinced it's nothing." He downs the last of his beer. "All this aside, we have a party to get ready for. The girls will be showing up soon to help get things ready, so let's get to settin' out tables and fire up the grills," Logan announces, chucking his empty bottle in the trash.

The ladies walk in not long after, with no Emerson. "I thought Emerson was ridin' with you ladies?" I ask.

"She said she was running late and would drive herself," Alba explains.

Bella walks up and pats my arm. "Don't worry, she'll be here in about an hour. She got held up at the hospital."

An hour later, Prez kicks things off with a speech. "Today, we celebrate adding a permanent member to our growing brotherhood. Grey started prospecting for our club over a year ago." He motions for Grey to step forward, and as he walks past he earns cheers and hollers from the entire family gathered here today.

That's also when I notice Emerson walking around the corner of the building and toward the women. Her captivating eyes meet mine as I follow her across the yard. The brief smile she gives me throws me for a loop and steals my heart from my chest. A clasp on my shoulder loosens the hold Emerson has on me.

"Claim her later, brother. Let's watch our brother get patched in first," Gabriel redirects my attention, and I reluctantly peel my eyes away from Emerson.

I listen as Prez continues his speech. "Son, from day one, you've earned this cut. You show up to every meeting, finish any and every task given. You've done it all while showing respect to this club and yourself. Time and time again, you have demonstrated your commitment to the club and your brothers with pride."

Taking his prospect cut off and given his fully patched cut, Grey slips it over his shoulders, the grin displaying how proud he is in the moment. He clears his throat. "After being allowed to hang around for a while and getting to know you guys, getting to see the tight-knit family you are, getting to experience the brotherhood you offered, I knew I wanted to be a part of it. I knew I was missing somethin' in my life—a family; a brotherhood." He looks down at the patch that bears his name. "I'll wear this with pride and with respect for my club and my brothers."

The backyard erupts with cheers. One by one, we all make our way to congratulate him personally. "How's it feel, brother?" I ask him and hand him a cold beer.

"Feels great." He takes the beer and clinks it against mine.

"You've earned it, man," I smile and raise my bottle.

The party has been in full force for a few hours now. Night has fallen. Music is playing through the giant speakers set up under the covered patio area off the back of the building, and everyone seems to be enjoying themselves. My eyes have been glued to Emerson all night, and those tight as fuck jeans she's wearing have caused me to sport a semi the entire night. Noticing she's gone MIA, I decided to go on a little treasure hunt and find her. Once making a loop around front to make sure her car is still here, I circle back around to the backyard and make my way through the sliding doors leading to the kitchen. As I'm turning the corner to head down the unlit hall leading to the downstairs bathroom, we collide. Emerson loses her balance, but my hand shoots out, wrapping around her slim waist and helping her stay on her feet. She sways slightly before her palm comes to rest on my chest as she steadies herself. Emerson has let her hair down tonight and has been thoroughly enjoying herself and maybe has had a little too much to drink by the looks of it. I keep my hands on her. Partly to make sure she doesn't fall, but mostly because I don't want to let go. The soft curves of her waist fit my hands like a glove. "Sunshine, you okay?" I ask her because she hasn't stopped staring at her hand, still placed on my chest. "Hey, beautiful." I place my finger under her chin, guiding her eyes to mine.

"Umm." She blinks a few times. "Yeah, I'm okay. Just a little tipsy is all," she tells me as her eyes fall to my lips, then she licks hers. The need to kiss her becomes unbearable. "Quinn," she breathes my name, and the soft melodic sound of her voice draws me closer to her.

"Sunshine, unless you want me to claim those sweet lips of yours, I'm gonna need you to stop lookin' at me like I'm your favorite candy." My voice drips with lust as I dangle by a thread.

"What if I want you to?" Emerson whispers, and I think my heart skips a beat and my cock twitches with her admission. My eyes close, but only for a moment. "Babe, I won't make a move unless you say so." I pull her body flush against mine, letting her feel the effect she has on me. "What do you want?"

"You."

I waste no time capturing her lips with mine. I breathe her in like she's my dying breath. She clenches my shirt. Dropping my hands lower, I scoop her off the floor, and her legs wrap around my hips. Not breaking the connection, I press her back against the wall and hold her there. I pull back, leaning my forehead against hers. "Fuck, Sunshine. You don't know how long I've waited to taste your mouth." Her hands run through my hair snagging the hair tie in the process as she pulls it free. The way her nails drag across my scalp sends tingles down my spine. Her hips rock, rubbing against my raging hard-on. I grin. My woman is feelin' bold. *I like it.* Leaning down, I run my lips across the sensitive flesh on her neck and kiss my way down over her shoulder. She grinds her hips again creating agonizing friction. The heat I feel from between her legs adds fuel to my fire. Instantly my lips are on hers. Grinding my hips against her, we make out in the dark hallway.

"Quinn," Emerson pants, wanting more of me. Needing to give her what she wants, I drop her feet to the floor and run my palm under her shirt until my thumb caresses the underside of her breast. "You aching for more?" I ask her and tug on her earlobe with my teeth.

"Yes." She runs her small soft hands under my shirt, splaying her fingers across my abs before roaming higher finding my nipple piercings. She bites her lower lip as she lightly tugs on one watching my reaction to the sensation it creates. I pull the strap of her bra over her shoulder and run my palm over her breast as her eyes never leave mine. Imagine my sweet surprise when I discover her pierced nipple and I tug on it. Her head leans against the wall as a moan of pleasure escapes her lips and my cock throbs with excitement. "Fuck. You're full of surprises, aren't you, Sunshine?" I pull the hem of her shirt up, dip my head and take her taut pink nipple into my mouth causing a deep throaty moan to vibrate off the walls. Her body is tense. Tense in the way she needs a release, and I'm about to give it to her. I run my finger along the waist of her jeans and gauge her reaction as I unbutton them. Not once does she waver. Her look gives me the green light, and I go for it. I slip my hand down past her panties finding her swollen clit. "You're soaked." I kiss her and block her body with mine in case someone happens upon us. I move my hand further down, sliding my fingers through her slick folds then drag them up and start massaging her clit, instantly finding her sweet spot. I build her up to the point her hips start to take over. "You ready to come for me, Sunshine?" I sink two fingers into her tight pussy and rub her clit with the heel of my palm.

"Oh god." Her nails dig into my shoulders, and she buries her face in my chest to muffle her moans.

"Come for me, beautiful," I whisper across her ear. Her pussy clamps down on my fingers and continues to pulsate as she rides out her orgasm. Claiming her mouth again, I wait for her body to relax into mine before I'm unable to resist any longer. Wanting to taste her, I bring my fingers to my mouth and suck them clean.

"Quinn," she says, her voice barely a whisper as she attempts to get her breathing under control.

I lean against the wall, my arm above her head. I can't stop staring at the beautiful woman in front of me. She has no idea how deep I've fallen for her. I brush the hair from her face with the back of my hand and tuck it behind her ear. "Yeah, babe?"

"Take me home."

6

EMERSON

I can't believe I'm going through with this. For one night, I'm going to throw caution to the wind and give in to what I have been craving for the past couple of years. Riding on the back of Quinn's bike with my arms wrapped tightly around his waist and my palms pressed flat against his hard abs feels right. It feels like this is where I am supposed to be. Resting my chin on his shoulder, I close my eyes, breathe in his intoxicating scent, and enjoy the moment. A shiver runs down my spine when he reaches back and runs his hand up my leg then grabs it pulling me flush against his back, and I can feel the heat of his skin through his clothes. Deciding to be bold, I lean in and brush my lips against the crook of Quinn's neck, and my actions have him turning his eyes away from the road as he gives me a heated stare. It causes a familiar tingle between my legs, the same one I get every time he looks at me. When his eyes return to the road, he begins picking up speed, ignoring the red light he just ran. I'd be lying if I said I didn't get a thrill out of Quinn wanting me desperately enough that he's willing to ignore the laws of the road.

Pulling up in front of my apartment, neither one of us says a word as Quinn parks his bike and we climb off. Taking my hand in his, he leads me from the parking lot and up the stairs to my door. The whole time I feel as if my heart is about to beat out of my chest. "Keys," he says with a husky tone, holding out his hand. Reaching into my pocket, I pull out my keys and place them in his palm. Still holding my hand, he unlocks my apartment door and leads me in. I don't get two steps inside before the door slams shut and my body is pressed against the wall as Quinn's mouth comes crashing down on mine. Grabbing my ass, he lifts me off the floor, and my legs wrap around his torso. His taste is electrifying. When his mouth is on mine, and his hands are on my body, I lose all senses. All that exists is us, and everything else around us fades away. "You feel it don't ya?" he asks, breaking our connection.

"Yes. I feel it," I admit, my voice barely a whisper.

Sliding down Quinn's body, I let out a small moan when I feel his impressive erection, and he growls. Taking hold of his hand, I take the lead this time, guiding us down the hallway to my bedroom. Once we are standing at the foot of my bed, I gently push against his chest urging him to sit. Allowing me to continue my lead which is something I never do, but thanks to liquid courage I don't hesitate, Quinn complies. I can tell by the set line in his jaw and his clenched fist he is fighting not to take over. With a smirk, I step back and decide to tease him a bit, see how long he can last before he takes what he wants. Grabbing the hem of my shirt, I slowly pull it off over my head exposing my sheer yellow bra that leaves nothing to the imagination. I smile when Quinn's eyes drop to my pert nipples that are visible through the sheer material. "Fuck, Sunshine," he hisses. Moving forward, I unbutton my jeans and slowly slide the zipper down. I then hook my thumbs into the waist and shimmy my hips while gliding them over my ass and down my legs revealing my matching yellow thong. It's in the exact moment I shed my jeans when Quinn's will power snaps and he can no longer hold back. In a flash, he is up off the bed taking one long stride to stand directly in front of me. Without a word, he begins to undress, starting by toeing off his boots. Next, he removes his cut and lays it on top of the dresser directly behind me. Quinn then grabs the back of his t-shirt and pulls it off over his head. By this time, my breaths are coming out in pants, and I become even more hyper-aware that this thing between us is finally happening. My finger twitches at the need to touch him. As if knowing what I want, Quinn speaks, "Touch me, Sunshine. Take what you want."

Swallowing past the lump in my throat, I lick my lips and do just that. I place my hands on his shoulder then bring them down over his chest and down along the hard ridge of his six-pack abs. By Quinn's labored breathing, I can tell he too is as affected by this moment. "Ask me, Emerson," he demands. "Tell me what you want."

Without a second thought, I answer him, "I want you to take me."

"With fuckin' pleasure, Sunshine." Scooping me up in his arms, Quinn strides to the bed, then lays me down. I watch as he strips off his jeans, and I gasp at the sight in front of me. Quinn has a frenum piercing—a barbell just above the head of his cock. I begin to rub my legs together imagining how it's going to feel inside me. "You like that, don't you, Sunshine?" Quinn asks while stroking his dick. "You can't wait to see how it feels when I fill your tight pussy?" At the sight of him stroking his cock, I slide my hand into the front of my panties wanting to ease the ache I have between my legs. When my finger comes in contact with my swollen clit, I close my eyes and let out a groan. "Eyes on me," Quinn barks. "You keep those beautiful eyes on me while you play with your pussy." Our actions come together in perfect synchronized motion. Just as I feel myself about to fall over the edge, Quinn is on me, tearing my hand away from my body.

"Your orgasm is mine."

As soon as those words leave his mouth, he rips my panties from me and latches his mouth onto my pussy, sucking my clit into his mouth, giving me no choice but to scream out his name as my orgasm consumes my entire body. Quinn continues to lap up my essence until the last tremor has left my body, leaving me completely sated.

Bringing his body flush against mine, I wrap my arms around his neck as he claims my mouth. His tongue coaxes mine to open, and when I do, I can taste myself on him. Breaking our kiss, he rests his forehead on mine, "Tell me you're mine."

"I'm yours." As soon as the words leave my lips, he fills me with one slow thrust. My nails dig into his back at the burning as the exquisite sensation of being so full takes over. I lift my hips seeking more of him. There is a hunger in me fueled only by Quinn. "More!" I cry out.

"No," he says, denying me what I ask for. "I'm going to take my time with you. I've waited too long for this to be over so fast. I'm going to fill this hungry pussy, and I'm going to take all night doing it."

I have no doubt Quinn will make good on his promise. So, I decide not to fight it. I let him set the pace while I revel in the way he makes me feel. "I knew it would feel like this," he tells me, angling his hips in a way that takes him deeper than he was before.

"Like what?"

"Like coming home," Quinn admits, looking at me like I mean something to him—like I'm everything. His gaze is so intense I can't help but look away.

"Eyes," he demands again with sheer dominance. This time when I comply, no more words are spoken. Quinn lets his body; his actions do the talking. Moments later, I feel another orgasm building and Quinn must feel it too because he bends his head down and takes my nipple in his mouth. I don't even remember the moment he rid me of my bra. As soon as he bites down on my piercing, it sends a jolt of electricity straight to my clit, and bright flashes of light fill my vision. "That's it, Sunshine. Come—come all over my cock and take me with you."

I do just that. On his command, I come. I come harder than I ever have before. As I'm coming, Quinn scoops me up into his arms so that we are now chest to chest with my legs wrapped around his waist and his cock buried deep inside of me. We come together with his name on my lips, and the *mine* roaring from his.

Minutes pass, and neither of us makes a move. We stay in the position of Quinn holding me as my breathing settles, and my body goes lax. There is a moment right before I fall asleep while we lie facing each other chest to chest that I feel our hearts beating together as one, and I wonder if he can feel it.

"I feel it, Sunshine," I hear Quinn say just before drifting off to sleep.

BLINKING MY EYES OPEN, it takes me a moment to remember last night's events.

The soreness between my legs is all the reminder I need. Stretching out my limbs, I realize an arm is halting my movements. Looking over my shoulder, I see Quinn fast asleep with his arm draped across my stomach. I didn't expect him to be here still. I figured he would have left last night after I fell asleep. Glancing at the clock on the table beside my bed, I see it's only four o'clock in the morning. My shift doesn't start until six o'clock but I decide I'd rather not deal with the "morning after" awkwardness, so I'm going to head to work early. I'm sure Quinn can show himself out. Carefully slipping his arm off me, I slide out of bed hoping I don't wake him. Once I see he's dead to the world, I quickly throw on a pair of scrubs then grab an extra pair, throwing them in a bag along with a few things from my bathroom. I can take a shower at the gym before my shift. I might as well get a workout in since I have some time to kill. After I've gathered all my things, I slip out of my apartment. Thankfully the Uber I called is already waiting on me to take me to get my Jeep. For a brief moment I worry Quinn will be pissed I left without telling him but then brush it off. He'll probably be relieved. I'm sure now that he's gotten what he's been after for so long he's done. Quinn got one night, and now I'm out of his system. A knot forms in the pit of my stomach at the thought. "You sure this is the place ma'am?" the driver asks me, stopping in front of the clubhouse. "Yeah, this is it," I say as I step out of the car and walk up to the gate.

"What ya doing here so early, doc?" Sean asks me.

"Just come to pick up my car."

"Why didn't ya have Quinn bring you, sweetheart?" he asks, pointing at the Uber that just left. *Of course, he noticed I left with Quinn.* I'm sure he's not the only one either, but I am not ready to answer anyone's questions. Seeing the look on my face, Sean shuts his mouth and lets me in the gate to get my Jeep.

Later that day, I'm sitting in the doctor's lounge, finishing the last of my paperwork for the day when Dr. Givens walks in. "How's it going, Emerson?" she asks, making her way to her locker.

"It's been a busy day. I didn't even get a break for lunch, but luckily all is quiet now." I smile.

Looking at her watch, she replies, "You only have thirty minutes left of your shift. Why don't you knock off early? I'll cover for you."

"Really? Are you sure you don't mind?"

"Not at all. Go on down to the cafeteria and get you something to eat before you pass out. You look dead on your feet, Emerson."

"Alright, thanks," I sigh. "I owe you one."

Leaving the lounge, I make my way down the hall to the

elevator, and I'm met with a familiar face and smile. "Hey Christy, how are you?" Christy is a social worker. I met her during my first week at the hospital, and we became quick friends. She is usually the social worker sent when the hospital has the misfortune of needing child services. She is the best social worker in Polson if you ask me. Christy doesn't just treat children as if they are her job. She cares about those kids and will go above and beyond when it comes to their well-being. She's also the same social worker who I called in a favor for Bella and Logan when they wanted to adopt Breanna. She had a big hand in making sure Breanna was placed with them while waiting on the adoption process.

"Hi, Emerson. You on your way out?"

"Yeah, but I was going to stop by the cafeteria and grab a bite to eat."

"Mind if I join you? I was headed back to the office, but since I have a mountain of paperwork, I doubt I'll make it home in time for dinner."

"I'd love for you to join me."

After making our way into the cafeteria, we grab our food and decide to sit at one of the tables outside since the weather is warm, and there is a gentle evening breeze. We eat in silence for a minute before Christy speaks up. "Something is different about you, but I can't put my finger on it. You look, I don't know, relaxed and glowy."

"Glowy? Really?" I giggle.

"You know what I mean." She nudges me with her elbow.

"So, how's your husband?" I ask, trying to change the conversation.

"Oh no, you don't, Emerson. Come on, you can tell me."

Rolling my eyes, I give in. "It's nothing. I just had a good time this weekend with some friends."

"Was one of those friends a man? Come on, tell me, who was it?"

"His name is Quinn."

"Quinn Beckett?" she asks, and I snap my head in her direction. "You know Quinn?"

"Of course. He volunteers down at the youth center. He has for as long as I can remember. He's a great guy and great with the kids." I sit stunned for a moment at the realization at how little I know about Quinn, though not surprised at all the good he does. Christy brings me out of my thoughts when she stands and tosses her trash in the bin. "Well, I need to be going if I want to make it home to my husband at a decent time. But don't think this conversation is over. I want to hear all the juicy details about you and Quinn later."

Waving my hand dismissively, I tell her, "There's nothing to tell, Quinn is only a friend." The words taste bitter on my tongue the moment they leave my mouth. Christy looks at me like she doesn't believe me but doesn't say any more about the subject. Once Christy and I part ways with a promise to catch up with each other again later this week, I round the corner of the front entrance of the emergency room toward the parking lot when I see Quinn sitting on his bike next to my Jeep. My steps falter. The look currently directed in my direction is one I have not seen before. Quinn looks pissed. Forcing my legs to work, I walk in his direction. Stepping in front of him, I go to open my mouth only to have him swiftly shut me down. "Don't," he grits out. "I don't know what's goin' on inside that pretty head of yours, babe, but apparently between the time my cock was buried deep inside your pussy last night to this morning when you snuck out of bed you forgot that **you are mine.** So, the only thing you're going to do right now is get your ass on the back of my bike, so I can take you home and remind you."

I stand there staring at him in silence until he thrusts his helmet toward me and growls, "Now, Sunshine." Doing what he demands, I put the helmet on, place my hand on his shoulder, and climb on the back of his bike. Once settled with my arms wrapped around his waist, Quinn turns his head slightly and looks at me over his shoulder. "You pull another stunt like you did this morning, I'll redden your ass so good you'll carry my mark for a week."

My breath hitches at the promise as he fires up his bike and takes off in the direction of my apartment.

QUINN

There are no words to describe how pissed off I am right now at my woman, and she *is* my woman. I didn't do a good enough job last night proving to her she now belongs to me. I lied when I told her I didn't know what was going through her head when she snuck her ass out of her apartment this morning. I know what she was thinking. Emerson thought last night was a one-time deal, but she is very fuckin' wrong. I'm about to show my Sunshine how wrong she was.

As we both walk silently up to her apartment with me trailing behind her, she keeps tossing nervous glances over her shoulder. When Emerson unlocks her front door, I follow her inside and kick it shut with my foot. The sound of the door slamming shut vibrates off the living room walls, and it causes her to jump. "Room!" I bark. Setting her bag and keys down on the kitchen counter, Emerson, without so much as a peep, makes her way down the hall and into her room with me on her heels. Once we're standing in front of the dresser, she turns to face me, and when she goes to open her mouth, I cut her off. "Clothes off now."

"What?" Emerson sputters, "Now? I thought we were going to talk?"

"Nope. It appears talking doesn't work. I told you last night you were mine. You don't believe me, so I'm going to show you. Now strip."

I watch as Emerson contemplates her next move but only for a second before she does what I say. My cock grows harder and harder with every piece of clothing she sheds, and a wicked thought comes to mind. "Where is your white coat? The one you wear at work?" Standing before me completely naked, Emerson licks her lips and answers with a confused look.

"At work. I usually leave it in my locker."

Taking two strides, I come to stand toe to toe in front of her. Reaching up with my left hand, I grab a fist full of her blonde hair and force her head to tip back to where she is looking at me. I then take my other hand and cup the heavy weight of her full breast using my thumb to tweak her piercing, my actions causing her to whimper. "Next time you go to work, I want ya to bring it home. I want to fuck you in nothing but that white coat." I wouldn't be surprised if the girls have told Emerson about my little fetish. It's not something I need, just something I enjoy from time to time. Nothing wrong with being a little creative and having some fun. The thought alone of having Emerson ride my cock while wearing that white coat and a stethoscope around her neck has me ready to come in my jeans. By the look on my woman's face, I'd say she likes that idea too. *Fuck, I knew she would be perfect for me.*

"Turn around and place your hands on the dresser," I instruct, letting go of her hair. Doing as I say, she places both palms flat on the dresser and meets my eyes in the mirror as I come to stand behind her. Taking my cut off, I turn and lay it in the bed. Next, I pull my t-shirt off and watch Emerson's pupils dilate at the sight of my bare chest. I then move on to my jeans and pop open the button and unzip them but keep my throbbing cock under wraps for now. Grabbing Emerson's hips, I thrust them out toward me and rub her ass on my jean-covered erection. "Fuck," I hiss. "I can feel the heat of your pussy through my jeans. Tell me, Sunshine, is your pussy greedy for my cock again?"

"Yes," she moans while she shamelessly grinds on my dick. Emerson lets out a whimper when I step back, slightly breaking our connection.

"Well, your pussy is going to have to wait, babe, because right now, my cock wants your mouth." Without a moment of hesitation, Emerson spins around and drops to her knees. "I see your mouth is as hungry for my cock as your pussy is, isn't it, baby?" Her only response is licking her lips as she reaches into my jeans and pulls out my dick. She doesn't waste any time taking me in her warm wet mouth. It's all I can do not to come right then. I have imagined this moment hundreds of times, but my dreams have nothing on the real thing. "God damn baby, your mouth feels like fuckin' heaven." Several beats later, I begin to feel a tingle at the base of my spine, so I fist Emerson's hair and pull her off my cock. "That was so fuckin' good, but when I come, I'm going to do it inside you. Now get on the bed— on all fours."

As Emerson climbs on the bed, I toe off my boots and shuck my jeans. Before tossing them to the floor, I reach into my pocket and retrieve what I picked up at the store earlier and throw it to the bed beside her. Snapping her head in my direction, she gives me a wild yet nervous look. Settling myself behind her, I run my palm down her back and between her ass cheeks, brushing my thumb over her forbidden spot, and I feel her tense. "Has anyone ever taken you here?" I ask, already knowing the answer.

"No," she answers with a bit of apprehension in her voice.

"I want to claim all of you. Will you let me?" When her breathing picks up, and she doesn't answer me right away, I try to soothe her worries. "You know I would never hurt you right, Sunshine?"

"I know you wouldn't, Quinn. I trust you."

Emerson's words and trust in me fills my chest with something I've never felt before. Leaning over her body, I pepper kisses along her neck and shoulders while rubbing my cock through the wet folds of her pussy. Retrieving the bottle of lube, I pop the cap and pour a generous amount in my hand and rub it all over my cock. I then use the same hand to rub over her backside. My fingers glide from the top of her ass down to her pussy, getting her nice and ready for me. "I'm going to take this slow," I soothe as I start to penetrate her tight barrier with my thumb.

"Oh God," she says, her breath hitching.

"Relax, baby. I promise it's going to feel good." After working my finger in and out a few times, I feel her body slack, and she starts to thrust back seeking more. Taking that as my green light, I remove my thumb, grab the base of my cock, and guide the head into her tight hole. Reaching around her hip, I find her swollen clit and begin to rub.

"Yes," she moans. I use small thrusts, and with each one, she takes more and more of me inside her until I am fully seated. "Fuck, you're perfect," I grit.

"I feel so full." Gripping the sheets, Emerson turns her heated eyes to me. "I need more Quinn. I need you to move."

Growling, I pull out then surge forward, giving her what she needs.

"Yes!" she screams.

"You like my cock in your ass, don't ya?"

"Stroke your clit, baby. Take yourself there and bring me with you."

As soon as she brings her hand between her legs and strums her swollen bud, she flies over the edge, screaming my name, and her cries of pleasure have me falling over with her.

Thirty minutes later, after I carried a sated Emerson into the shower and proceeded to worship every inch of her body as I washed it, I carry her back to bed. Now we both lay here with her draped over my chest and I ask her a question about something I've wanted to know the answer to for over a year. "Why a peacock?" I remember the first time I saw her tattoo. We were at one of the kid's birthday parties, and Emerson was in a bikini with her tats on full display, shocking everyone.

"A peacock is proud, confident, and not afraid to show their colors. That's what I aspire to be like," she tells me in an almost sad tone.

"What do you mean? What are you afraid of?"

"I'm afraid of disappointing people. Mainly my parents."

What the fuck? Emerson's admission has me sitting up in bed. Following my movement, she straightens herself while keeping the blanket clutched to her chest.

"How could you say something like that? You could never be a disappointment. And fuck anyone who doesn't agree with what you do. You're a doctor for Christ sakes babe; you don't get much better than that."

"Not according to my parents," she sighs. "Look, my mom and dad are great. They love me, and I had a good childhood, but they push too hard, you know. They feel I could be doing more with my life."

"Like what?" I spit out.

"Well, like where I work, for example. My parents feel I should be putting my skills to use at some well-known fancy hospital and eventually work my way up the ladder just as they have."

"And what do you want, Sunshine?" A big smile takes over her face at my question.

"I want my own small family practice. I'd like it to be here in Polson. I love living in a small town. I want something slower paced—more personal. I love helping people, but I also love getting to know them. I want to know their stories. Working in the ER, everything is fast-paced. I don't even have time to learn my patient's name. You know what I mean?" Shaking her head, she looks down with a somber look on her face. "Sounds stupid, don't it?"

Using my finger, I tip her chin, bringing her eyes to look at mine. "It doesn't sound stupid at all, babe. Sounds like a pretty kickass plan to me. I think you should go for it. Open your clinic. That's just the kind of place Polson needs. This is your life, Emerson. You shouldn't give a fuck what anyone thinks, your parents included."

"What about you?" she asks, turning the subject around on me. "Were your parents upset at your decision to join the MC?"

"Hell no. My parents supported my choice from day one. We moved from California to Polson when I was in high school. My mom is a psychiatrist, and her mentor had offered her a job working with her. High school is where I first met Logan and Reid. Some douchebag bully was kickin' my ass in the bathroom at school one day. Logan and Reid saw what was going on and stepped in. From that day forward, I latched on to those two like white on rice. Fuckers didn't have a chance in hell of gettin' rid of me after that. I designated myself as their new best friend. It didn't take them long to accept what was," I say with a smirk.

"Yeah, I think I'm beginning to learn you don't give up too easily," she teases.

"Not when I know something is worth it, I don't," I level her with a look letting my words sink in before I continue.

"Anyway, that very same day I began hangin' with Logan and Reid they started bringing me around the club. That's when I met Jake and everyone else. I knew right away the club was where I belonged. I can't explain it."

"I get it," she says, cutting me off. "The club is amazing. I can see why you chose to be a part of it."

Grinning, I lean down and take her mouth with mine. "I knew

you would be perfect for me. I've known for a long damn time, Sunshine."

"Oh, really? When did you know?"

"The second time I saw you. When you walked into Alba's hospital room, I knew right then you were supposed to be mine. Fate brought you to Polson and me. One thing my father taught me was when God brings the right woman into your life, you do whatever necessary to make her yours. My dad should know, he chased after Mom for months before she finally gave in, and they've been together ever since. Close to thirty years."

"Will you tell me about them? About you and them?" Emerson asks nervously. Only she shouldn't be.

"You talkin' about my adoption?"

"If it's something you don't like talking about, we don't have to," she is quick to throw out. Leaning back against the headboard, I snag Emerson around her waist and haul her up with me, letting her rest her head on my chest.

"My adoption is not a sore subject, Sunshine. It's very simple. My birth parents were young when they had me, still in high school. Both knew they would not be able to provide for a child. So, they figured adoption was best. Mom and Dad tried for several years to get pregnant, but her doctor said their chances were slim to none. Long story short, they adopted me."

"Have you ever met your birth parents?"

"No. I know who they are and where they live but have never had the desire to meet them. They are both married to different people and seem happy. Plus, I'm happy. I have two of the greatest parents anyone could ever hope for." We sit in silence for a beat while she soaks in the information I just handed before she asks her next question.

"What about your sister?"

A huge smile takes over my face at the mention of Kat. "Kat was a surprise. My parents were blown away when they discovered my mom was pregnant. I was already in high school when she came along. Katalina is smart, beautiful, sassy, and has me wrapped around her finger."

"I'll bet she does," Emerson says, letting out a yawn.

Tucking her in closer to my side, I kiss the top of her head. "That's enough storytellin' for now. Let's get some sleep. I'm going to want your pussy one more time before work tomorrow." My comment earns me a giggle from Emerson. Silence fills the room a minute before I ask. "Emerson?"

"Yeah?"

"Give me the words."

"I'm yours."

"That's my girl."

"Goodnight, Quinn."

"Night, Sunshine."

THE NEXT MORNING I'm walking into work after dropping Emerson off at the hospital when Jake walks out of his office with a grim expression on his face. "What's up, Prez?"

"I want you to go down to Charley's. He just called. Said he had a couple of bikers in there, and they were not any of ours." His new-found information has me on high alert, and I think back to the incident I had with the fucker who almost ran me off the road. "On it, Prez," I say, turning on my heel and make my way back out to my bike. "Gabriel is going to meet you there," Jake adds. Gabriel and I arrive at Charley's at the same time. We acknowledge each other with a chin lift as we walk into the bar with the intention of seeing who the hell these motherfuckers are.

Charley steps around the bar when he sees us walk in. "They're gone. High-tailed their asses out of here about five minutes ago. They might have suspected something when they saw me on the phone. Anybody who's anybody knows my loyalty lies with The Kings. Any respectable club would know not to show up on another club's territory without proper notice."

"You recognize either one of them?" I ask while Gabriel remains silent as he looks around the bar on high alert.

"No, I never saw them before. They had Satan's Reapers cuts on. I will tell you this, though; there's trouble there. I felt it in my bones as soon as they strode their asses into my bar."

"Fuck," I curse under my breath. "Alright, Charley. Thanks for lettin' us know. Did you get that feed for us? I'll pass it along to Reid. See what he can dig up."

"Sure do. Here ya go," he says, handing me the USB with today's security feed on it.

"You want me to send one of the guys down here to watch over the place?"

"That won't be necessary, son," he tells me, lifting his flannel shirt, revealing his piece strapped to his side.

Smirking, I clap Charley on his back. "We'll catch ya later, man. Call us if ya need anything." With that, Gabriel and I make our way back out of the bar and to our bikes. We share a look. A look that says that shit is about to hit the fan here in Polson. These sons of bitches don't know who they are fuckin' with, but they're about to find out.

8

EMERSON

I'm standing at my locker in the lounge at work when my phone alerts me to a text. Pulling it from my pocket, I smile, and my stomach is overcome with butterflies when I see who it's from.

Quinn: *Miss me?*

Me: *Maybe.*

Quinn: *Admit it, Sunshine.*

Me: *Don't flatter yourself.*

Quinn: *I know that sweet pussy of yours misses me.*

I feel my cheeks flush at his last text. He's not wrong. My lady bits start to tingle at the memory of the dirty things Quinn did to my body last night.

Quinn: *I'll take your silence as a yes.*

Me: *Is there something you needed?*

Quinn: *I want you to come straight to the clubhouse after work. I know your shift ended ten minutes ago. I'll see you in fifteen.*

Me: *What if I had plans?*

Quinn: *You do. With my cock.*

Me: *On my way.*

Giggling to myself, I shove my phone back in my pocket. No way am I going to argue with that because let's face it, he's not wrong. Opening my locker, I take the large manila envelope my brother had delivered to me earlier and place it in my bag. Then I slip my lab coat off, but when I go to place it on the hanger, my mind drifts back to what Quinn requested last night, and with a grin, I fold it and put it in my bag as well.

Fifteen minutes later, I pull up outside the clubhouse to see Quinn leaning against the wall waiting on me. He wastes no time striding to my Jeep, pulling open the door and hauling me into his chest, and searing my mouth with a brutal kiss. Quinn kisses me as if he craves my taste. Once he's had his fill, he sets me down on my feet and takes my hand in his. "Come on, babe. Let's go inside."

I walk beside him across the clubhouse parking lot hand in hand. When I scan the lot, I see Bella's car, and Alba's truck is here. I suddenly become nervous because this will be mine and Quinn's first public display. When we walk inside together, holding hands, it will show everyone we are together. It makes this thing between us feel more official. As if he senses what I'm thinking Quinn squeezes my hand and I look up at his handsome face only to see him grinning from ear to ear. "How come you look like a little boy with a shiny new toy who can't wait for show and tell?"

"Because I've been waitin' for this moment for a long fuckin' time. I've claimed my Sunshine, and now everyone is going to know."

Damn, when he puts it like that, I can't help but smile back. With unfaltering steps, we walk inside. The slam of the door behind us grabs the attention of everyone in the room. Both Bella and Alba look at me knowingly while Logan, Gabriel, Reid, and Jake bang their beer bottles on the bar and cheer.

"Your ass owes me fifty bucks, son," Jake announces, clapping

Logan on his back. Pulling out his wallet, he takes out some cash and slaps it on the bar.

"What the hell are you two assholes bettin' on?" This came from Quinn. It's Logan who speaks up. "Prez and I had a bet going on how long it would take you two to finally get your shit together. I said it would take your ass at least another year to seal the deal, but Prez here said three months. That was two months ago."

"What about your grumpy ass?" Quinn asks, turning his attention to Gabriel, who has remained quiet. All we get is a grunt in response, then see Alba walk up to her husband with her hand held out. Quinn's mouth falls open when Gabriel passes Alba a few bills, and she tucks them away in her pocket with a triumphant look on her pretty face. "His bet was with me."

"Well, I'm glad to see some of ya have some confidence in me."

"Don't go gettin' all sensitive on us, brother. We knew it would happen eventually," Logan chimes in.

"So, what are your plans tonight?" Bella asks, cutting in. "You two want to come to the house for supper?"

"Hell, yeah, darlin'! You know I won't turn down your cookin'," Quinn says, rubbing his hands together.

"I can't tonight," I throw in. Digging into my bag, I pull out the envelope my brother sent earlier. "And if all of you all are game, I have somewhere I'd like to take you."

Quinn looks at me with confusion. "What you got in there, babe?"

"Tickets to go see East of Addiction in Missoula."

"No fucking way!" Logan booms jumping up from his bar stool. "How the hell did you get those? They've been sold out for weeks."

I shrug my shoulders, "I have my ways. So, what do you guys say? Can you get someone to watch the kids?"

"Already taken care of," Bella announces, holding up her phone. "Sofia and Leah have agreed to watch the kids at mine and

Logan's place." Turning to Jake, she continues, "I even called Grace, she's taking Remi over there now, and she will meet us here, and since Alba and Gabriel's kids are already there, then everything is settled."

Everyone looks at Bella with an amused expression. "Don't look at me like that. Momma needs a night out on the town. Now let's get moving people. Alba, Emerson, let's go upstairs and get ready." With that, she turns on her heel and makes her way upstairs. Alba and I share a look before shrugging our shoulders and follow behind.

An hour later, we're cruising down the road headed for Missoula with Jake leading the way. Directly behind him to the right is Logan, next to Logan is Reid. Behind Reid is Quinn and me, and riding beside us is Gabriel and Alba. Quinn explained to me earlier this is the formation they ride in when they are all together. It's a sight to see how they ride together in sync. The way they follow their fierce leader and command the road is beautiful. An hour later, heads turn as we pull into the parking lot of the outdoor amphitheater, my brother and his band are playing. I'm amped with excitement to see him. It's been months.

"How good are our seats?" Alba asks, climbing off Gabriel's bike. When she takes her helmet off Alba shakes out her long blonde locks, and draws the attention from several red-blooded men walking by. One dipshit, in particular, walks pass and comes a little too close for Gabriel's liking. So close that the six-foot-four Cuban steps in front of the unsuspecting guy causing him to crash right into Gabriel's chest. Stumbling back a few steps in shock, the poor kid finally takes in his current surroundings and notices the man that has blocked his path and the cut he is wearing. "If you want to keep those eyes of yours, I suggest they not look at my woman again," Gabriel warns. Frantically nodding his head, the guy looks at Jake, Reid, and Quinn who have gathered at Gabriel's side. After agreeing, the guy makes a hasty retreat. Hopefully, he'll spread the word, and we can avoid another incident. I look over at Alba to see her rolling her eyes. I'm sure she's used to her husband's protectiveness by now.

"To answer your question, we're front row," I say after the show of dominance has ended.

"No shit, Sunshine? How'd you pull that off?" Quinn asks, snagging me around my waist.

"I told you I have connections. Now come on. I have backstage passes too." With that, I take Quinn's hand and lead my friends through the seating area and around the corner of the stage toward the back. Arriving at a long hallway filled with staff members, roadies, and barely dressed groupies, I spy a familiar face.

"Em! Is that you, girl?" Teddy, a huge burly man who is a part of my brother's security greets me. "Hi, Teddy! Have you seen..." I don't get to finish my sentence when my brother, shouting my name, answers it. I see him walk out of a room at the end of the hall with a massive smile on his face that mirrors my own. I break away from Quinn and run as fast as my legs will carry me and jump into Easton's waiting arms, and we hug the shit out of each other. A minute later, our happy reunion is broken up when Quinn snatches me from my brother's arms and stands toe to toe with him.

"Want to tell me what the fuck is going on here?" His enraged voice vibrates off the walls.

I nervously look to my brother, but he doesn't back down and rewards Quinn with an arrogant smirk. Easton knows all about Quinn, and if I know my brother, he will use this opportunity to mess with him. The last thing I want is a fight to break out and for someone to end up hurt or in jail, so I quickly step in. Placing my hand on Quinn's chest, I bring his attention to me.

"Quinn, I'd like you to meet my brother Easton. East, this is

Quinn." At the mention of the word brother Quinn loses the rage that was in his eyes moments ago and visibly relaxes.

"Brother?"

"Yes. Easton is my twin brother, and he's the lead singer for East of Addiction."

"Holy shit!" I hear Logan say from somewhere behind us.

"Why the hell didn't ya tell me this before, babe? Instead, you had me thinkin' I was about to have to rip someone's head off!"

"I was. I planned on introducing you tonight."

"So, you're telling me not only do you have a brother, but he's your twin, and he also happens to be the singer for one of the hottest bands in the world right now?"

I shrug. "Um, yeah, that's what I'm saying."

"Always full of surprises, aren't you, Sunshine?" Quinn teases, then turns his attention to my brother and offers his hand. "Nice to meet ya, man."

"You too, Quinn. Em hasn't stopped talking about you. Every time we talk, it's Quinn this, and Quinn that. Oww!" Easton grunts when I punch him in his stomach.

"No, I do not, East! You better quit lying," I fuss, but the damage is already done. No way is Quinn going to let this shit go. I'm proven right when he opens his mouth.

"Oh, really? Tell me, baby, what kinds of stuff you tellin' him? You tell him how much of a sexy motherfucker I am?" he taunts, and my face flushes with embarrassment.

Pointing my finger at my brother, I give him fair warning, "You'll pay for this, asshole!"

"Looking forward to it, Sis," Easton says as he retreats, walking backward. "You guys enjoy the show."

I look around at all the people crowding the hall and the dozens of groupies who are lined up outside my brother's dressing room door with the hopes of being the lucky chosen one he beds tonight. Then a wicked thought comes to mind.

"Mr. Evans!" I shout, getting Easton's attention. "As your doctor, I highly advise you to refrain from all sexual activity until the rash and inflammation has cleared up. Also, don't forget to take those antibiotics I prescribed!" Now it's my brother's turn to be embarrassed. The hall goes completely silent, and several of the skanky women who minutes ago were waiting to get chosen, look at him with horror then make a hasty retreat as fast as their hooker shoes will carry them.

Narrowing his eyes at me, Easton declares, "This means war." Then he disappears into his dressing room while I double over in laughter.

After the best concert I have ever seen, Easton invites everyone back to his hotel suite for drinks. I love how my brother doesn't even bat an eye at four large bikers standing in his room. He's completely unjudging. About an hour into our visit, Jake receives a phone call that changes his entire demeanor, and it doesn't go unnoticed by the guys who are suddenly on high alert.

"There a problem, Prez?" Quinn asks.

"Time to roll out," is all he offers in a clipped tone. Without question, Logan, Gabriel, and Reid move into action with their woman in tow.

"Time to go, babe," Quinn tells me. "Go on and tell your brother goodbye." Nodding, I walk over to Easton, who has a concerned look on his face. "Everything alright, Em?"

"Yeah, we just need to get going."

My brother looks over to Quinn, who has come up beside me. "Should I be worried about my sister?" he asks, getting straight to the point.

Quinn answers him with genuine conviction in his tone. "Never. Emerson is always safe with my club and me. I promise ya that."

Seeing the truth in Quinn's eyes, my brother offers his hand,

and Quinn accepts. "Then we're cool. She's the most important person in my life."

Quinn nods. "That makes two of us."

We make it back to the clubhouse in record time and are met by Bennett and Lisa. Immediately, the men go straight to the room they hold church in while we women sit at the bar and wonder what the hell is going on.

9

QUINN

"Babe, stop fidgeting. You have nothing to be nervous about."

"Quinn! You said we were going to hang at Charley's for a bit when you called this morning. You failed to mention we were going to visit your parents too," Emerson fires back, crossing her arms over her chest.

I called Emerson this morning, saying I wanted to take her to Charley's for lunch and drinks. When I picked her up at her apartment in my car instead of my bike she didn't think anything of it until she climbed in and I informed her that I needed to stop by my parent's house and drop off some car parts I ordered for my dad while pointing to several boxes sitting on my back seat.

"I can't believe you would spring this on me. Scratch that, yes, I can. This is such a Quinn thing to do," she grumbles. "Always pushing boundaries. I don't see why you can't just drop this stuff off, then come back for me, or I can meet up with you at Charley's when you're done."

"Hell no, it's time for you to officially meet them, babe. Besides, they've known about you for a long time."

"What! What do you mean they know about me? This thing

between us just started," Emerson says, gesturing back and forth between us with her finger.

"We might have just become official, Em, but you've always been mine. My mom and dad have always known about my feelings for you. Hell, my dad is the one who encouraged me to keep going after what I want. My dad practically stalked my mom until she caved."

"Great, now I know where you get your crazy from," she remarks, rolling her eyes.

"Admit it. You like my crazy, don't ya, Sunshine." Ignoring my question, she huffs out a frustrated breath and turns to look out the window. My booming laugh only pisses her off more, and she ignores me the rest of the drive there.

When we arrive at my parent's house fifteen minutes later, Emerson and I are greeted by my sister running down the steps of the porch and heading in our direction. I don't make it two steps out of my car before she launches herself into my arms. "How's it goin', KitKat?"

"Good," she says when I set her back down on her feet. "Hi, Ms. Evans," Kat greets Emerson with a wave. They met months ago at the club when we were on lockdown. She even met my parents then, so I don't get what she's so nervous about.

"Hi, Kat. Please call me Emerson." She smiles.

Taking hold of Emerson's hand, I lead her across the lawn and up the porch steps just as my mom and dad walk out the front door to greet us. My mom is the first to speak. "It's good to see you again, Emerson." She pulls her in for a hug.

"You too, Mrs. Beckett."

"Oh honey, please call me Vicky, and you remember my husband Quinten?" She gestures to my dad.

"Of course. It's nice to see you again."

"Mom, why don't ya take Em inside while Dad helps me with the parts I ordered him?"

"Sure, sweetheart. Come on, honey. I just put some coffee on."

I give Emerson a wink and walk off with my dad as she looks at me with pleading eyes.

Two hours later, we are back on the road after leaving my parents' house and headed to Charley's. "It wasn't so bad now, was it, babe?"

"No, and I really like your mom. I've never been in a serious relationship and met the parents before. This is all new to me."

"This shit is new to me, too, Sunshine. I've never dated anyone seriously or met a woman's parents before either. I know there will come a time when I meet yours too." At the mention of her parents, Emerson visibly tenses. *Fuck, maybe she doesn't want me to meet them. Maybe she is embarrassed because I'm a biker?* Pushing the thought away, I decide not to question her about it. The way Emerson spoke about her parents before has me thinking they are a sore subject, and I don't want to ruin a good day by bringing them up.

"Quinn, my boy. How ya doing?" Charley asks when we walk into the bar. "And who's this pretty young lady you got with ya?"

"Hey, Charley. This is my old lady, Emerson. I told her you make the best Philly Cheese Steak sandwiches, so we thought we'd come by and fill our bellies up."

"You come to the right place, sweetheart. Let me grab you guys a couple of beers, and I'll go fire up the grill."

After Charley delivers our beers, I turn to Emerson. "I'll be right back, babe. I've got to hit the head." Several minutes later, I finish my business. When I walk out of the bathroom, I come to a dead stop, and an icy chill runs down my spine before the devil himself lights a fire under my ass because standing at the bar flanking my woman are two bikers, and they don't belong to The Kings.

Adrenaline takes over, and in two seconds flat, I have the barrel of my gun pressed against the back of some piece of shit's head.

"I'm thinkin' you must be lost motherfucker. Either that or you're stupid for thinkin' you can waltz up into Kings territory. My bet is on the latter," I grind out, my voice dripping with venom. I can't help but notice the look of pure fear on my Sunshine's face. Cocking my gun, I pray the pussy tries something stupid so that I have an excuse to paint the bar with his brains.

Stepping around the man in front of me, I grab Emerson by the arm and bring her to my side. It's then I get my first look at the fucker's face. I instantly recognize who he is. The son of a bitch in front of me is the prospect who rode to Polson with our Louisiana chapter a while back. The same prospect who tried to rape my woman. He goes by the name Twiggy. The fucker is scrawny as hell and has stringy, greasy hair. "I see I didn't teach you enough of a lesson last time we met." I snarl, "I should have blown your head off when I had the chance."

Hearing Emerson cry and the vile things coming from some motherfucker's mouth as I walk around the corner of the clubhouse has me seeing red. It's when I hear the audible sound of her being slapped that had me drawing my gun and ready to paint the wall with his insides. Once Emerson was in my sights, I could tell by her behavior something wasn't right, and there was a good possibility she had been drugged. She was out of it. I've never known Em to drink more than one or two beers in a single sitting.

Logan knew I was about to kill the prospect for what he had done. He gave me a look that told me it wasn't my place because the guy belonged to Riggs. Thirty minutes later, the prospect was sent packin', but that alone wasn't good enough for me. Not after what he did to my Sunshine. Leaving out the back door, I make my way around the front of my bike. A few people are milling around, but nobody questions me leaving. I make it about five miles down the road when I spot the prospect pushing his bike. He stops and turns around when he hears me pull up behind him. I see a flash of fear cross his face before my fist connects with his jaw, and I feel his bones shatter at the contact. I deliver blow after blow until he is nothing but a bloody, unrecognizable heap of shit lying at my feet.

When I return to the clubhouse, I take a seat at the bar and down a cold beer. Logan notices my bloody and swollen knuckles but doesn't say a word. I could get into some serious shit for what I just did because Riggs handled the situation the way he saw fit. I know what my brother was thinkin'; he would have done the same thing had it been Bella. Consequences be damned.

I'm brought back to the present when I hear Emerson gasp. I notice the other biker out of the corner of my eye about ten feet to my left and take in the blade he has in his hand. "Get down!" I holler to Emerson the same time I push her to the floor against the bar as I use the butt of my gun to clock the guy in front of me in the back of his head, then raise my left arm to block the blow from the knife coming at me from the other guy. Just as I'm about to aim my gun at the fucker holding the knife, the prospect lands a barstool across my back, bringing me to my knees, and I hear Emerson scream my name. Two gunshots ring out, and I am back on my feet with my gun raised, searching for my target only to come up to an empty bar. Looking behind me, I see Charley with a shotgun in his hand pointed at the now blown-up door. "I called Jake. The guys are on their way," Charley announces.

I go to make my way to my woman, but she beats me to it. "Oh my God, Quinn! Are you okay? Let me look at you," she cries and goes into doctor mode.

"I'm okay, baby. It's nothing I can't handle."

"You just had some asshole break a bar stool over your back, Quinn!" Pulling her into my chest, I wrap my arms around her and hold her close. As soon as Emerson's head meets my chest, she breaks down into sobs.

"Everything is going to be okay, baby, I promise." Seconds later, I hear the rumble of Harleys, letting me know my brothers are here. The energy in the room turns electric when Prez,

Logan, Gabriel and Reid walk in. Prez takes in Emerson who is still softly crying in my arms then cuts his eyes around the room taking in his surroundings. "You okay, son?" he asks with concern.

"Yeah, Prez, we're good."

Jake strides over to Charley, and they exchange a few words before he barks out orders. "I want all the women and children at the clubhouse now. Charley is going to close the bar for a few days. I called Grey over here to fix his door. I expect to see all of you back at the clubhouse in an hour for church. For now, I only want women and children on lockdown. Once we assess the threat, then I'll choose whether to extend it to the rest of our family." Turning his attention back to me, Prez asks, "Those cocksuckers say anything to you?"

"Not a word, brother."

"Um..." Emerson interrupts. "One of them spoke to me. The one that hit Quinn with a stool."

"What did he say, sweetheart?" Jake asks her in a soft tone.

"He said tell your old man he'll get his. All of them will." A moment of silence follows before Emerson speaks again. "It was him," she chokes out on a sob.

"Who?" Logan asks.

"The guy who drugged me at the clubhouse at that time. I don't remember his face, but I'll never forget his voice. It was him."

"That true?" Prez grinds out, looking at me.

"Yeah, Prez, it was him. I was going to wait until church to bring it up because I didn't want to say anything in front of Emerson. I didn't think she remembered him." Tuning out the collective rounds of 'motherfuckers' coming from my brothers, I take Emerson's face in my hands. "I'm so fuckin' sorry, Sunshine. I should have killed the bastard when I had the chance."

"It's okay, Quinn. It's not your fault." Her hands reach up and cover mine.

"No, but it's my job from now on to protect you, and I promise that son of a bitch will never hurt you again."

Peering up at me with tears pooling in her eyes, Emerson whispers, "It's not me I'm worried about."

JAKE WENT and picked up Grace from the bakery, and together they went to Remi's school to check her out. Logan went back to the garage, closed it down, and has Bella and their two little ones with him. The same goes for Gabriel and Reid.

Roughly an hour later, all the brothers have made it back to the clubhouse with their women and kids in tow. The women have worried looks on their faces, but don't ask questions. I'm sure once we're in church, Emerson will fill them in on what little she knows of the events that have transpired today.

Walking into church, I take my seat and light up a cigarette just as Prez slams the gavel bringing everyone's attention to him. "As some of you have already heard, there was an incident at Charley's involving Quinn and two men from an unknown club. Quinn was able to get a good look at the fucker's cut. They call themselves Satan's Reapers. The same bikers Charley has been telling us about. I've never heard of them before, so my guess is they're new. At first, we had no idea why they were suddenly so interested in Polson or what their agenda was, but that has changed. It turns out one of those men is the same prospect Riggs brought with him on his last visit. The same one that got kicked out of the club for drugging and trying to force himself on Quinn's woman."

By the time Prez has given a rundown on the shit storm at hand, the room erupts into fury. We haven't had to deal with a rival club since the Los Demonios. Slamming the gavel, Jake brings the room back to order. "I want Logan, Gabriel, and Quinn to hit the road ASAP lookin' for anything you can find. We haven't got a clue where this club is held up or what their numbers are.

Reid, I want you on that computer of yours seeing what you can find from the security feed we got at Charley's." Leaning back in his seat, Prez continues, "Meanwhile, I'm going to put a call into Riggs down in Louisiana and see what he can tell me about his former prospect. For now, the garage will remain closed and so will Gabriel's shop. I'll have Bella reschedule all appointments until next week. The problem at hand takes top priority. I'm not taking any chances on anything happening to our women and children." Prez's eyes land on me. "Quinn, I want you to get with Emerson and see if she can take some time off work. Now, I know how she can be. She's likely to put up a fight, but I hope you can make her see reason."

Finished with his orders, Prez brings the gavel down once more, ending church. I remain in my seat as the room clears out. A few of the brothers clap me on the back when passing and express how glad they are that Emerson and I are okay. All the while, the only thing I can dwell on is the fact this shit wouldn't be happening had I ended the prospect's life when I had the chance. Now the fucker has hooked up with another club and has sworn vengeance on The Kings. Jake has worked too hard the past few years to bring the club out of shit like this and make sure our families stay safe.

Walking up behind me, Prez lays a hand on my shoulder. "You want to know what sets you apart from the other men in this club?" he asks out of the blue. "It's your heart, son. The other men get to feeling guilty about certain things that are beyond their control. They let that shit go to their heads, and it makes them wild with anger. But you, Quinn, you let it go to your heart, and it makes you shut down. Something you need to realize now is that you have a woman who is depending on you. What happened today and what happened months ago with that prospect was not your fault. Did he deserve a bullet to the head along with the ass beatin' you gave him after he walked off our property that night? Fuck yeah, he did. But it also wasn't our call."

"So, you know about that?" I ask a little surprised.

"Yeah, son. I know what you did. I know everything that goes down in my club. The reason I never said anything was because I would have done the same damn thing. Now here is what you're going to do. You get the what if's out of your head and go take care of business."

10

EMERSON

I'm sitting on the sofa in the main room of the clubhouse where just moments ago, Bella, Alba, and Mia, along with their children, were hustled in by their husbands. Bella made a promise to return in a few minutes to check on me after she got the kids settled in the playroom. I waved her off and told her I'm okay and to take her time. Making sure the kids are alright and not scared or suspecting anything is more important than my frazzled nerves.

I thought I was over the incident that happened months ago at the clubhouse party with the prospect of the Louisiana chapter, but hearing his voice in my ear brought all that back to the forefront of my memory. The way he forced me to kneel before him on the ground, and the vile things he was demanding of me right before he smacked me across my face.

The memory sends a cold chill down my spine, making my body shiver. I thank God every day the guys thought enough to check on me. I don't want to imagine what would have happened had they not shown up when they did. Jake apologized a thousand times and assured me his club and the men he surrounds himself with would never treat a woman in that manner. I already knew that though and expressed to him what happened wasn't his or his men's fault. You can't always control the people around you. The President of the visiting chapter even came to me the next day before leaving and apologized. I told him he was lucky he found out sooner rather than later what kind of man his former prospect was. I'm sure the guy would have brought a heap of trouble to his club in the future.

Hearing a noise, I turn to see Raine and Ember walking into the room with Ember carrying a tray. When she sits it down in front of me, I notice a sandwich, some fruit, and a cup of tea. "Raine and I wanted to come and check on you. We also thought some food or tea might help settle your nerves a bit," she says.

I don't know much about the two women in front of me, only that they are the club girls. The thought alone brings a sinking feeling in my stomach. Raine and Ember have been living at the club for a while now. Quinn and I have only been together a week. *Oh God, what if he's slept with these two women?* Will I be able to see them daily knowing he's shared a bed with them?

"I know what you're thinking," Raine admits as she comes to sit down next to me while Ember takes a seat in the chair across the table from us.

"Your face does your talking for you," she chuckles softly.

"Ember and I both want you to know Quinn has never shared our beds. Even though technically, you two were not together, we always looked at Quinn as if he was yours, and you were his."

Ember's admission has me in a state of shock, and it's all I can do to keep from staring at her with my mouth gaped open. I knew they had the respect of all the other old ladies, and now they have mine. Continuing Raine adds, "Despite what society says about women like us, Ember and I are not the kind of women to act catty nor do we have the desire to break up a family or stand in the way of love. Not only are the married, engaged and involved men off-limits but so are the men who are clearly in love with another woman. We both could tell from the very first day we entered this clubhouse Quinn was yours. Therefore, he became off-limits."

"Thank you both for telling me that," I say sincerely. When Ember and Raine are finished with their confession, Bella, Alba, Mila, and Grace walk back into the room. Bella is the first to take me in her arms, hugging me.

Standing from the sofa, Ember addresses the old ladies. "Raine and I will go entertain the kids while you all catch up. We picked up a few new board games that we promised them we would get and we've been looking forward to playing with them."

Bella gives her a warm smile. "Thanks, ladies, you're lifesavers, and I know the kids will be happy to see you both."

Once Ember and Raine have left the room, I look to the girls. "Damn it's hard not to like them." We all burst out laughing. I laugh until my laughter turns into a full-blown sob. "Fuck being with one of these men sure does bring a lot of chaos, doesn't it?" I say to no one in particular, but it's Grace who answers. "No, but being with one of us is no picnic either," she chuckles.

"No, I suppose it's not," I agree.

"They're worth it, though," Alba adds softly.

"She's right," Mila chimes in. "Sure, the men and their club come with tons of baggage, but so did all of us. Think about it. Think about how Logan stood by Bella and all she went through. Look at what Alba and Gabriel have overcome. The same goes for my fucked-up family and how Reid stood by my side. Then there is Jake. He did not once give up on Grace and how he stood up to her past. If they can be there for us, then we owe it to be there for them."

"Are you having second thoughts about being with Quinn?" Bella asks with concern.

I snap my head in her direction. "God, no! I'm just wondering if maybe he's going to start thinking I'm too much trouble. I mean it's because of me the club is having to go on lockdown."

"What are you talking about because of you?"

"You remember the party the club had a while back to celebrate the arrival of the Louisiana chapter?" When all the ladies nod, I continue, "You also remember the asshole prospect of theirs, the one who drugged me and tried to force himself on me?" Looking at Bella, I still see the guilt she carries around for what happened that night.

"Yes, I remember," Bella adds.

"Well, that's the guy who started this fight with the club. He was at Charley's today with another biker. I'm guessing he's hooked up with another club, and now he wants revenge on Quinn and The Kings."

Shaking her head, Bella protests, "None of what happened is your fault, and nobody blames you, Em."

"I won't be able to live with myself if something happens to one of you or the guys because of what went down that night," I cry. I don't think I have cried as much in my life as I have today. This whole week has been such a whirlwind. Mine and Quinn's little tug-of-war has finally come full circle. Taking the club to meet my brother who I miss more than anything, the god-awful dinner at my parent's house last weekend, Quinn taking me to his parent's house, him declaring me his, and then the fiasco at Charley's this afternoon. I don't know how much more my emotions can take.

"What the hell? What's wrong, Sunshine?" Quinn's voice booms, which causes me to jump.

"She's had a rough day, Quinn. She's allowed a mental breakdown from time to time. Take it easy," Bella fusses, and by the amused look on her face, she's not at all offended by his outburst.

Squatting down in front of me, Quinn rubs the palms of his hands up and down my legs. "Come on, babe, let's go to my room and get you settled, okay?" Nodding in agreement, I stand and allow him to lead me up the stairs toward the back of the clubhouse and down the hall to his room.

"I'm sorry, Quinn. You know me, and I'm not usually a mess like this. It's just the past week has been a lot to take in, and my emotions are playing catch up. As Bella said, I needed a good cry. That and I'm exhausted."

"I'm sure you are, baby. The adrenaline from before has worn off. How about a nap?"

Plopping down on his bed, I let out a heavy sigh and rub my tired, scratchy eyes with my palms. "A nap sounds good."

Striding toward me, Quinn steps between my legs. "Stand up, babe."

I do as he says.

"Shoes off." Once I've toed off my shoes, Quinn goes down to his knees in front of me, unbuttons my jeans and peels them off. "Arms up, baby." Raising my arms above my head, I allow him to pull my t-shirt off. Next, Quinn reaches around and unhooks my bra and tosses it to the growing pile of clothes on the floor, then pulls back the blanket on the bed. "Climb in, Sunshine."

Crawling into bed, I let my head hit the pillow, and it smells of Quinn—like pine mixed with the crisp smell of laundry detergent and something else I can't explain. All I know is that he has the most addicting scent, and once I breathe him in, my body instantly relaxes. The last thing I remember is Quinn kissing my lips before falling asleep.

11

QUINN

I wake to Emerson safely tucked into my side. Knowing Prez needed us in church again before the start of everyone's day this morning so we can go over what the next steps the club should take against those other bikers, I try to slide my body from the bed without disturbing her. Just as my arm is almost free from under the pillow she has her head on, Emerson wiggles her tight round ass across my morning stiffy.

"Mmm, don't go. Stay a little longer," Emerson rasps. Her needy tone causes my dick to twitch.

I run the palm of my hand over the curve of her hip and pull her closer, pressing my cock against her backside. "How can I say no," I knead her ass-cheek in the palm of my hand, "when you wiggle this ass against my cock like that, woman?" I press my lips against the warmth of her skin and kiss my way across the top of her shoulder, then to the curve of her neck. Stopping there, I breathe her in.

Reaching her hand back, Emerson turns her head, takes hold of my hair, and brings my mouth to hers. Slowly I caress her skin. My hand glides from her hip, past her lower abdomen, and makes contact with her bare pussy. Moving my finger in circles, I begin to manipulate her clit. Laying on her side, with her back to my front, I lift Emerson's leg, opening her up to me. I press the tip of my cock to her entrance, close my eyes, and relish the feeling of her tight heat as I slowly sink into her. "Fuck, Sunshine. Your pussy squeezes my cock just right." Bringing her leg back to rest over my hip, I pull out then thrust into her once again.

"Oh god, Quinn," she moans.

"You like that?" I pull out, leaving only the tip of my cock inside her for a moment then thrust upwards with so much force the headboard slams against the wall. My hand reaches for hers, and I bring it down helping her stroke her swollen clit beneath our hands. "I wanna watch you touch yourself while I fuck you, Sunshine." Letting go, I watch her take over.

"I'm close, Quinn," Emerson pants.

Pure need for her pleasure—to satisfy her, pumps through my veins. Grabbing her leg under her knee, I lift her leg higher. "Give it to me, Sunshine," I demand of her, fucking her harder, causing her pussy to flutter before clamping down on my cock, sending me over the edge right along with her and we climax together.

Gaining control of our breaths, we lay still for a moment. It doesn't take long for my cock to be thirsty for more, and it starts to swell once again. Rolling Emerson under my body, I sink into her pussy. This time I make love to her, slowly taking my time with her already sensitive body. With my lips never leaving hers, I bring her to another release.

After several minutes of holding each other, a relaxed and sated, Emerson's wispy breaths tell me she has fallen asleep. I smile for a moment and watch the hairs that have fallen across her face move with each exhale, and I admire the greatest treasure I've ever held. Just as quickly anger bubbles inside me because of the presence of a dirty motherfucker; someone who has had his filthy hands on my woman before; someone who dares to call himself a biker—a man. He and a few of his no-good buddies have come to town stirrin' up shit and making threats. *With my last breath, I'll protect what is mine.*

This time I make it out of bed without waking Emerson. Throwing on some clothes and lacing up my boots, I shrug my cut on, quietly leave the room, and head downstairs.

It's no surprise to me either when I make it to church and walk in and find the rest of the men waiting on me.

"Good of you to finally join us," Prez grumps, a little irritated at my lateness.

I can't help but wear a shit-eatin' grin as to my reason for being late this morning. I swear I'm in a perpetual state of always sporting a hard-on because of my woman. Looking around the room, I notice my brothers sportin' shit-eatin' grins of their own. They know what I was up to. Hell, most of them probably had their fill this morning too. Remembering the look on Prez's face and the fact that we do have more pressing things to deal with, I squash my instinct to make a joke and plant my ass in my seat next to Reid and instead offer an apology. "Sorry about that, Prez. I'll try not to let it happen again."

Crackin' a grin of his own, Prez eyeballs me. "Make sure that you don't." He lets out a deep sigh before addressing the room. "I've decided we need to have a sit down with the Satan's Reapers. I believe the only way to deal with this is head on straight through the bullshit. I'm not about to beat around the bush with these dickheads."

The rest of us look to one another, all knowing this is the best course of action. The Kings don't back down. Not from anyone.

"I found out they've been camped out in an RV park located on the other side of Flathead," Reid informs us all.

"Alright." Prez turns his attention toward Gabriel, who's sitting with his arms crossed over his chest. "Gabriel, get the word out that I want a sit-down with whoever is calling themselves their leader. I want this to happen today." His finger taps the tabletop as he barks his order.

"Somethin' tells me these fuckers aren't going away quietly, Prez." Logan scratches the beard he's been sporting for a few months now.

"I smell trouble too," I add. *The vibes I get from those grade A assholes are not good ones.*

"Quinn," Prez grabs my attention, "Go with Gabriel. For safety reasons," he looks at each of us, "I don't want any brother on the roads alone. We only know of a few that are in town, but we don't know if there may be more. Eyes open and have each other's backs." The gavel cracks against the wooden surface of the table, bringing church to a close.

Being on semi-lockdown puts a kink in all our day to day lives. We all have jobs. Club members' kids have school, and when shit like this goes down, it disrupts everything. Knowing all this, I head off Gabriel, asking him to give me thirty minutes to check in on my woman. Knowing he wants to do the same with his family, he gives me a nod, and we go our separate ways. I make my way back up the stairs toward my room. Quietly, I open the door and slip in only to find Emerson up and dressed; her hair still dampened from grabbing a shower while I was gone. She looks up from tying her shoes as the door clicks closed behind me.

"Oh, hey." She smiles.

"You tryin' to go somewhere, Sunshine?" I ask her, cocking my head to the side.

Letting out an exasperated sigh, Emerson stands. "I'm needed at the hospital."

I calm myself. Everything in me wants to keep her safe, especially today, but her job is saving lives, and that's one thing I can't change or turn my back on. "I have to take care of club business today, but since I know you need to go, I won't stop you."

Emerson makes her way toward me and wraps her arms

around my waist. "Is this something you can't talk about?" She stretches on her tiptoes and presses her lips to mine. Tightening my hold on her, I deepen the kiss.

"Not yet. But—" I say after pulling back and looking into her eyes. Her eyebrow raises, waiting for me to finish.

"But?" she inquires.

"One of my brothers will take you to work today and hang around."

She rolls her eyes in annoyance. "Why?"

"It makes me feel better." I shrug my shoulders but stand firm on the issue, then decide to give in just a little. "I'll make sure he stays outside and out of sight," I finish.

Her full lips lift in a smile that reaches her eyes, and her face lights up, causing my heart to skip a beat.

"Good. Thank you, Quinn."

A few minutes later, I make arrangements for Blake to drive Emerson to town and to stick around until she texts or calls stating she is ready to leave. Until we know how this whole meeting is going to play out, I won't risk leaving her vulnerable in any way.

I find Gabriel outside sitting on his bike waiting. "Let's do this, brother," I say as I throw my leg over my bike.

It takes us thirty minutes or so to make it to our destination on the other side of town. Making a left turn, we enter the RV park. Gabriel and I find one of the fuckers sitting on top of a picnic table next to an old Winnebago toward the back of the park in a secluded wooded area. He immediately jumps down, looks around, and sticks his hand inside his cut. Gabriel and I slow to a stop but leave our engines running. With Gabriel's focus on the one guy we can see, I scan the area looking for signs that there may be others and find none.

"My Prez wants a meeting with your Prez. The abandoned Super Inn motel on the edge of town at six o'clock tonight," Gabriel's voice booms, making sure the shithead hears him loud and clear. The guy gets the bold nerve to smirk and tries his best to intimidate us by slyly showing his weapon without completely exposing it to a couple of people milling about nearby.

"Message received," are the only words he offers, giving us a seething, toothy grin.

If looks could kill, the guy would be dead by the way Gabriel is cutting him down with his stare. I ease my bike up a few feet coming in between the two men. I give Gabriel a look, hoping he will let it go; for now. His nostrils flare with rage before looking forward.

The whole exchange takes only a couple of minutes. With my eyes trained on the dumbass who has sat back down in the spot he was before, I wait for Gabriel to signal us leaving and fall in behind him until we get on the open road and ride side by side back to the club.

The remainder of the day, everyone goes on with business as usual. Prez decided, for now, a complete lockdown wasn't needed. The Reapers haven't posed a threat to anyone other than us men so there is no need to disrupt lives any further. Being vigilant is a top priority though, and you can bet your sweet ass if they mess with my family they will pay. With their lives.

We've had the entire day for adrenaline to course through our veins as we anticipate all the ways this meeting can go down this evening.

All the guys, including myself, have met up at the shop to have a quick walkthrough of how Prez wants to go into this mess.

"No information has traveled back to me or anyone else to confirm these pussies will show up. Either way, we ride. I want every man to check your weapons. Keep a visual, have each other's backs. Check yourself before walking out that door, men. I know we are all worked up over this bullshit, but level heads prevail," Prez finishes, retrieving his pistol from the holster on his side, inspecting it then placing it back into the holster.

We all do as we are told and check. I watch each man hold their weapon of choice. All of us have our favorites, but mine; mine is old school. A Dirty Hairy style revolver. *That's how I roll*—a .44 Magnum. Nowhere near ideal for concealing, but it belonged to my dad, and it feels good in my hand.

Truth be told, I have a particular bullet—I tap the inside pocket of my cut, making sure it's tucked away. This bullet is for the motherfucker that put his hands on my woman. The man who should have eaten the bullet a while back. If ever the situation arises, and I get the chance, he'll taste the end of my barrel just before I blow the back of his head off.

Walking out of the building, we make our way to our bikes and mount up. "Alright, brothers, let's ride," Prez commands, raising a fist in the air.

Making sure my brothers stay safe, I remain vigilant, my eyes scanning every building, every alleyway as we make our way through town. Just before reaching the abandoned motel, I flag Gabriel, motioning for him to ride ahead with me to scope the area before the rest of our brothers join us.

When we pull up to the run-down building, we both circle the area on our bikes before backing up in front of what used to be the central office of the motel. Leaving our bikes, Gabriel and I clear each room—20 in all, in the single-story building. The only things we find are evidence of hookers, druggies, and probably a few homeless people that have been here.

Once we're satisfied, and the area is secure, I call it in. Ten minutes later, the rest of the club rolls in, filling the empty atmosphere with sounds of thunder.

No words are exchanged between us as we wait. The sun itself begins to set before hearing the distant sounds of bikes approaching. In my position at the end of the building facing the highway, I count five riders. Quickly making my way back to the group, I tell my brothers. Making sure our families were safe, I designated Blake and Austin to stay behind to keep eyes and ears open while the rest of us are gone.

Doc is with us, along with Grey, making it seven to their five. The Satan's Reapers pull into the parking lot, stopping several yards in front of us. The guy out in front, the one I'm assuming is their President, dismounts first. It will be the first time we get a look at the son of a bitch leading their merry band into our town; on our territory. He's a big motherfucker. Not just in height but girth as well. He's sporting a Fu Manchu mustache, and the guy has a gut on him the size of a tractor tire. I'd be surprised if he can find his dick. The other riders I recognize and immediately zone in on the greasy fucker I'd like to get rid of; permanently.

"So, you wanted to meet with me?" The Satan's Reapers Prez lifts his chin, his breath heavy with the sour stench of cheap beer as they come to stand a couple of feet from us.

"That's right." Our Prez folds his arms over his chest and stares at the burly man in front of him. "You see, some of your men are causing problems in town—our town. And this—" his arms spread wide to gesture, "this meeting is the final warning my club will give you and your men to get the fuck out of Polson." Prez takes a step closer, showing he means every word he is saying by invading the other guy's personal space.

I can finally see his patch from where I stand, and he goes by the name Boulder. Unfazed, he's quick to square his shoulders, showing no signs of backing down or cooperation. "Do we threaten you?" He smirks, stepping into Jake's space a bit more. "Cause we ain't going anywhere."

This guy has a big set of balls.

Prez slightly shifts his weight to his right foot as he takes a step back. I recognize the stance he is making.

"Wrong fuckin' answer," I mumble under my breath.

Before anyone can react, Prez brings his arm back, swings, and cracks the son of a bitch with a right hook across his meaty chin causing the big motherfucker's knees to buckle. Boulder hits the ground and proceeds to spit blood and teeth onto the cracked asphalt beneath him.

One of the Satan's Reapers reaches into the left side of his cut and goes to pull his weapon, which sets off a chain reaction.

Every man standing now has the end of someone else's barrel pointed at him.

Mine is trained on the sorry fucker I desperately want to go toe to toe with, waiting for him to make one wrong move. Wanting him to give me a reason to pull my trigger. It's no surprise his gun is aimed in my direction as well.

Boulder, as he's called, wipes the blood from his mouth with the back of his hand and stands. A look of pure murder from being blindsided blackens his stare, and he's probably pissed as hell he has two fewer teeth in his head.

"You're outnumbered, so you may want to rethink what you might be contemplating. Now before my men and I start having your men dig a shallow grave for your body, I advise you to get the fuck out of town," Prez growls, ready to go rounds with the big guy.

12

EMERSON

It's been over a month since the blow up at Charley's with the mysterious club which has yet to show their faces in Polson again. Not that I've seen or heard anyway. I get the feeling the guys know more than they are telling. I questioned Quinn once about the topic, and his only response was 'It was club business.' I have learned enough from the girls over the last couple of years to know we are not to meddle in club business. So, I accepted his answer and moved on.

It's also been five weeks since Quinn and I became us. It's weird how completely comfortable I am with him and how we fell into our relationship so easily. It feels like we have been together for years instead of mere weeks. Quinn crawls into bed with me each night, and I wake up in his arms every morning. I keep waiting for the moment he wakes up and realizes this is all too domestic for him and bolts, but he hasn't yet. He's proven all the fears I had before, and the misconceptions I assumed about him in the past were all wrong.

Quinn has been upfront with me about his history, about how he enjoyed the company of a different woman and had never found anyone that made him want to settle down until me. He confessed he's always wanted to find the perfect old lady and the past few years he's envied what his brothers have with their women. Quinn said he never intended to give up on me because he knew I was that woman. I sometimes find myself wondering where we'd be now had I not been so afraid and given in to him long before I did.

Using the back of my hand, I wipe away the sweat dripping down my forehead as my feet pound the treadmill I am currently on. Glancing to my left, I see Quinn sitting outside on his bike. Every day since the fight at the bar, he follows me from work to the gym, but I refuse to let him come inside.

Three weeks ago, I had my Muay Thai class with Rhett. The sport at times is very hands on and even though Rhett has been nothing but respectful and professional Quinn about lost his shit when seeing another man put his hands on my body. Thank God Rhett took the whole situation in stride. Since then, I have banned Quinn from coming into the gym with me. Now he spends the hour I'm here working out sitting outside sulking like a little kid. It probably doesn't help that I made the mistake of telling Quinn about Rhett asking me out in the past. I thought for sure I saw steam coming out of his ears, but quickly assured him that I politely declined the gym owner's offer. However, I am still friends with Rhett and will continue working out here and continue with my classes. He is just going to have to trust me just as I have to believe him when it comes to other women, considering his past is a hell of a lot more active than mine ever was.

Hearing two women on the ellipticals next to me talking and giggling catches my attention, especially when they both keep cutting their eyes toward the entrance where I can see Quinn leaning against the window smoking a cigarette and talking on his phone. So, I bring the speed of my treadmill down to a slow but steady walk to try and catch what they are saying.

"Girl, look at him. God, he's sexy," blondie says to her big-boobed friend.

"Hell, yeah, he is. I bet he has a big dick too. I could ride him all night."

"You should go for it, girl," blondie encourages, causing me to see red.

Oh, hell, no! Stepping off the machine, I stride up behind the two bitches just as Big Boobs begins tugging on her top, pulling it down to expose her cleavage. I'm about to tap the little whore on her shoulder and confront her when an arm snags me around my waist, and Quinn's intoxicating smell instantly calms me.

"Ready to get out of here, Sunshine?" he rumbles loud enough for the two women to hear, and they turn their heads in our direction.

"I sure am." I smile smugly at big boobs. "I was going to shower first, but we can do that at home," I add for good measure while enjoying the way the slut looks at me with envy before she huffs and walks off.

"I love when you get all territorial, babe. Makes my dick hard as a rock," he rasps in my ear. He's not lying. I can feel his erection digging into my back. I swear I don't recognize the person I am right now. I don't act catty ever, and I don't get jealous. "I love how you're this prim and proper doctor on the outside, but on the inside, you're a hellcat."

Rolling my eyes, I wiggle out of his embrace. "Can we go now before your head gets any bigger?" I remark dryly.

"First admit you were jealous. My hellcat was about to unleash her claws because another woman was lookin' at her man."

Fuck! I know Quinn is not going to let this go, especially not after the way I got on to him about being jealous over Rhett.

"Come on, babe. It's only three little words," he teases.

Crossing my arms over my chest and gritting my teeth, I swallow my pride and give him what he wants. "I was jealous. You happy?" I try to sass, but my words fall short when he steals my breath by taking my mouth with his in one of the most toe-curling heated kisses I have ever experienced. When Quinn breaks our kiss, he looks down at me with mischief in his eyes. "Let's go home and play doctor."

Two hours later, I untangle myself from Quinn's arms, climb out of bed, snag my white lab coat off the floor, and slip it on over my naked body. I must confess I love Quinn's adventurous side.

"Where are you going, babe?"

"I'm going to the kitchen to get some water, I'll be right back," I say while taking the time to rake my eyes over his body as he lies in my bed with his back propped up against the headboard. Quinn doesn't have as much ink has his brothers do. Along with his club piece on his back, he has a full sleeve on his left arm. His sleeve consists of a motorcycle piston, skulls, and a large compass that takes up almost his entire forearm. Gabriel does beautiful work. I've been considering letting him ink me.

"Thought you were going to get some water?" Quinn teases, calling me out on my blatant ogling.

Ignoring his arrogant smirk, I turn and make my way to the kitchen. Opening the refrigerator, I pull out a bottle of water, twist the cap off, and down half the contents. A second later, my front door opens, and I am stunned by who just barged in and water spews out of my mouth. "Mom, Dad, what are you two doing here?" When neither of them answers, I notice my dad is looking everywhere but at me and my mother's mouth is hanging open in shock. It's then I realize what I'm wearing. Shit! Just as I am pulling my coat tight around my body to cover up as much as I possibly can, Quinn makes himself known at the worst possible moment.

"Oh, Doctor Pretty. I'm ready for my physical now," he sing songs as he struts into the kitchen wearing nothing but his birthday suit and my stethoscope around his neck. I silently pray the floor will open up and swallow me because this is by far the most embarrassing thing to ever happen to me. Not only did my father see me nearly naked, but my boyfriend is standing in my kitchen with all his pierced glory swinging in the breeze. My mother looks as if she's going to pass out and my father is on the verge of a coronary.

"Oh, shit—my bad," Quinn says, quickly covering himself with his hands then slowly begins walking backward toward my bedroom.

"Perhaps you should join your friend in putting on some clothes," my father suggests.

With nothing to say, I hightail it out of the kitchen. When I make it to my room, I slam the door behind me before leaning up against it and closing my eyes. "This cannot be happening. When I open my eyes, I will see this was all just a dream," I chant. Counting to five inside my head, I open my eyes to see Quinn's amused face right in front of mine.

"Sorry, Sunshine. You're not dreamin'." He chuckles.

"Why are you laughing? There is nothing funny about what just happened! Those are my parents," I tell him.

"Yeah, babe, I got that."

"They just saw your dick, Quinn!" I shout. "Nothing is amusing about that."

"They're doctors, babe. I'm pretty sure they've seen a pecker or two in their time." He pauses a moment. "Well, probably not one as fuckin' perfect as mine." He grins.

"Oh my god," I breathe, feeling lightheaded.

"The way I see it, babe, we're up a shit creek without a paddle," he says, grinning, and I give him a warning glare that has zero effect on him as he continues, "luckily I'm a shit creek survivor. We have to suck it up and face the music because there is no way out of this one, Sunshine." He steps closer. "Look, I know this is not the ideal way to be meeting your folks for the first time, but look at it this way, it will make for one hell of a story to tell our kids."

Stepping around Quinn, I walk over to my bed, plop down and put my head in my hands. "Nothing you're saying right now is helping, Quinn. I wasn't ready for this."

"Ready for what? For me to meet your parents? Why not, Emerson? You ashamed of me?" he asks with a little bite in his tone.

I quickly snap my head in his direction. "Of course not. I could never be ashamed of you."

"Then what is it? We've been together for nearly six weeks and have yet to bring up the subject of me ever meeting your parents. I haven't said anything because I didn't want to push, but I've started to get the feeling you're embarrassed by me and my lifestyle. I feel like you're hiding me."

I don't miss the small look of hurt on his face. Pushing off the bed, I go to him, wrap my arms around his middle and look him in the eyes. "I am not embarrassed or ashamed of you or the club. You and the club mean a lot to me. You are all like family." When Quinn sees and hears the sincerity in my words, he loses the look he had on his face and relaxes his tense body. It's in this exact moment I realize I no longer have the same fear I had weeks ago of what my parent's opinion of Quinn and the club will be. Whether they choose to accept him and our relationship will be up to them, but their decision will have no bearing on my choice to be with him. Being with Quinn has made me the happiest I have ever been in my life, and I refuse to give him up for anyone.

Walking back into the kitchen, my parents stand from where they were sitting at the kitchen table. Quinn is the first to speak by offering his hand to my dad.

"Mr. Evans, it's nice to meet ya."

My father looks at him for a long second before reluctantly taking his hand, and my mom follows suit. The four of us take a seat at the table. Quinn sits next to me and casually rests his arm over the back of my chair. Several tense moments later, my mother is the first to break the silence. "So, what exactly are you two and how long has this been going on?"

Just as I open my mouth to answer, Quinn cuts in. "Emerson is my old lady." At the term old lady, I know what question my mother has next.

"Is that what the men in your gang call their girlfriends or wives?" She raises a judging eyebrow.

This time I'm the first to answer. "The Kings are not a gang. They're a club," I bite out, my tone shocking my mother.

"I've heard rumors about this so-called club. I would say our assumption of them being a gang is pretty accurate," my father adds, causing Quinn to sit up straighter in his seat. "I can also see the kind of influence this club has had on you. Don't think I didn't notice all those tattoos you have."

I can see by the set line in Quinn's jaw he's about to snap.

Only I'm about to handle the situation for him. Rising from my seat, I place my palms on the table and lean my body in the direction of my parents. "Let me tell you something. Quinn is my man. His club has become like a family to me. If you think I am going to allow you to come into my home—unannounced, might I add—and disrespect the man I love you are sorely mistaken. For your information, I got my tattoos back in college before I ever met Quinn and his club. Now, I think it's time for you two to leave, and do not think about coming back until you can treat Quinn with the respect he deserves."

"Emerson," my mother sputters. Holding up my hand, I cut her off. "No. There is nothing else to say. Please leave."

"Come on, Brenda, let's go. Our daughter is not thinking clearly," my father says taking my mom by the arm and leads her to the door. Just as they are about to walk out, my mom delivers the blow I was already expecting. Only this time I don't give a shit.

"I am very disappointed in you, Emerson."

With my head held high, I look at both my parents. "Really? I could say the same thing about you two. I'm embarrassed to say I have two of the most stuck-up and judgmental parents. All you care about is judging a book by its cover. Not once did you ask me if I'm happy. You have never cared about what made me happy. All you have ever cared about is what YOU wanted for me and what made YOU happy. I'm the one who is disappointed. I'm disappointed in you both." I walk over to where Brenda and Martin Evans are standing in my doorway and shut the door in their faces.

Holy shit! I can't believe I just did that. I have never stood up to my parents like that before. My body is shaking, and I feel like my legs are about to give out, but before they do, Quinn has me in his arms and his mouth on mine. Our tongues battle each other as he slams me up against the door and I wrap my legs around his waist. In a race to rid each other of our clothes, I rip his shirt off over his head at the same time he sets me down long enough to take my jean shorts off. Palming my ass, he lifts me back up, and my hands shake as I frantically unbuckle his belt and free his thick cock. Placing his swollen head at my entrance, he wastes no time surging forward burying himself to the hilt. His mouth swallows my cry. Breaking our kiss, Quinn rests his forehead on mine. He pulls out almost all the way then slams back in with so much force the door behind me rattles.

"Say it again," he growls, never losing momentum.

"Say what?" I moan when he swivels his hip, making his piercing rub just the right spot.

"Tell me you love me. I want to hear you repeat it."

His plea brings me out of my fog, and Quinn stills with his cock buried inside me. "Tell me you meant it. Tell me you love me."

Cupping his face, I say the words he's desperate to hear. The words I know with all my heart and soul to be true. "I'm in love with you, Quinn Beckett."

Quinn closes his eyes as if he's soaking in my confession. A second later, he opens them and makes his own. "I'm in love with you too, Emerson Evans. I've been in love with you for two goddamn years."

As soon as those words leave his lips, I let out a sob. Kissing away my tears, Quinn begins to thrust, and my cries turn into moans as he fucks me into the door. Not once does he let up and not once does he take his eyes off mine. I can feel him pouring his soul into my body. At this moment, I give Quinn my heart.

13

QUINN

It's been a few days since we had our little encounter with Boulder and his men. And the fact we haven't heard a peep out of them should be a good sign. It should mean they've packed their shit and rode their sorry asses out of town as ordered, but it's not settling too well with me. We haven't heard of them being seen anywhere. Gabriel and I made a trip back out to the RV park they had been held up in only to find no sight of them. The camper was gone. The fuckers don't seem like the type that would be smart enough to overlook the fact their Prez ate a fist sandwich. The pure lack of disrespect the guy had already displayed by stepping foot on our turf and puffin' his tail feathers, pretty much declaring he wants something that doesn't belong to him clearly shows they don't follow any biker code. That leads me to believe they have nothing to lose. And when someone has nothing to lose, they live life giving little to zero fucks how they go about taking what they want. It's turds like those bikers that give MC's a bad name.

I stand in front of the bathroom mirror and study my face. It's early. Peering across the room, I watch Emerson for a moment as she sleeps. Turning my head, I examine myself again. Rolling my neck a few times, I try to work out the tension in my muscles, but it doesn't work. I'm tired, and sleep hasn't been easy with all this shit on my mind. I get lost in thought, standing here.

I smell her before she touches me. Emerson comes up behind me, wraps her arms around my waist, and splays her palms across my bare abs. "I love you." Her soft lips press against my back, and her hot breath causes my skin to prickle.

"I love you too, Sunshine." Exhaling, I push my thoughts away for now. Emerson dips her head under my arm, putting herself between me and the bathroom sink. Tilting her head back, she looks at me. Her beautiful grey eyes lock on mine.

"Are you okay? You've been restless. I don't think you've slept at all the past two nights," she says with worry.

"I'm good, babe." Brushing her unruly slept in hair from her face, I run the pad of my thumb over her cheek. "You don't have to worry about me," I look at her knowing my words aren't sinking in.

"You can't tell someone who cares about you not to worry and expect them not to worry." Her lips lift in a half-smile. "I understand you can't tell me everything that's going down with this other club. I'm also very aware after being involved with the MC for a while now you men don't talk outside the member circle about things, but something's eating at you." She scrunches her nose, causing her forehead to crease as she makes her point. "I've never seen you this way, and for me, that's enough cause to worry."

There is a lot of shit we don't tell the women and our other family members. To keep them safe. The less they know about some of the shit we encounter from time to time, the better. Plausible deniability. If they don't know, it can't be used against them. When something needs to be said, we keep it to a minimum. Sometimes that can be hard as hell when the one person you want to tell all your secrets to is stressed out. Not for herself, but for me. "Sunshine." I zone in on her full lips that have a little pout too them. "Everything is good. Promise." Leaning down, I kiss her forehead before touching my lips to hers. Her hands clench at the waistband of my sweatpants. Pulling away, she looks at my face again, her cheeks flushed. Emerson clears her throat.

"Nice try—" she reaches up, putting her hand on the back of my neck. Her fingers start to play with my hair. "But I can't shake this feeling I've been having lately. The feeling that something awful is going to happen." Her eyes start to gloss over with emotion.

"Babe." I grab her other hand and place it over my heart. "You feel that?" I ask her. She nods. "It beats for you, Sunshine. It beats for us. We can't live in the future. Not when we haven't lived for right now. At this moment." Placing my hands beneath her ass, I lift her. With her palm still over my heart, she wraps her legs around my waist, and I carry her to the bed. Laying her on her back, I hover my body over hers, covering her hand on my chest with mine. "That's what we focus on. We live for today; for this moment." Emerson bites her bottom lip to keep from crying. "I love you, and nothing else matters right now but you and me." The rest of the morning, I make slow love to my woman.

It's mid-afternoon and Logan and I are knee-deep in a massive rebuild at the shop when my phone rings. Assuming it's Emerson who usually calls on her lunch break, I half-ass wipe my hands down the front of my jeans, grab my phone from the top of the workbench next to me, and swipe my thumb across the screen leaving a light smudge on the surface. "Hey, beautiful. You miss me?" I say playfully, hoping she says yes.

"Quinn?" My mother's shaky voice is barely audible coming through the speaker of my phone, causing every muscle in my body to go rigid. "Mom, what's wrong?" I say a little too loud, and it catches Logan's attention. Standing, he walks over and stands beside me. My mom sniffles at the other end of the phone.

"Sweetheart, Dad had an accident at work. They're en route to the hospital now—" she pauses for a moment. I can hear her take a deep breath. "I'm in my car heading that way now."

All the air gets sucked from my lungs. "Did they tell you anything else?"

"No, just that I need to get to the hospital. Honey, I need you there with me if—" Her voice breaks.

"I'll be there," I tell her before ending the call. Knowing Logan heard every word, I haul ass, running out the bay door. I know he will cover all the bases, and in no time, my brothers will follow suit and be standing right beside me.

After weaving in and out of lunchtime traffic, I make it to the hospital and find my mom's car already in the parking lot. Racing to the entrance of the ER and through the automatic doors, I immediately scan the waiting room looking for her. I don't see her. Maybe she's back there with him. I walk over to the small exam room where the triage nurse is and knock on the open door. Her head lifts from the papers on the table in front of her. "Can I help you?" she asks with a smile.

"A patient was brought in, Quinten Beckett."

"Yes, I took his wife to the back only moments ago." She stands. "Are you family?"

"I'm his son," I inform her as we walk out of the exam room.

"I was instructed to take your mom to the chapel. I'll take you to her."

The chapel? My stomach sinks. The nurse notices the look of concern on my face, and just before the double doors open leading to the back, she pauses. "The doctors are with your dad right now. The chapel is a quiet place for the family to wait," she tries to assure me. It does nothing to ease my nerves. Just as we pass the nurses station, Emerson walks out of an exam room, her arms clasping her laptop to her chest. She looks up, surprised to see me, "Quinn?" Quickly her eyes shift to the nurse beside me. "What are you—"

I interrupt her. "My dad was brought in. Something happened to him at work."

"Dr. Evans, I was taking Mr. Beckett's son to the chapel to wait with his mother," the nurse explains. "Dr. Chamberlin is with the patient now."

"Thank you, Tracie." Emerson faces me and places her hand on my arm. "I'll go see what I can find out. Right now, go comfort your mom."

Giving Emerson a quick hug, I follow the nurse. Upon opening the doors to the chapel, I find Mom sitting on the small front pew with her face buried in the palms of her hands. "Mom," I say softly, trying not to make her jump out of her skin. Her tear-stained eyes break my heart as she lifts her worried face to mine.

"They haven't been in to tell me anything. Not knowing is the worst part for me right now." She wipes the wetness from her face with a tissue she has in her right hand. Sitting beside her, I bring her close and wrap my arms around her.

"Dad's strong. Whatever happened, he'll pull through," I do my best to soothe her.

The door to the room creaks. Turning my head and looking over my shoulder, I see Emerson making her way in. Following her is a tall, dark-haired doctor.

"Mrs. Beckett?" he says, stopping in front of us. Squatting, he brings himself level to talk with my mom. Emerson sits beside me, her hand resting on my thigh.

Wringing her hands together, my mom addresses him with a plea. "Please tell me the love of my life is going to be okay."

Dr. Chamberlin's face softens with understanding. "Your husband is going to be okay. He suffered a gunshot in the kidney region. We've confirmed the bullet went through the left kidney, so he's being prepped for surgery and I'll be the surgeon taking care of him."

"Shot?" my mom asks in a state of shock.

"Mrs. Beckett," Emerson speaks. "I talked with the guy who rode with him. Bob, I believe he said his name was."

"That's a coworker of his. They've worked together for years," I clarify.

"He said that Mr. Beckett rode out to investigate a potential poacher on the property that someone had called in this morning. An hour later, he received a distress call over their hand-held radios that your husband was shot," Emerson finishes with the information she was able to find.

"But, he is going to be okay? Right?" my mom wants Dr. Chamberlin to confirm.

He looks from me back to my mom, settling his attention on her. "Yes. All his vitals looked good. He's fit and healthy for his age. I have no reason to believe otherwise," he states. Placing his hand on his knees, Dr. Chamberlin stands, and I stand as well and put out my hand.

"I'll take care of him." Dr. Chamberlin assures, shaking my hand.

"Thank you," I tell him.

He gives me a nod and leaves the room. Suddenly the air is a lot less thick, and we all breathe a sigh of relief.

"Unfortunately, I need to get back to work." Emerson stands. "I'll take you two to the family waiting area and get you some coffee. As soon as he's out of surgery, I'll come get you." Mom and I stand, and Emerson steps closer and embraces my mom and rubs her back as she hugs her. "How about some coffee or some warm tea?" she offers as we exit into the hallway.

"Tea sounds nice," my mom conveys.

After walking us to the waiting area, Emerson makes a quick trip to the cafeteria then reappears with a cup of tea in one hand

and a coffee in the other. I take the offered coffee from her as Mom sips on her drink. "Cream and sugar, just the way you like it," Emerson says, smiling. I pull her close to me so that I can feel the warmth of her body against mine.

"Thank you, Sunshine." Leaning in, I kiss her.

"I'll see you soon," she whispers as I let her go.

A couple of hours later, Dad is in recovery, resting comfortably, with Mom by his side, holding his hand. They couldn't repair the damage to the kidney caused by the bullet so now he's left with one. My brothers showed up too. Jake closed the shop early, and even Gabriel shut down and rescheduled clients for the rest of the day to be here. Every one of them sat out in the waiting room waiting to hear the final word after surgery before leaving.

"Quinn, honey, would you pick your sister up from school and stay home with her tonight? I want to stay here, and once she finds out about Dad, she'll be upset," my mom says while stroking my dad's hair with her fingertips.

"No problem." I walk over, lean down and kiss her cheek. "Call me if you need anything. Do you mind if Emerson stays too? She's about to clock out for the day," I ask.

"Of course, sweetie. Emerson is always welcome," she says, sitting down in the chair beside the bed looking exhausted.

I leave the room and make my way toward the elevators, pushing the down button. The door slides open to reveal my woman standing inside, looking back at me.

"Hey, you," she says.

"Hey, you," I echo.

An hour and a half later, the three of us pull into the driveway of my parent's home. After Kat calmed down from hearing the news about Dad, we took her to get pizza and ice cream, and now she's feeling a little better. Emerson staying over seems to have helped. It went from her staying the night with me to having a pajama party with my sister. The talk of painting nails and doing each other's hair was all Kat could talk about on the way home. I smile at how easy my baby sister and Emerson get along. "She's my woman," I tell my sister. "Besides, what if I want a pedi too?" I chime in, interrupting girl talk as I put Emerson's Jeep in park.

"Ooh, you can wear Dad's Christmas onesie I got him last year. I think it's still in the box." Kat laughs.

"Hell yeah. I'll rock that motherfucker," I boast, unlocking the front door.

THE FOLLOWING MORNING, I wake to my phone ringing. Leaning over the side of the bed, I rummage through my clothes on the floor only to realize it wasn't my phone it was Emerson's. "Babe, here." I pass her phone to her as she rolls onto her back and stretches her arms above her head, causing the sheet to fall exposing her breasts. She swipes the screen and immediately calls whoever it was back. Trying to distract her, I flick my tongue across her taut nipple then take it into my mouth.

"Quinn, stop," she whispers and tries pushing my face away. "I'm on call, I have to see if the hospital needs me."

I tune out the fact she is on the phone with someone from work and continue by kissing my way down her body before diving under the sheet. Before my lips make it to my destination, Emerson blocks me with her hand. "Quinn, I've got to go." She jumps from the bed and pulls her clothes on in a hurry. "They have some accident victims being brought in." As she's tying up her shoes, she looks over her shoulder at me. "Don't you need a ride?"

I roll onto my back. "Naw, babe. I brought my car out here a few weekends ago to have my dad's detail guy clean it for me, so it's sitting out in the garage."

Snatching her keys and purse from the dresser next to the

bedroom door, she walks over and leans down. "I'm sorry I gotta go."

"Go save lives, Superwoman." I swat her on the ass after she kisses me and turns toward the door. "We'll pick up where I left off later." I wink.

Blowing me a kiss, she's out the door, and a minute later, I hear her Jeep start. Getting myself out of bed, I head to the kitchen to make some coffee. When it's finished, I pour a cup and carry over to the big window that overlooks the backyard and the side of the house. From the corner of my eye, I catch movement near the garage and notice the door moving back and forth with the breeze. *The fuck?* The door was closed when we got home last night. And the way it locks there is no way it can open on its own.

Placing my mug on the counter, I look out the living room window toward the driveway. Nothing. Making sure the front door is locked, I go back to my room and grab my gun. I peek in on my sister who's fast asleep. Thankfully she sleeps like a rock. Easing out the back door and locking it with the code pad, I inch alongside the house until I reach the corner. With my gun in my hand, I turn the corner of the house and walk over to the garage. Sure as fuck, the lock has been pried off. Thinking I might catch whoever it may be off guard, I charge in with my gun held out in front of me ready to defend myself and flip the overhead light on only to find my car vandalized. Tires and interior have been slashed, and red spray paint covers every inch of the body. It's the words painted on the hood that causes my blood to boil.

YOU'RE NEXT

I waste no time getting back to the house. The only call I make is to Prez. I need to get my car out of here before anyone else gets the chance to notice. *Something isn't adding up. First, my dad, then this.*

14

EMERSON

"Great save in there, Evans," Doctor Collins says, sitting down on a chair next to me at the nurse's station with his laptop.

"Thanks," I reply as we both continue to type away, entering our notes for the trauma that we both finished working on moments ago. A mother and son were brought in after a truck t-boned their minivan. Luckily the little boy was in his car seat and had only minor injuries. His mom, on the other hand, suffered a broken arm, and a deep gash on the left side of her neck due to broken glass, and she had a twisted piece of metal lodged in her left side puncturing her kidney. By the time she arrived at the emergency room, she had lost a lot of blood and had a weak pulse. She is upstairs in surgery and is expected to make a full recovery. "Did anyone locate a family member for the little boy?" I ask.

"Christy is in with him now. She was already here on another case and has agreed to contact the father. She's going to stay with him until his dad arrives."

"Do you want to talk to him about his wife or you want me to?" I ask.

Looking down at his watch, Doctor Collins shakes his head. "No, your break is soon. I got it."

"Thanks," I say, closing my laptop and standing. "I'm going to peek in on the little boy and see how he's doing before I go to lunch."

When I walk into the room where the little boy is being held, Christy is sitting beside the hospital bed, and I see the little guy has fallen asleep. "Hey," I speak quietly. "How's he been doing?"

"He was a little scared and worried about his mom. I was able to get his dad on the phone, and once he talked to him, he settled down and went to sleep. How's his mom doing? I heard she was pretty bad?"

"It was touch and go, but she's going to be fine. She should be out of surgery soon. I called up and told them her husband was on his way. They will send someone down to get him as soon as he gets here."

Slumping back in her seat, Christy lets out a deep sigh of relief. "That's good."

"So, how have you been? How's your husband doing?" I ask.

"Oh, you know, same old same old. The better half is doing good. He needs to talk to Quinn. He found an old 1966 Pontiac GTO for sale. It doesn't have a motor or anything, but he says the body is in decent condition. He figured Quinn would be interested. I won't see him until Friday when he comes to the center, though. The old man selling the car said he has another interested buyer but is willing to hold off a day or two for Quinn to look at it."

"How do you know Quinn and I are together? The last time we talked, I admitted I liked him, but we weren't an item."

Christy waves her hand at me, "Oh, girl, please. Quinn has made sure the whole town of Polson knows you belong to him. I mean, this is Quinn we are talking about."

Thinking about it for a second, I roll my eyes and agree, "True."

Looking at the clock on the wall, I realize I only have forty-five minutes left of my break. "Well, I'm going to get going. I'm starving. I'll be sure to relay your message to Quinn." After Christy and I say our goodbyes and I step out of the room, my phone rings. "Hello," I answer.

"May I speak to Emerson Evans?" the voice on the other end asks.

"This is her."

"Ms. Evans, this is Beth with Dr. Spear's office. We are calling to remind you of your appointment today. We were expecting you thirty minutes ago. Dr. Spears had a couple of cancellations and said she could see you now if you can make it."

Shit! I forgot about my appointment with my OBGYN today.

"Yes, I can make it. I'm on my way up now. Thanks for calling me." I head down the hall and make my way to the elevator and up to the third floor. Thank God, Dr. Spears is a friend. I worked alongside her when I first transferred to Polson.

"Good afternoon, Emerson," Dr. Spears greets me as she walks into the exam room. I'm only here for my birth control shot, so hopefully, I can get this taken care of and still have time to grab a snack from the vending machine. "How's it going, Dr. Spears? I'm sorry about missing my scheduled appointment time."

"It's okay. That's the life of a doctor. We're too busy taking care of others that we often forget to take care of ourselves. I see here you missed your last injection," she says, looking down at the tablet in her hands. "So, before I can administer another, we'll need to do a pregnancy test. Just as a precaution."

Confused, I hold up my hand, cutting her off. "What do you mean I missed my last injection? I came to that appointment." *Didn't I?*

Dr. Spears furrows her brows and looks back down at her notes then back at me. "No. I'm positive you missed that appointment. You called the next day and rescheduled to today," she reminds me.

Sitting on the exam table stunned, I think back to a few months ago. *Fuck, she's right.* I wasn't having sex at the time and didn't see it as a big deal missing my next shot. Suddenly I feel nauseous, and I clap my hand over my mouth. How many times have Quinn and I had sex in the past six weeks? Too many to count, that's for sure.

"Emerson, are you okay?" Dr. Spears asks, placing her hand on my shoulder. "I'm going to guess by your reaction to what I just said a pregnancy test is definitely in order?"

Closing my eyes and unable to speak, I nod my head in confirmation. Ten minutes after taking the test, the doctor returns to the room, and the look on her face confirms what I already knew. "I'm pregnant," I state before she has a chance to open her mouth.

"Yes, Emerson, you are pregnant. I want to do an internal ultrasound to see how far along you are. Are you okay with doing that now?"

"Yes."

At my agreement, Dr. Spears walks over to the ultrasound machine and places it next to the exam table. She steps out of the room, allowing me to prep myself. With shaky hands, I remove my scrub bottoms and panties then climb back on the exam table and use the provided paper cloth to cover myself. A minute later, she returns and flips off the lights before sitting down on a stool next to the machine. "You ready?"

"Yes," I say, not able to hide the shakiness of my voice. Once the ultrasound wand is in place, Dr. Spears clicks away at the keyboard, and suddenly the room fills with the whoosh, whoosh sound of a heartbeat—my baby's heartbeat. The moment feels so surreal. But in this very instant with mine and Quinn's baby's heartbeat filling the room, my priorities shift.

"Here he or she is," Dr. Spears says, pointing at the screen to an image the size of a pea. "You look to be about six weeks." That confirmation tells me this baby was most likely conceived the first time Quinn and I had sex. Of course, he would accomplish impregnating me on his first go. Knowing Quinn, he's probably going to brag about it too.

My body runs on autopilot for the rest of my shift. After finishing up with Dr. Spears and her giving me a prescription for prenatal vitamins and scheduling me for a follow-up appointment in four weeks, I grabbed myself a juice and chips from the vending machine since I missed my lunch. Now I'm sitting in my Jeep in the hospital parking lot staring down at the ultrasound picture in my hand. I can't help but question if I'm ready for this. Can I be someone's mom? At least I don't have to worry about Quinn's reaction. He has made his feelings about us having children clear. Even before we were together, he made comments about us having kids, or as he once said a litter.

One thing I know for sure about that man is that he jokes a lot about the subject, but he means every word he says. I know he'll be crazy happy about this news. Shoving all my fears about motherhood into the back of my mind, I place the ultrasound pictures in my bag, start my Jeep and head home.

When I pull up to my apartment, I see Grey on his bike parked a few spots over. Quinn texted me earlier saying he had club business and that Grey would see me home. Walking into my apartment, I head straight for my bedroom. I strip off my clothes that smell like the hospital and toss them in the hamper. All I want right now is a hot bath. I need time to relax and absorb the life-changing news I received. I even called my supervisor Dr. Brewer and told her I needed to take the next couple of days off work due to a family emergency. I've never taken so much as a sick day off of work, so she was understanding and said my taking two days wouldn't be a problem. But in all fairness, I'd say this situation constitutes a family emergency.

Sinking into the tub, I close my eyes and let out a deep sigh and think of all the changes about to take over my life and body. At the last thought, I run my hands over my still flat tummy. I can't believe there is a life growing inside of me right now. I may be uncertain of a lot of things at this moment, but there is one thing I'm sure of, and that is, I love Quinn, and he loves me. As long as I have the comfort of him and his love, I'll make it through anything thrown my way.

"What the hell are you doing!?" I hear, and I startle awake with water splashing all around me. I'm about to scream when through my water-filled eyes, coughing, and sputtering, I see Quinn in front of me, lifting me out of the tub where I must have fallen asleep. Wrapping a towel around my body, he carries me over to my bed and sits me down. Taking a knee in front of me, he begins drying me off. "Don't ever do that shit again, Emerson. Who knows what could have happened had I not come in here and found you? You could have drowned," he grits through clenched teeth.

"I'm fine, Quinn. It's not the first time I've fallen asleep in the tub," I say, trying to tease only for him to level me with a hard look. The look on his face says he is mad, but his eyes show I truly scared him. "You're right. It's dangerous. I'll be more careful from now on," I say, cupping his cheek. Nodding his head, Quinn goes about drying me off. He then walks over to the dresser and pulls out one of his t-shirts. They are my favorite thing to sleep in. "I thought we were going to the clubhouse for dinner tonight."

"No. We're going to stay in tonight. Pizza will be here soon," he informs as he slips his shirt on over my head.

"Is everything alright?"

Hearing the worry in my voice, Quinn kisses me gently on the lips. "Everything is fine. Just figured we needed to talk, Sunshine."

Taking my hand in his, he leads me out to the living room and guides me to sit on the sofa. Before Quinn has a chance to relax, the doorbell chimes. "That's probably the pizza." After paying the delivery guy, Quinn sets the food on the table in front of the sofa. The smell causes my mouth to water and my stomach to grumble. "Since you missed your lunch today, I want you to eat first, then we'll talk," he orders.

"How did you know I missed lunch?"

Taking a large bite, Quinn answers me around a mouth full of cheese pizza. "Max told me. Said he saw you scarfing down a juice and a bag of chips. I'm going to tell you right now, babe, there will be no more skipped meals. Even if I have to bring your lunch every day, you will eat."

Chucking my food back into the box, I turn my body toward Quinn and level him with a look. "Who the hell is Max? Do you have people spying on me at work, Quinn? Because if you do, that is not cool."

"First of all, babe," he says, grabbing me by the waist and bringing me over to straddle his waist. "I don't have people looking in on you because I don't trust you. I have you watched to protect you. You are the most important person in my life. I'll always have someone watching you and protecting you when I can't." Knowing this is something he feels strongly about, I decide to drop it, but not about who he has watching me.

"Fine, but that still doesn't answer my question on who this Max person is."

"Babe, you work with Max Collins. Also, the guys and I went to high school with him. He decided to come back home to Polson after med school and got back in touch with me when he did. I still grab a beer with him at Charley's a few times a month. He's a good guy," Quinn finishes with a shrug.

Still confused, I ask, "Max Collins as in Dr. Collins?"

"The same, babe."

"How come neither one of you mentioned you knew each other?"

"I wasn't trying to hide it from you. I honestly thought you knew."

Changing the subject, Quinn asks, " So, are there some other things we need to talk about, Sunshine?" he asks running his hands up and down my legs and suddenly, all thoughts of earlier today come flooding back. The baby.

"Yes, I have something I need to tell you," I confess while looking down and fidgeting with the hem of his shirt. My mouth has gone dry, and my heart feels like it's going to explode out of my chest. Placing his finger underneath my chin Quinn coaxes me to look at him.

"You don't have to be scared to tell me, Sunshine. I already know."

"Know what?" I choke out.

Quinn shakes his head. "Nope. I want to hear you say the words, Emerson. I want you to say the words I've been waiting two years to hear. Words that will make me the happiest man in the world," he rasps, resting his forehead on mine, and I begin to cry. In this moment with me in Quinn's arms, his face a breath away from mine and with his beautiful blue eyes on me I know that this baby I am carrying is meant to be. So, I give him what he's waiting to hear. "I'm pregnant."

"Yeah, you are," he says before claiming my mouth with a brutal kiss. A soul-consuming kiss that wipes away every fear I had about the future and replaces it with hope.

Breaking our connection, I ask, "How did you know?"

"It was little things over the past two weeks that gave it away. For one, you started drinking milk like it was water. You used to drink orange juice. Then one day, I came home, and you had five jugs of milk in the refrigerator, and you drink it morning, noon, and night. Then I noticed these," he says, cupping my breast.

"They're bigger and more sensitive," he tells me as he plucks my nipple through my shirt and I gasp. Quinn's right. My breasts are more sensitive. "Another thing that clued me in was you hadn't had a period in six weeks. I would know because I have fucked you every day of those six weeks."

"I can't believe you noticed all those things about me, and I didn't."

"I know every inch, every detail about you and your body, Sunshine. I have been patiently waiting for you to find out for sure and then come to me with what I already knew. When I called Max to check on you, he told me since returning from your lunch break, you seemed off. He also may have mentioned you spent about forty-five minutes up on the third floor."

"I don't know whether I should be happy Dr. Collins is your friend, and he looks out for me or creeped out by it."

Chuckling, Quinn shakes his head, "Max is a solid guy, babe. He's only reporting back to me as a favor."

A minute later, we both fall silent. We are content at the moment with him holding me. Quinn begins to rub lazy circles on my back. That and the rise and fall of his chest is all that is needed to lull me to sleep.

15

QUINN

I'm awake again in the early morning hours because I can't sleep, so I lay on my side, staring at my woman's beautiful face. My hand rests palm down, with my fingers splayed over her lower abdomen as she sleeps.

Holy shit balls, I'm going to be a dad.

My heart races. It may be a huge cliché, but as I lay here next to the mother of my unborn child, I can't help but put a different perspective on just about every damn aspect of my life. For the past couple of years, I've watched my brothers become fathers. And I'm not ashamed to admit the envy I felt because I wanted that for myself. And now it's happening for me. My life belongs to them now; belongs to Emerson and the child she carries.

Emerson begins to stir in her sleep. Her hand comes to rest over mine. With a long moan, she turns over on her side and faces me. "Can't sleep again?"

"Too excited to sleep," I tell her, which is partially correct. It's true, I am excited, but other things on my mind have kept me awake as well, but that's for me to worry about, not her. Emerson needs to focus on herself and the baby.

"I'm surprised you didn't call everyone last night," she softly giggles. Closing her eyes, she snuggles her face into my chest, her warm breath brushes across my skin, and I allow my eyes to close comforted by her warmth.

"It was our moment, babe. I didn't want to share it with anyone but you."

Emerson responds by placing her hand over my heart. "It beats for us," she whispers.

Rolling onto my back, Emerson rests her cheek on my chest. Kissing the top of her head, I hold the center of my universe as she falls back to sleep.

"YOU SHOULD FIND something safer to drive other than this Jeep now that you're carryin' our baby," I mention as I drive us to the clubhouse this morning. We need to take care of the whole car vandalization that happened the other day, but first, I'm going to have lunch with my brothers.

We've all been a little busy since my dad has been in the hospital recovering. My mom has been relying on me to help with my sister, so we haven't gotten the chance to sit down and figure any shit out yet. Jake assured me, though, he and the guys would handle things because I was needed elsewhere.

The good thing is my old man gets to go home tomorrow. Not to mention, I wanted Emerson to be with me when I told my brothers the news. This morning before leaving the house, Emerson said she wanted to wait until my dad got home from the hospital to visit and tell them they were going to be grandparents. I can't wait to see the look on their faces when we tell them.

Emerson whips her head in my direction. "What? There is nothing unsafe about my vehicle. I love my Jeep. I'm not getting rid of it."

Waiting for the light to turn green, I glance in her direction to find her arms crossed under her breasts. My eyes fall to her cleavage, and I forget what I was about to say. I become blinded by boobs. Then I start to think about how I'd like to fuck them. I visualize sliding—

A blaring car horn sideswipes my fantasy, bringing me out of my thoughts. My eyes finally rise to meet Emerson's.

"You done?" She raises her eyebrow, but her stare gives away the fact that my eye-fucking has turned her on. "By the way," she says, clearing her throat, "you're drooling, handsome." She grins.

Unfolding her arms, she reaches across the center console and uses the pad of her thumb to wipe some drool from the corner of my mouth. Her leaning in my direction only gives me a much better view. "I'm gonna slide my cock between your luscious tits one day, Sunshine," I confess my dirty thoughts. Another car's horn blows as the driver behind us becomes impatient.

Sitting back in her seat, Emerson laughs. "You're insatiable."

ONCE WE MAKE it to the clubhouse, I park under the tree next to the other women's vehicles.

"It will be nice to see the girls today, even if it's only for a couple of hours. Did they bring the kids too?" Emerson's smile grows, anticipating spending time with her friends.

"Yeah, as far as I know, the rugrats are here too, Sunshine." Unbuckling I climb out and meet my woman on the other side, helping her climb out.

"Quinn, I'm pregnant; not broken or made of glass," she fusses as her body slides down mine.

I kiss the tip of her button nose. "Get used to it." Taking her by the hand, I lead her inside.

What Emerson doesn't know is I contacted Lisa yesterday and asked her if she and the other women could whip together an early lunch today because she had to work, and I didn't want her to miss out. The other reason is, I want my brothers—my family to know she's having my baby.

As soon as we walk in, the smell of fried chicken engulfs my nostrils. "Oh my god, it smells so good in here." Emerson inhales deeply. Crossing the room, we stop at the bar where everyone is sitting.

Peeling herself from Logan's hold, Bella walks up and pulls Emerson in for a quick hug. "I'm so glad you could come by today."

"Me too." Her stomach growls loudly, causing laughter between the two of them. "I'm also starving," Emerson adds.

"Good, cause Lisa made her famous fried chicken today. I craved it almost every day when I was pregnant with Jake. It's so good," Bella brags, then looks up at me, her eyes softening. "How's your dad today?" she inquires.

"Doing good. He should get to go home tomorrow."

Bella smiles warmly, "With that good news, why don't we all fix a plate of food and eat outside at the picnic tables? It's such a beautiful day not to enjoy it. The kids are already out there with Raine and Ember."

I'm burstin' at the seams; I can't hold it in any longer. "I'm pregnant!" *Shit that came out all wrong.* Everyone freezes, and their eyes land on me. "My super swimmers knocked up my woman. I'm gonna be a daddy!" I can't stop grinnin' and place my hand over Emerson's flat stomach. "I finally get to be a dad." I look down at my woman who is biting her bottom lip. The entire room goes silent, but not for long.

"Super swimmers? Really?" Emerson shakes her head.

"Super swimmers, baby batter, dick spit." I shrug my shoulders. "Whatever you want to call my seed."

"Damn, brother, you didn't waste any time puttin' a bun in the oven, did ya?" Prez is the first to say as he walks up and places his hand on my shoulder. "Congratulations," he tells us both then hugs Emerson. All my brothers follow suit.

"I'm happy for ya, brother. You'll make a great dad," Logan says to me.

Reid makes his way over as well. "Congratulations, brother."

"Thanks." I take the beer Reid offers me and watch Emerson's face light up as the other women huddle around her and gush over the new mom to be—her happiness lighting up the room.

"How's it feel?" Gabriel asks when he comes to stand beside me.

It's everything I've wanted for two years. I give Gabriel my honest answer. "Fuckin' great, brother."

LUNCH WAS GOOD. For a couple of hours, we let go and enjoyed the day. When it comes time for Emerson to leave, I asked Austin to follow her to the hospital. "I love you, Sunshine." I lean down and kiss her lips that still taste like the cherry pie she ate earlier.

"I love you too," she says back.

I help her into her Jeep. "Text me when you get there. I'm gonna run by the youth center this evening and help Liam with his bike, but I'll be waiting on you when you get off work. Don't leave until I get there to follow you home. Got it?" Grabbing the back of her head, I pull her in for one more kiss after she has fastened her seatbelt.

"Got it." her nails dig into my scalp when she pulls me in and presses her lips against mine once more. This time the kiss is different. Deep and desperate.

She pulls away too soon, leaving me wanting more. I stand outside and watch until I lose sight of her and Austin before walking back into the clubhouse.

"Church," Prez announces just before downing the beer in his hand when the door behind me slams shut.

Once we've all taken our seat around the table, Prez speaks. "This shit with your car. It's not sitting well with me." His eyes cut to mine.

"It hasn't set well with me either, Prez. Something's truly fucked up with the sequence of events lately. First, my run-in with the fucker who put his hands on my woman. Second, we have to run him and his new-found biker buddies from town, then my dad gets shot—" I look around the room. "I don't believe my old man was shot by accident, and I don't think a poacher did it either. That message left on my car was personal." I let my words resonate with my brothers.

"You thinkin' it was Twiggy? You think he's been holdin' a grudge against you ever since you fucked him up?" Reid's arm folds across his chest, and he leans back in his chair.

"He's made it known more than once he has a hard-on for my ass since showing his face in our town. And somehow, he made his fight their fight," I finish.

Logan leans forward, resting his forearms on top of the table. "From what we have learned about the Satan's Reapers reputation, they don't need much coaching or reason to pick a fight with anyone. For them, it's more for sport than survival."

Tension builds in my neck, and a headache starts to develop. Rolling my neck from side to side, I try and loosen my muscles. Every damn thing is linked. My gut says so. The problem is proving it when there have been no signs of the bastards for more than a week now. One of those motherfuckers messed with my family.

"Here's the thing. We've had our men along with some of our known contacts in town keeping their eyes open and ears to the ground, trying to find these fuckers. We've turned up nothing," Logan adds.

I think back to my dad and where he was when he got shot. "What if these assholes went off the grid? We have a shit ton of mountains around here. It's one place they could hide. Plus makes it damn near impossible to find someone unless you know every area like the back of your hand." I throw the theory out there. It makes sense, and I don't know why I haven't thought of it before.

Prez scrubs his hand down his beard. "If that's the case, it would pose a problem for us. We don't have the manpower to send trekking through the thick, dense woods around here. If they are hiding in the shadows of the trees, it makes it that much easier for us to not see them if we go in to investigate. What extra men we have are already keeping tabs on our women and children." The wrinkle on his forehead deepens while deep in thought.

Doc, whose sitting alongside the wall shifts in his chair. "Jake, you still keep in touch with Ian?"

"From time to time. I haven't talked with Ian in a few months." Prez leans forward. "I see where you're going with this."

I, like the rest of the men, wait for him to divulge more, but he leaves us hanging. "Listen up. I'm gonna make some calls. For now, let's keep things as they are. We have eyes posted throughout town. The women have been instructed not to go anywhere without a brother with them, so I'm going to keep it that way. Quinn—," Prez pauses and focuses his attention on me, "Reid has a guy putting the finishing touches on security over at your parents' home. I advise you to let them know what's going on, or I will."

I nod my head in agreement. Knowing is half the battle. I fuckin' hate it, but they need to know our suspicions. I regret all this shit leads back to a grudge held against me.

"Get out of your head, son. None of this shit is your fault. These fuckers were lookin' for trouble. It just so happens Twiggy took up with them," Jake deadpans. "Humiliating their Prez in front of his men added fuel to the fire," he adds, rubbing his knuckles and grinning.

After a few moments of silence passes, the gavel hits the table.

Most of the men head out toward their homes. I head toward town riding alongside Reid because he's riding in the same direction since him and Mila still live downtown. We part ways at the intersection, him turning right, me turning left in the opposite direction heading toward the youth center. One thing about our youth center is they keep their doors open 24/7. They always have at least one staff member on-site, because the need for help of any kind knows no timeframe.

Pulling around to the backside of the property where the garage is located about twenty yards from the building, I park my bike alongside Liam's silver truck.

The doors to the work shed are open, and rock music is playing from inside, indicating he's been here for a while. I scan the area and double check my surroundings making sure it's secure. Liam is hard at work when I walk inside, having already broken down the entire engine with every part neatly laid out on a clean blue tarp across the floor. "Shit, kid, you've been busy." I hover over him.

"Hey, Quinn." He stands, turns the radio down, and wipes his hands on a shop rag. "Yeah." He removes his hat, runs his fingers through his hair then places that cap back on his head. "I didn't have any other plans, so I've been here most of the day. By the way, thanks for coming," he says with appreciation.

"No problem, kid. Let's see what we can get done before it gets too late." Working side by side, we clean all the motor parts and start to reassemble everything. We've almost got it together when I peer outside into the darkness. "It's getting late. You want to head on home? Don't need you gettin' into trouble," I mention as I wipe my forehead with the back of my forearm.

"Could you grab the gasket set out of the back of my truck really quick?" he asks.

"You got it," I offer.

Squatting, Liam bends over to inspect the motor parts we've

assembled, and I pivot around heading to his truck parked outside, and grab the parts box from beside the fender wheel. Turning the box over in my hand, I inspect it making sure he has the right gasket for the bike, which is why I don't notice anything is wrong when I step back inside the shed—until it's too fuckin' late.

"Stop right there, motherfucker."

Stopping mid-stride, I raise my eyes, finding Liam standing stock still with the barrel of a gun pressed against his temple. The filthy fucker holding him? None other than Twiggy.

"You done fucked up," I inform him.

He laughs. Signs he's high as fuck on something evident by his dilated pupils and sweat beading on his forehead. His trigger finger twitches. *Fuck.* "Throw the piece I know you're carrying to the floor before I blow this kid's brains out."

My eyes shift to Liam. So far, he's staying calm, which is good. This guy is already unpredictable. With him doped up on something, it makes him more so. The slightest movement from Liam could cause the guy to react without thought. Tossing the box I'm holding to the ground, I slowly raise my hands. With my right hand, I reach into the left side of my cut and pull my pistol from its holster, keeping my eyes on him the entire time.

"Don't fuck with me. Toss it. Now," he seethes. I do as he says, tossing it to the floor, then use my foot to kick it, causing it to skid across the floor midway between us. I keep my hands up.

"The kid has nothin' to do with this. Let him go." I keep the tone of my voice even and chill. His chin lifts as he says, "Your life for his. That's the deal. That's the only way he gets to live another day."

There's no hesitation in my response. "Deal."

The prick whistles. *Shit.* I hear boots crunch the loose gravel behind me. I know it's coming, yet I keep my eyes trained on Liam. His face is finally showing a hint of emotion. His eyes are pleading with me to do something, anything but sacrificing my own life for his. I receive a sharp blow to the back of my head. I don't fight it. A boot to my knee sends me to the floor before the two fuckers haul me up, each holding my arms at my side.

My patience is runnin' thin. "I'm not resisting asshole. Now let the kid go," I demand.

"Tie him up," he orders, which they do by placing my hands behind my back. Several zip ties dig into my flesh. "On the floor. Facedown," he orders, and I comply. He's smarter than I gave him credit for. He's made it much harder for me to try anything in this position. The other assholes snatch Liam, and Twiggy strides over and kneels near my face and places the barrel of his gun against the back of my head. The others put a gag over Liam's mouth. He struggles against it, earning a quick blow to the ribs.

I clench my teeth as I watch them land blow after blow to the kid's face and body. "You motherfucker, you gave your word you would let him live. My life for his."

Leaning down, he brings his mouth close to my face. The vile stench of his breath, making me want to gag. "I said he would live. I didn't say he would live unscathed."

With every blow, I cringe. Lifting a cheetah pipe off the workbench beside him, one guy raises it above his head and swings, bringing the steel down hard, breaking Liam's arm, leaving it to dangle in an unnatural position.

Suddenly I feel a prick to the inside of my left arm. *This asshole did not just stick me with a needle.* My body jerks, and immediately, I try to roll away. Other than the occasional joint I've smoked through the years, I've never touched any other drugs in my life.

His laughter grates at my ears like nails scraping a chalkboard. "Only the best for you, my friend." He and one of the other guys sit me on my ass. I zone in on Liam's beaten body lying motionless on the garage floor. Blood covering his face. The gag still in his mouth. Passed out but still breathing.

"You'll start feeling it in a second. You'll feel yourself levitate. It's fuckin' great," Twiggy tells me.

I fight it. I don't know what he injected me with, but my vision starts to blur around the edges. I shake my head, trying to clear my head. I'm finding it hard to keep any train of thought or even hold my head up. My whole body feels heavy, like gravity is pulling me into the ground trying to swallow me. The last clear-minded thought I have before completely being pulled under by the drug coursing through my veins is of Emerson.

16

EMERSON

Bracing my hands on the side of the bathroom stall at work, I stand on wobbly legs, wipe my mouth with the tissue in my hand and flush the toilet. Two days ago, morning sickness hit me like a battering ram. And the throwing up is not just in the morning; it's all damn day. I wake up feeling like I have a hangover and the only difference is there was no alcohol or good time the night before to make up for feeling like shit the next day. When I step out of the stall, I'm startled when I see Christy standing by the sink with a worried look on her face. I didn't hear anyone come in, though I wouldn't have over the sound of my retching.

"Emerson, are you okay? That sounded pretty bad in there."

Waving my hand, I stroll over to the counter, where I tossed my purse in haste a few minutes ago. "Yeah, I'm fine," I insist while unzipping my purse in search of the toothbrush and toothpaste I now keep in there.

"Are you sure? How long have you been sick? Have you seen someone about it? I know how you doctors are always taking care of others, but stubborn as hell when it comes to taking care of yourself," Christy huffs, crossing her arms over her chest.

I know by her stance she's not going to let me off the hook. Christy is the most obstinate person I know. Working with children and teenagers all day every day makes her that way. Hell, I've seen Christy make some of the most arrogant, pigheaded doctors around here bend to her will a time or two when it comes to the kids she cares for, so I'd expect nothing different for someone she considers a friend. I wouldn't put it past her to drag me out of this bathroom kicking and screaming insistent I see a doctor.

Once I've rinsed my mouth and splash water on my face making myself feel somewhat human again, I chance a glance at Christy. Yup, still standing there with her arms crossed and head cocked, waiting for my answer. Sighing, I turn and lean my butt against the counter. "I don't need to see anyone. It's just morning sickness," I confess.

The 'mom' look she had moments ago is replaced with one of shock followed by a full-fledged smile. "You and Quinn are going to have a baby?" she asks, and I nod.

"This is wonderful news. Congratulations." She beams. "I have to say I'm shocked I haven't heard about this sooner. You know with Quinn's big mouth and all." Christy giggles. "I mean, shouldn't he be on some rooftop pounding his chest and announcing it to the world?" she asks with amusement. I throw my head back and laugh because she hit Quinn's mark with that one.

"No rooftop declaration of fatherhood yet, but he did waltz into the clubhouse earlier today and announce to everyone there, and it did include the mention of his super sperm."

Christy shakes her head and grins. "Why am I not surprised."

Peering down at my watch, I groan when I see I still have a couple of hours left of my shift. I don't get off until ten o'clock. Quinn called me earlier, saying he was working late with one of the boys from the youth center, but he would be here in time to follow me home. "What are you doing here so late anyway?" I ask

Christy as I pull my lab coat back on, grab my purse and we make our way out of the bathroom and to the doctor's lounge down the hall.

"I was on my way out when I stopped by the restroom. There is an eighteen-year-old upstairs who I have been counseling that just gave birth."

Shoving my purse in my locker, I ask, "How is she doing?" I couldn't imagine being so young and having to face the kinds of obstacles some of these young people have today.

"She's holding up. Had a healthy baby boy," Christy tells me.

"Does she have any family with her?"

"Yeah, her aunt is with her. The girl's parents kicked her out when she became pregnant. Her boyfriend bailed. She was living at the shelter in town when Lisa called and told me about her. I helped her finish her GED and got her a job at the grocery store. They have a new manager now, and the woman hired Violet on the spot. She even worked out a paid maternity leave," Christy adds.

"That's great. Is she still at the shelter?"

"No, I set Violet up with New Hope House, and Sofia has helped her get into an apartment along with getting her everything she would need for the baby. Sofia is upstairs with her now. They have become good friends, and she has been with Violet every step of the way."

I found out weeks ago that not only did Christy know and work with Quinn, but she works with Lisa, Bennett, and Sofia. Christy is one of the few people who genuinely know how fantastic the club and their family is. Just as I am about to open my mouth to speak again, the door to the lounge bursts open, and Dr. Collins eyes land on me. "You're needed now Dr. Evans. Male approximately eighteen years of age was just brought in by ambulance. Suspected assault and is currently unconscious," he shouts.

Jumping into action, I slam my locker shut and rush out of the lounge and follow Dr. Collins to curtain two where the EMT's and nurses are transferring the kid from the stretcher over to the bed. The first thing I notice is he's nearly unrecognizable due to the amount of blood and swelling that has taken over his face. I also know by the odd angle of his right arm that it's broken.

After cutting away his shirt, nurse Kim goes about splinting the boy's broken arm while nurse Sarah takes his blood pressure. Dr. Collins starts his assessment of the boy's belly and ribs while shouting out a series of tests he wants to run on him. After checking the patient's heart, I use my penlight to check his pupils. With the patient's unconscious state and the dilation of his pupils, I suspect he has a concussion.

"I want a CT scan stat!" No sooner do I get those words out of my mouth when the boy proceeds to vomit, and I roll him to his side to prevent him from choking. When I push him back over, I see he has his left eye open. He can only see out of one since his right one is completely swollen shut. "Hey, sweetheart," I say in a soothing voice. "Can you tell us your name?"

"Liam."

"That's good, Liam. You're going to be okay. We're going to take you upstairs for a CT scan. That's where we take a picture of your brain."

Releasing the breaks for the bed, I lift the side rail and begin wheeling him out of the room toward the elevator. "I'm going to stay with him," I say to Dr. Collins.

"Okay, I'm going to see about finding his parents," he informs me just as I notice Christy waiting by the nurse's station. "Hey, Christy. Will you help Dr. Collins locate his parents?" I asked, gesturing toward my patient.

"Of course," she agrees, walking up and suddenly stops when she looks down at the boy lying in bed. "Oh my God, Liam!" She gasps.

"You know him?"

"Yes. I know his mom too. I'll call her now. Listen, I'll bring her to you when she arrives." Christy rushes out, wasting no time getting on the phone.

With that part taken care of, nurse Kim and I continue to the second floor for the CT scan. An hour and a half later, I walk into Liam's hospital room, where he will be staying for the next few days. The scan proved my suspicions were correct and that he has a concussion and an Orthopedic surgeon has been by to look at his broken arm which will require surgery.

Sitting in a chair on one side of his bed is his mom, Beth, along with Christy standing behind her and on the other side is a police officer. Everyone stops talking as I enter the room. My eyes immediately go to my patient who, under the circumstances, looks a bit better and more alert which is a relief. Next, I meet his mother's gaze, and she returns a tired but polite smile. Then there is Christy. A pinch of guilt fills my stomach because she was supposed to have gone home hours ago, but here she is making sure this young boy and the family she works with are going to be okay. The woman works just as hard if not more than the doctors and nurses in this hospital. Lord knows she spends just as much time here.

"Everything okay in here?" I ask, and Christy is the first to speak.

"Yes. The officer here was just about to take Liam's statement on what happened tonight."

"Well, alright, I'll leave you to it. I just wanted to check on you before heading home."

"If you don't mind, Dr. Evans, I'd like for you to stick around. I need to speak with you after I finish questioning Liam."

"Sure officer," I say, taking a seat next to the window on the other side of the room. When I notice it's nearly eleven o'clock, and I haven't heard anything from Quinn, I pull out my phone and fire off a text. He said he would be here by ten o'clock to follow me home. It's not like him to be late or at least contact me if he was going to be. I'm just about to text Austin since he's the one who is on hospital watch today when Liam says something that not only catches my attention but also sends a cold chill down my spine.

Standing from my seat, I walk over to the edge of the hospital bed as dread seeps into my stomach. "Did you say you were at the youth center tonight when you were assaulted?" I ask, interrupting the officer's questioning.

"Yes. Quinn and I were working on my bike. He said he was going to stay late and help since it wasn't a school night. He wanted me to get home so I wouldn't miss curfew. It was around nine o'clock when we decided to call it a night. Quinn was getting some parts from my truck while I began gathering up the tools."

"What happened next?" the officer questions.

"I was putting tools away when two dudes grabbed me. After that, everything happened so fast. One of the men holding me had a gun. He told Quinn if he didn't go with them, they were going to kill me." At his last statement, Beth lets out a sob. The officer begins to speak again, but I can't hear anything past the whooshing sound in my ears. It's taking everything I have to choke down the bile rising in my throat. I know what's coming next out of Liam's mouth, yet I'm not prepared to hear it.

"Quinn gave himself up for me," Liam chokes out. "He gave himself up, and then they made him watch as they beat the shit out of me."

"Can you tell me what these men look like?" the officer asks.

"No, sir. I don't remember," Liam curtly replies.

Suddenly my vision blurs, and my legs feel as they are about to give out. Thankfully, Christy comes up behind me and catches me before I fall and guides me over to a chair.

"Is she okay?" the officer inquired, standing from his chair.

"She's fine officer, just a little stomach bug," Christy lies. "Emerson, look at me."

Fighting back nausea and tears threatening to spill out, I look at my friend who's kneeled in front of me.

"You have to call the club right now," she says in a hushed tone, so the cop doesn't hear us. "You have to call Jake and get them here now."

Drawing every bit of strength I have in me, I quickly stand and excuse myself from the room. I don't want to alert the officer to what I am doing. My loyalty is to the club, and right now, the man I love is missing. I have a feeling the shit that has been happening with the other bikers has something to do with Quinn's abduction. If that's true, the cops won't be any help. Running down the hall, I slip into the stairwell, and with shaky hands, immediately dial Jake.

"Doc?" Jake's husky voice answers, and I can no longer hold back my anguished sob.

"Jake."

"Emerson, sweetheart?" His voice now gentle but alert. "What's wrong?"

"You and the guys need to come to the hospital—now," I cry. "Some guys took Quinn." I hear some rustling in the background, along with Jake barking orders followed by the sound of his motorcycle starting.

"The guys and I are on our way, sweetheart. Be there soon." Then the line goes dead.

Swiping the tears off my face, I take a couple of deep breaths. "Get your shit together, Emerson. Quinn needs you to stay strong," I say to myself. By the time I calm myself down and decide to walk outside to get some fresh air, I hear the rumble of Harleys as they pull into the parking lot. Led by Jake is Logan, Gabriel, Reid, and Bennett. Every one of them with the look of murder in their eyes, and it's that look that gives me hope. I provide the guys with a brief rundown of what Liam said went down earlier tonight.

"I want to talk to the boy," Jake demands, and we all make our way up to his hospital room. When we walk in, the officer is still here, and he stands.

"Delane. You and your boys need to leave. The cops will handle the situation."

"I don't fuckin' think so. One of my brothers is missing, and if you think me or my men are going to go home and sit around with our thumbs up our asses, then you have another thing comin'." Jake squares off with him.

"Don't make me have to take you all in for obstruction," the cop spits.

I hear a growling noise come from Gabriel.

"We're not obstructing shit," Jake fires back.

When the cop opens his mouth to say something, Beth interrupts, "Jake and his men can stay. If my son remembers anything else, we'll be sure to give your department a call."

The cop reaches into his pocket and gives Beth a card with a phone number. "Call me if he remembers anything else."

I can tell by the officer's red face he doesn't like the fact he was dismissed, and Jake got his way. As soon as the cop disappears out of the room, we turn our attention toward Liam.

"Satan's Reapers," he says. I realize he lied to the cop, telling him he didn't remember who took Quinn. I look to his mom to gauge her reaction to her son lying to the authorities, and she doesn't look the least bit upset. That goes to show the kind of impact Quinn has had on this boy's life. He and his mom are choosing to give their loyalty to the club rather than the police. Jake turns and gives Gabriel and Reid a signal and the two of them burst out of the room. He turns to Bennett and barks, "Lockdown."

"I'm sorry, Mr. Delane," Liam apologizes. "I should have fought harder, but those men were too strong."

Walking over to the hospital bed, Jake places his hand on the kid's shoulder. "None of this shit is your fault, son. Quinn did what any of us would expect him to do. If he were here now, he'd kick your ass for feeling guilty about it. Now, we're going to head out and let you get some rest."

It's at this moment I see why Quinn and the guys admire Jake so much and what makes him a good President. His brother is missing, and only God knows what's being done to him right now, but here he is keeping his cool in front of this kid and reassuring him not to place blame on himself.

I follow Jake and Logan out of the hospital and to the parking lot where I watch Bella climb off Grey's bike and head straight for me. Her tears mirror my own, making me aware she's heard the news by now, and I realize Logan most likely summoned her here for my sake. These people have become my family, and right now, I need them more than ever.

Bella's steps never falter as she makes her way across the parking lot toward me. As soon as I am within arm's reach, she pulls me in for a hug. I cling to her and finally let the tears that I have been holding back fall.

"It's going to be okay, Emerson. They'll find him." A second later, Grey pulls up beside us in my Jeep and hops out.

"Angel, I want you to drive Emerson back to the clubhouse. Jake and I will lead, and Grey will tail," Logan orders.

Knowing we don't have time to waste, I climb into the passenger seat of my car while Bella gets in on the other side. When we pull up to the clubhouse, the first person I see rushing out the door toward Jake is Quinn's mom Victoria. I watch Jake gently grab her by her shoulders and murmur something to her. A second later, she lets out a blood-curdling cry just before Jake scoops her up and carries her inside.

My body is numb. I sit in my Jeep, unmoving. I don't know where to go from here. *What do I do?* I've never felt so helpless in all my life. *How could God be so cruel? Why would he bring me the love of my life only to take him away so soon?* A rapping on my window brings me out of my fog.

I turn my tear-filled eyes to see Blake standing next to my passenger door. When I don't move, he opens the door for me. "Come on, Doc. Let's get you inside."

With a slight nod, I take Blake's hand and make my way into the clubhouse to face my reality.

17

QUINN

A dull throb accompanied by ringing in my ears seems to be the only thing I can focus on at the moment I start to come to my senses. My eyelids feel heavy, but I try prying them open when I feel my body jostle from side to side. The sensations I'm feeling—the vibrations and humming of wheels running along asphalt brings me to the conclusion that I'm in a moving vehicle.

I lick my lips. *Fuck,* my mouth tastes like I ate a bag of cotton balls. After several attempts, I crack my lids. The smell of paint and paint thinner is overwhelming. Lying still, I home in on the low murmured voices coming from somewhere in the vehicle, but after a few minutes, they fall silent. Unfortunately, through my brain fog, I can't make out a word.

Still secured behind my back, I wiggle my hands that are now numb from the lack of blood flow due to the tightness of the bonds. *Shit.* Lifting my head slightly off the floor, I do my best to glance around. No windows. Painters supplies like ladders and white tarps clink on the other side of where I lay. I have no idea how long I've been passed out, but from the little to no light in here, I have to assume it hasn't been for very long.

"Well looky here, fellas. It looks like pretty boy decided to join the party," the detached voice drifts from the farthest end of the van, followed by the strike of a lighter setting his face aglow as he lights a smoke. My eyes fixate on the orange-red glow of the burning end of the cigarette as he takes a drag. The fucker sure was quiet this whole time sitting in his little corner.

"Aww, shucks. I'm flattered you find me attractive, but my dick doesn't swing that way," I taunt him. Not that it's in my best interest to fuck with the asshole, but what the hell, there's nothin' better to do at the moment. As expected, I get a rise out of him. The toe of his heavy boot makes direct contact with my balls, sucking the air from my lungs and leaving me with a deep resonating guttural pain equivalent to feeling like I could shit myself at any moment. *God damn*, I'd rather get punched in the face than get kicked in the balls. *Hit where it hurts, right?*

"Who's laughing now, asshole," the guy spits.

"Sit the fuck down, Smokey. We need him to walk on his own unless you plan on carrying his ass the whole way there!" the voice I recognize as Twiggy hollers out from behind me, so he's either driving this heap or sitting in the passenger seat. Smokey, as he calls himself, sits back down, but not before thumping his lit cigarette ashes onto my face.

Bracing my foot against a stack of paint cans, I maneuver myself to sit in an upright position, pushing my back against the ladder on the opposite side. The van falls silent. It gives me a clear-headed moment to figure out how I'm going to get out of the mess I'm in. By now, Emerson will have been trying to find out why I never showed up to follow her home from work. Then my thoughts shift to Liam. The poor kid. They worked him over well. I just hope someone finds him.

The ride becomes bumpier after a few minutes before coming to a sudden stop. No one exchanges words until the back doors swing open, allowing the dim moonlight in.

"Time to go. Prez wants shit done before daybreak," Twiggy orders. With force, the guy riding in the back along with me grabs me by the collar of my leather cut, shoving me out the double doors. With no way to catch my fall, I land on my knees, a mixture of sand and rock beneath them, sending dull throbs of pain through both joints. Glancing around, I try to make out our location. We've stopped a few yards away from a bridge. The reflection of the moon lights the water below. *Shit.* I don't see any signs or markers. It's too fuckin' dark.

"Stand his ass up," someone's told.

"Stop being a bossy prick, Twiggy. No one was left in charge of this little adventure." They start to argue amongst themselves. The one who kicked my baby makers hauls me up from my kneeled position. My patience runnin' thin, I proceed to kick his feet out from under him. Lifting my foot, I bring it down, crushin' the heel of my twelve-inch boot between his legs to see how far I can shove his balls up his ass.

"How's that feel, motherfucker?" I grind harder before my body is slammed against the side of the van with a gun pointed at my face. Turning his head, Twiggy addresses the other guy who is picking himself up off the ground holding his pint-sized dick in the palm of his hand. "Get rid of the van."

Ushering me toward the edge of the tree line he warns, "Try some stupid shit like that again I'll shoot you where you stand."

My attention shifts to the engine of the van revving before watching as it barrels toward the bridge railing then plunges into the water below. His two biker buddies take off into the woods, and Twiggy waves the barrel of his gun in their direction. "Get to walkin'."

With two leading the way—one shining a dim flashlight to guide us through the darkness and another behind me—we begin making our way through the dense trees. Tilting my head back, I glance at the night sky, hoping maybe the position of the stars might give me some idea of the direction we are walking in. Sadly, between the cloudy skies and the thick tree canopies above us, I can't make out much of anything.

With their ease of navigation, my theory that they might be held up in an area such as this proves accurate. They know where they are going.

Here's the thing. I'm still alive. Which means, they have an agenda. For now, that's good. It gives my brothers time to try and find my ass. It's also bad, unfortunately, because that means they have plans for me. They get to toy with me. Bad because the deeper we hike into the woods, the harder it will be for the club to find me. I value my life. I have everything to live for. I'm not about to throw it all away and risk dying just yet.

Thankfully, the three of them are so focused on where they are going, they let me be. One thing I happen to notice, which is completely stupid on their part but beneficial to me is I've watched one of the guys pluck what looks to be fruit candy from his pocket—and often. When he does this, he tosses the wrapper to the ground. Ten times. I've kept count. I'm hoping one of the others doesn't catch on or may be too dumb to give a shit that he's leaving a crumb trail. Granted, the possibility of someone—one of my brothers hiking into this section of the mountain is slim.

Never say never. Right?

While trying to keep my mind from wandering—keep myself from overthinking about Emerson and my unborn child, and what she must be going through, I start counting to help me keep track of time. We've walked for a good two hours or more since I began to count not long after disappearing among the cover of the trees.

Up ahead is a small clearing. The guy in front with the flashlight stops and casts the light down at his feet and starts looking for something by kicking leaves and branches from side to side. A heavy thick rope comes into view. Squatting, he grips the string into his hand and lifts. *What the hell?* A piece of old as fuck plywood lifts off the forest floor, and I'm staring into a dark hole. Is this where they plan on keeping me? I feel like I've dropped into a real-life Deliverance scene and pretty soon, I'll hear banjos playing in the background.

Just as I get the idea I'm about to be pushed into the abyss and left to rot, the flashlight reveals steps leading down to hell.

"Get in." Twiggy pushes me forward with a hand between my shoulder blades. Again, the one with the light goes down first, followed by me and the other two. Once we've descended several steps, my feet touch the bottom.

Holy shit. I'm in an underground bunker of some sort. From what I can make out in the cover of darkness, it looks like the inside of a large shipping container. Solid steel all around. How the hell did someone get this big ass thing here in the first place? It's like walking into one of those weird reality shows.

"I get it. You guys are like those doomsday preppers you see on TV or somethin'? You believe we all die in a zombie apocalypse?" That earns me a sharp blow to the side of my head with the heavy end of a gun. *Shit, that stung.* Squeezing my eyes shut, I shake it off. Dim lights flicker before illuminating half of the space, bringing part of the room into view. At the far end of the container with his arms crossed over his broad chest, Boulder, their president, sits on a chair, a sinister grin on his face. Another one of his men sits across from him.

Shits about to get real.

"Ah, our guest has arrived." He stands. My head turns from left to right, taking in my surroundings. "Impressive huh?" he states, walking over to a small fridge retrieving a bottle of water from the inside. I have to agree with him. It is impressive. How the hell do they even have electricity, isolated out here? Then I spot a collection of car batteries stacked on a shelf to my left. Boulder jerks his head, gesturing for his men to move me toward a chair with leather straps attached to the arms and legs. Next to the chair sits a table draped with a tarp to hide whatever lies underneath.

Smokey pulls a knife from his boot and cuts the zip ties from my wrist, slicing my skin in the process. The sting is nothing compared to the relief my fingers are feeling as my blood rushes back to the tips and the prickles of numbness start to fade. Forcefully pushed down into the chair, they strap me in leaving one hand free.

Boulder shoves an unopened bottle of water at me. Eyeballing him for a moment, I snatch it from him. I'm no dumbass. I need to stay hydrated as often as I can get it because I have no idea how long this whole ordeal will play out before my brothers find me. Hopefully, I'll have the opportunity to escape, or—they kill me. Either way, they want to keep me alive for now, and that's the way I'd like to keep it.

Letting out a heavy sigh of thirst after gulping half the water down my dry throat, I address the elephant in the room. *Me.* "Alright, boys, let's get this show on the road. You can do what you want with me, but know this—I'm not talkin'. I'll die for my brothers; It's something called loyalty—something you don't know anything about. Let's see what you got."

He motions with a look for someone to take my water and secure my free hand. Holding my chin high, I stare the fucker down. He glares.

That's right, fucker, bring it.

"Oh, well, we don't want much. Just everything your club has. That's it," he boasts as he pulls a cigar from a pack resting inside his shirt pocket and lights it. Tilting his head back, he blows a puff of smoke toward the roof. "I want your town." Striding to the table next to me, he lifts the tarp exposing what he plans to use on me and picks up a rusty ice pick. "I want your President to tuck tail and run. I want blood. You will break. Your club will break. One by one, I'll take and shatter everything all of you hold dear. Starting with you." I brace myself as he rams the blunt tip of the pick into my right thigh. I grit my teeth, absorbing the pain that spreads down my leg as he twists it.

I chance a deep breath before every man in the room takes his turn landing blow after blow. At some point, Twiggy takes his turn at me. The pussy slaps me across my already bloodied face. Lookin' at him, I grin and taste my blood dripping from my busted lip. "Is that all you got? My baby sister hits harder than you—you fuckin' pussy." I spit blood at his feet. Closing his fist, he strikes me again. This time across my left ear that I can no longer hear out of after taking blow after blow from the others already.

"Sweet lookin' little thing—that sister of yours," he taunts.

He wants my attention. Now he's got it. My blood boils. I narrow my eyes into slits. "If your filthy fuckin' hands ever touch her, I'll kill you and everyone you share blood with, motherfucker." Forgetting I am strapped down to the chair; I try flinging myself toward him.

He laughs in my face. "Maybe I'll finish what I started with that feisty doctor lady of yours," he says, reaching down and grabbing his crotch. "Show her what a real dick feels like as I shove it down her throat and make her choke on it."

Two men grab my upper arms, keeping me in place as I attempt to break free of my restraints so I can kill the son of a bitch with my bare hands. Fuck the bullet. I want to feel the life drain from him.

Reaching into his cut, he pulls a hypodermic needle from the inside pocket and holds it up between his fingers. "I wonder if she will love you all strung out. Will she love an addict? After a few days, your body will start to crave it—need it to get by." He walks toward me. The others hold me tighter as I watch him take the cap off the tip. Gripping my arm, he presses the needle against the flesh of my inner wrist, breaking skin.

Breaking me with pain isn't their plan. The torture is strictly for shits and giggles. No. They plan on breaking my spirit another way. They plan on keeping me strung out on drugs.

My head falls back as warmth spreads through my body. The pain I was feeling seconds ago begins to fade away. Like in the garage at the youth center, my body relaxes to the point of weightlessness. The leather straps across my wrists loosen. I don't fight them as they rip my leather cut, covered in my blood off my body and toss it on the floor at my feet.

I fixate on my club symbol.

The very same tattooed across my back.

I fight to keep my eyes open.

The men of Satan's Reapers form a semi-circle in front of me. That's the last thing I remember before letting go—allowing the undertow to pull me under.

18

JAKE

Pulling into the clubhouse parking lot, I dismount my bike and cut my eyes over my shoulder to see Bella parking Emerson's Jeep. "Blake!" I bark when I see him striding in my direction after securing the entrance gate. "Help Emerson inside."

With a nod, Blake makes his way toward Emerson's car. No sooner does he turn around when Quinn's mom Vicky bursts through the clubhouse door and makes a beeline in my direction. "J.D., tell me it's not true!"

Reaching up, I grab hold of her shoulders to steady her before delivering the blow. "I'm sorry, sweetheart." This shit right here is the toughest part about being the club President. Having to deliver the news to a mother her son is missing all while everyone else around you is looking for guidance; looking at you like you have the answers to make the nightmare go away, only you're dying on the inside just like the rest of them wondering what the hell you are supposed to do. Hell, I know what I want to do, and that's tear this whole fuckin' town apart until I find every one of those sons of bitches, shove my gun down their throats and send them straight to hell. Those pussies will be begging for the devil's mercy by the time my club is through with them because that bastard doesn't have shit on the wrath The Kings will be dishing out. My brother is missing. Taken by some pieces of shit men who have the nerve to come into my town and fuck with my family. The woman in my arms lets out the most painful cry I have ever heard, and I haul her up into my arms and carry her inside.

When I walk in, all eyes are on me. Ignoring everyone's shocked and somber faces, I stride across the room, up the stairs and to the room I know Vicky is staying in. It's the room right across from Quinn's. No sooner do I set Vicky down on the bed, Bennett walks into the room with his medic bag and Lisa trailing behind him. He kneels on the floor in front of her. "Everything's going to be alright. Ya, hear me?"

"You bring my boy home, J.D. I want you to promise me right here, right now, you'll bring him home."

"You have my word, sweetheart."

Looking at Bennett, I give him the go ahead and watch as he pulls a syringe and vial from his bag. "I want you to let Bennett give you something to help you calm down. You stay here and rest. I'm going to send someone over to the hospital to stay with Quinten, and the girls will keep an eye on Kat."

Vicky lets out another sob and nods. Once Bennett administers the shot, I turn to Lisa, and she cuts me off knowing what I am about to ask. "I'll stay with Vicky. You men get shit done. Bring our boy home."

When I step out of Vicky's room, I come face to face with my boys, Logan, Reid, and Gabriel. All three carry the same look—one of retribution. No words are spoken as I stride past them. They fall in and follow behind me as I make my way back out to the common room.

Meeting Austin's eyes across the room, I signal him over. "I want you to get to the hospital ASAP. Your ass doesn't move from Quinten's room until he is discharged tomorrow. You put a bullet in the head of anyone not hospital staff or family, no questions asked."

Austin tips his head. "You got it, Prez," he says, then turns on his heel and leaves without another word.

Scanning the room, I see our entire family is accounted for. All our women and children, along with my parents, sit silently while looking at me. My eyes land on Rain and Ember who are on the floor in the far corner playing with the children. Reading my thoughts, Rain and Ember gather the children and usher them out of the room toward the back of the clubhouse to the playroom. When they pass us, I notice Remi holding Kat's hand in support. She doesn't know the details of what happened, but she knows something has happened to her brother. I halt Remi's movements and kiss the top of her head silently thanking her for comforting her friend.

Once the room is clear of children, I speak. "I'm sure you all know by now a little of what has happened. Quinn is missing." When those words leave my mouth, I hear sobs echo off the clubhouse walls. "You know I can't go into great detail about what's happening, but rest assured my men and I will be bringing our brother home, and those responsible will pay." I make sure to look directly at Emerson when I deliver my last statement. She is the one I worry about the most. Emerson is pregnant with Quinn's child. The stress and worry of this situation can be dangerous for her pregnancy. There is too much at stake right now.

Jerking my head toward the door to my left, I motion for the guys to follow as I walk into church. Slamming the gavel down, I bring church to order—the plethora of emotions filling the room right now is thick and heavy. The unprecedented events of today brought on a storm of epic proportions. Not once in the history of this club have we had to face the fact that one of our brothers has been taken. The Kings have seen it all and been through some of the most devastating circumstances regarding the women we love, but this is new territory. Quinn is our brother, a part of who we are. The Kings would not be The Kings without him.

"You ready, Prez?" Reid asks, bringing me to attention. At my nod, Reid syncs his laptop with the monitor on the wall and pulls up the security feed from when our brother was taken. The club is responsible for the security system at the youth center. When we arrived at Liam's hospital room and learned what happened, Reid didn't waste any time gathering the evidence we needed. As soon as he hits Play every eye in the room watches as a couple of men wearing Satan's Reapers cuts emerge from the shadows and grab Liam. Then we watch as Quinn steps into frame. What happens from there has me seeing red.

Jumping from my seat, I grab my chair and hurl it across the room and watch as it shatters against the brick wall. "Son of a fuckin' bitch!" I boom. Nobody says a word. The room goes silent and serves as, yet another reminder Quinn is gone. By now, he would have made some snide comments, and I would have threatened him with a bullet to his ass for it. With my hands resting on my hips, I close my eyes and rein in my temper. My men are looking to me for what to do next and losing my cool will not help the situation.

Once I've calmed, I turn, face my club, and deliver my orders. "Reid, get back on your computer and tap into every goddamn camera in Polson. See if you can catch sight of any one of those sons of bitches. Demetri, I want you and Nikolai to bring in some of your men to keep a watch on the clubhouse and our families. With my guys out looking for Quinn, I'll need some backup on the home front."

"You got it, my friend," Demetri agrees before he and Nikolai leave the room and start speaking rapid-fire Russian into their cells.

"Bennett, I want you to keep a watch on Emerson. All this

stress is not good for her and the baby. I want her checked on the hour every hour."

Lastly, I turn to Logan and Gabriel. "I'm going to put a call into the Louisiana chapter. We need all the manpower we can get. The more eyes, the better. In the meantime, I want you to get out there and tear the motherfuckin' state of Montana apart."

The second the room is clear, I sit back down at the table and make a call. It's time for reinforcements. Dialing the number, it rings twice before I hear Riggs' gruff voice coupled with loud music and a giggling woman.

"Jake."

"Riggs."

The tone of my voice must alert Riggs that something is wrong because I hear him bark out a few commands, and the background noise ceases.

"Talk to me, brother."

"That prospect you let go of hooked up with another club, the Satan's Reapers. Cock suckers snatched Quinn a few hours ago."

"Fuck!" Riggs hisses. "What do you need from me? Anything, and it's yours."

"I need you and every available brother you have to haul ass to Montana, brother."

"You got it, Jake. My men and I will be headed your way before sunrise."

"I owe ya one, Riggs."

"Hell, no, you don't. That's what brothers are for."

Running my palm over my weary face, I rest my elbows on my knees. Closing my eyes, I drift back to the day a scrawny mischievous kid with a busted lip, and black eyes walked into my clubhouse.

I'm tossing back a beer at the bar with one of the club girls, Suzy, perched on my lap dressed in a barely-there dress, and her fake tits pressed up on me when the door to the clubhouse opens drawing my attention. Turning on my stool, I see Logan and Reid strolling in from school with their backpacks slung over their shoulders. My brows furrow when I look at some blond-haired scrawny runt trailing behind them. Both Logan and Reid are acting as if this is the norm having some stranger walking in behind them and into my clubhouse. Tapping Suzy on her ass, I motion for her to get lost. I smirk when I see the newcomer's eyes go big as he watches Suzy sway her hips as she struts over to Sean, who is sitting on the sofa.

"Logan, Reid, you boys get your asses over here!" I holler.

"Mind tellin' me who the hell this kid is and why he's standing in my clubhouse droolin' over Suzy's tits?" I ask, thumbing my finger toward the kid.

"Followed us home from school, Prez," Reid answers. "He was getting his ass kicked in the bathroom at school. Logan and I stepped in and took care of the fucker wailing on him. Now he's declaring himself as our best friend or some shit. Followed us home."

"Fuck me," I mutter. "Hey, shithead," I call, getting the kid's attention. "Wipe your goddamn mouth and get your ass over here."

Without a care in the world or any fear, the kid steps to me, looks me straight in the face and gives a full-on grin. "I think I'm going to like it here," he says, beaming.

Chuckling, I ask, "You got a name, kid?"

"My name's Quinn Beckett."

"Well, Quinn, do you know where you're at?"

"Yes, sir. I'm at The Kings of Retribution clubhouse. I haven't lived in Polson for a very long time, but I've heard about you guys. Everyone knows who The Kings are."

"What would your folks say if they knew you were here right now?" I ask. "To most people in this town, we're nothing but dirty criminals."

Shrugging, Quinn answers. "Mom and Dad say you can't judge a book by its cover. They said you should never believe in rumors. It's best to get to know someone and make your mind up about that person. The way I see it, Logan and Reid saved my skin today. I've made up my mind."

From that day forward, Quinn was a daily presence at the clubhouse. The day he graduated from high school was the day he became a prospect for The Kings. I watched him as he earned his patch and took pride in watching him grow to be the man he is today.

The door behind me slamming open gains my attention and brings me to my feet.

"Prez, we need ya," Gabriel grunts.

"What's goin' on?"

"There's a kid at the gate. He has a package with him. Said he was told to bring it here."

Stomping my way across the clubhouse parking lot, I make my way to the front gate where there is, in fact, a boy no older than twelve standin' there next to a bike with a box in his hands.

"What's your name, boy?"

"M...mm...my name is Devan," he stammers.

"What are ya doing here on my property, Devan?"

"Some guy in town paid me fifty bucks to deliver this package." His voice cracks.

"Can you tell me what this guy looked like?"

"Um... he had black and grey hair. He had a big belly. He was also wearing a vest like yours; only it didn't say Kings."

"What did his cut say?" The question comes from Gabriel, and the boy's eyes got big, and he looks like he's going to piss his pants.

"It had Satan's something on it," Devan tells us.

"Fuckin' bastards," Logan hisses.

"Okay, son. I want you to put the box down on the ground. Then I want you to get on your bike and go home. If a man with that same kind of cut comes up to you again, I want you to run. Ya hear me kid?"

Nodding his head frantically, the boy jumps on his bike and

pedals his ass out of here like it's on fire. Those sorry fuckers have nerve, draggin' innocent kids into their business. Looking down at the box sittin' on the ground in front of me, my gut clenches because I know that whatever is inside is a message. By the looks on Logan and Gabriel's face, they know it too. Bending down, I rip the tape off the closed box then open the flaps. As soon as the contents inside are exposed, I hear a loud gasp behind me. When I whip around, I see Emerson with tears running down her pale face and her hand clasped over her mouth.

19

EMERSON

Collapsing to my knees, the gravel from the clubhouse parking lot sends sharp piercing pains up my shins as I begin to vomit what little bit of food I was able to hold down. But the pain in my legs doesn't compare to the pain in my heart. I wish with all I am that I could unsee what I just saw in that box. Moments ago, one by one, I watched as the men came out of the room they hold church. Each man walked through the clubhouse with fire in their eyes. Each one's body language spoke as if it were saying leave me the fuck alone—I'm on a mission. That mission being murder. Not two minutes after Logan and Gabriel walked out of the clubhouse, they returned. Only this time I couldn't decipher the looks that marred their faces. When they reemerged, this time with Jake in tow, I knew something was up. I wanted answers. Only I was not prepared for the response I got when I stupidly followed them out to the parking lot, where the guys were standing around a package sitting on the ground. I walked up behind Jake just as he flipped the top open. Inside—Quinn's cut covered in blood, accompanied by the very distinct smell of urine.

"Fuck!" I hear Jake hiss just before he hauls me up into his arms and carries me back inside. Through my drunken state, I feel Jake lay me down on a bed. An all otoo familiar smell tells me I am in Quinn's room. The scent causes me to cry even harder. It comforts me and causes my heart to ache all at the same time. I can't imagine not having his arms wrap around me ever again as I breathe in his scent.

"Sweetheart, I need ya to calm down. Take slow deep breaths," Jake says, and I realize I am on the verge of hyperventilating.

"Slow, doc. In and out. There ya go."

Blinking away my tears, I do as Jake encourages while keeping my eyes on his. After several cleansing breaths, the fog clears from my brain.

"I know what you saw was some fucked up shit, doc. I know it will do no good for me to tell you not to worry, but you need to get your emotions in check. Think about the baby."

Shit! He's right. Jake is right. This stress is not good for my baby.

"Quinn would kick my ass if I let anything happen to you or his baby. So, do me a solid, doc, and let's do what we need to do to make sure the two of you stay safe and healthy, yeah?"

Once I agree, he continues, "I want you to lay down and rest for a few minutes. I'm going to send Bella in here with something to eat. I know you're scared right now, sweetheart, but don't go gettin' inside your head. We can't go off the what-ifs. The what-ifs don't mean shit. You have people here who love you, Emerson. I want you to cling to them. We're your family and family are what's going to get you through this, ya got me?"

"Yeah, Jake, I got you."

Satisfied with my answer, he steps out into the hallway, where Bella is waiting. He mutters something to her, and she nods then walks off.

"Bella will be back in a minute. Close your eyes and rest."

Letting out a deep sigh, I squeeze my eyes shut and think to myself there is no way I can rest right now, but no sooner do those thoughts creep into my brain when a sudden wave of exhaustion takes over, and I fall asleep.

I wake sometime later to the sound of clinking glass, and when I open my eyes, I see Bella setting down a tray of food on the table beside the bed.

"Are you hungry?"

"Not really, but I know I need to eat something," I say, sitting up in bed and leaning back against the headboard. "How long have I been out?"

"About two hours. I came in earlier, but decided it was best to let you get some sleep."

"Bella, you don't have to fuss over me. It's late. The kids—" I begin to say when she stops me.

"The kids are fine. They're with Alba, Grace, and Mila." Picking the tray up off the table, Bella brings it over and sets it on the bed in front of me. The delicious smell of chicken noodle soup causes my tummy to rumble. Knowing Bella, the soup is homemade. None of that can stuff for her. Plucking the roll off the plate, I tear a piece off and dip it into the soup, then pop it in my mouth. Thank God my stomach doesn't protest.

"Soup was about the only thing I could keep down when I was pregnant with little Jake and feeling nauseous," she says softly.

"It's perfect. Thank you, Bella," I choke out. "It's funny, you know. Someone who was once the patient is taking care of the doctor," I observe.

Bella places her hand on my arm, squeezing gently. "No, it's family taking care of family."

A beat of silence later, she adds, "You'll get through this Em. The club will find Quinn. The guys will stop at nothing to bring him home."

"I keep thinking about what those men are doing to him. What he must be going through," I choke out. "They sent his cut, Bella."

"What are you talking about, sent his cut?"

"I followed the guys outside earlier. Someone delivered a package. Inside was Quinn's cut. It was covered in blood and piss."

"Oh, my God. I didn't know. Logan hasn't told me much of anything."

"If those men can beat the hell out of a child without an ounce of remorse, then imagine what they are capable of doing to Quinn. Them sending his cut is a warning or message. What I want to know is what they want."

"I don't have any of the answers, Em, but I have faith in the club, that they will take care of everything. Our job as their women is to keep it together and stay strong."

I finish the rest of my lunch in silence while mulling over Bella's words when the bedroom door opens, and Grey stands there with a look of shock on his face. My stomach plummets with the thought of bad news.

"Someone is here to see you," he says in a weird tone.

Who in the hell would be here to see me? I wonder to myself. My silent question is answered when my brother brushes past Grey. "This place does wonders for my ego, Em. You know you've made it when badass bikers are in awe of you." The smartass says waltzing into my room wearing his signature ripped jeans, a black t-shirt with the sleeves rolled up putting his tattoos on display, and combat boots.

"Oh my God, E! What the hell are you doing here?" I cry, climbing out of bed and launching myself into his arms. As soon as I'm engulfed in my brother's embrace, I feel a small sense of peace wash over me. Everything you hear about twins is true, and Easton fills a void in me that nobody else can.

"I called him," Bella confesses. "As soon as you arrived at the clubhouse, my gut told me you would need your brother, so I reached out to him."

"Thank you, Bella," I croak.

"You're welcome. I'm going to go and let you two catch up. If either of you needs anything, let me know."

Once Bella leaves, shutting the door behind her, I murmur into my brother's chest, "I can't believe you're here. How?"

"The band had a show in Albuquerque last night. My assistant gave me the message about an hour after the concert ended, saying some chick named Bella needed to talk to me. When I called her back, she gave me the watered-down version of what was going on. So, an hour later, I was on a plane to Polson."

"What about your tour?" I protest.

"We have a two-week break, but even if we didn't, I wouldn't give a shit. My sister comes before the band," he states with conviction. "I have to say, Em, you have some kick-ass friends. I'm kind of impressed that Bella chick was able to get my number."

"They have their ways."

"Come on, Em, the sun will be up in a couple of hours, and you need some rest and Uncle East needs his beauty sleep," Easton says and I shake my head at the idiot. Ten minutes later, I'm lying in bed next to my brother listening to him snore. Sleep escapes me the rest of the night but the uncertainty of what tomorrow will bring doesn't.

20

QUINN

The first snowfall has blanketed the ground outside, making it the perfect backdrop as Emerson and I enjoy the warmth from the fireplace while snuggled on the oversized couch in the living room of our home.

"I love you," Emerson's soft voice says while she runs her fingers through my hair.

My hands rest over her growing belly. Dipping my head, I let the warmth of my breath play across her neck when I whisper in her ear, "I love you," then press my lips against her skin.

"Did you feel that?" Emerson smiles and places her hand over mine.

"She's active today." I wait for her to kick my hand again.

Emerson giggles. "What makes you so sure our baby will be a girl?"

I don't know any other way to explain it. I feel it—I feel her. "Intuition, Sunshine. I have no other explanations. It's just how it's supposed to be."

Sitting forward, Emerson reaches for the fetal doppler sitting on the coffee table. "You want to hear the heartbeat?" She snuggles in between my legs and leans back against my chest. Lifting her shirt, Emerson exposes her round belly. Turning the doppler on, she moves it around searching.

Whoosh whoosh.

My face lights up. The rhythm of our baby's heart beating fills the room. I close my eyes and vividly picture her with blonde hair like me and her mother's captivating grey eyes. I place my hand over hers—over where our baby's heart beats.

Without warning, I'm torn away from the blissful moment. With a fist full of my hair, my head is jerked back. My eyes immediately fly open to find Twiggy keeping me from moving, while his President lingers over me with a white five-gallon bucket then proceeds to dump a torrent of water over my face.

I struggle for a breath of air only to be doused again. Four times—back-to-back, water is poured over my mouth and nose before it stops.

"Wake up." His laughter mixes with the sound of the high-pitch clunk of the bucket striking the floor.

I cough from inhaling stagnant smelling water into my lungs. My eyes water from the struggle to breathe seconds ago. Pulling in a deep breath, I fill my lungs with much-needed oxygen. My scalp stings after the other prick releases his grip on my hair. Shaking my head, I compose myself and reclaim my bearings. *Fuck. That will wake you up.*

I'm not sure how many hours I've been here now, but it has been long enough for the assholes to beat me, inject me with a drug, then wake me up and repeat the process several more times. If I took a guess, I'd say maybe a few days? The beatings did a number on me. The ringing in my ears is constant, and I can't breathe out the right side of my nose since they broke the damn thing. Taking deep breaths hurt like a motherfucker. Cracked ribs are most likely the cause. I'm pretty sure the wound from where I was stabbed in my thigh with an ice pick is infected by the sensation of radiating heat and pain I feel. That is, until the drugs kick in.

I know the club is trying to find me, but let's be real, how in the fuck will they find my ass? I'm in an underground bunker somewhere in the mountains of Polson. It will be like trying to find a needle in a haystack. Not that I don't have faith in them doing the best they can to find me. I'm realistic about the fact that I may be here for a while before they have the good fortune to stumble upon the place. And knowing Reid, he'll use his technical skills to find a way to pinpoint my whereabouts. *I hope.*

Scanning the room, I see Boulder and two of his ass kissers are the only men in this underground hotbox aside from myself. I watch as their President makes his way to a small table located near the other end of the bunker. Twisting on his heels, he heads back carrying a black duffle bag in his left hand. Hauling a chair across the floor, he stops. "Seems as if your brothers might need a little more motivation to realize I mean business." He drops the bag at my feet. Tilting forward, he brings his face close to mine, his breath smellin' like he ate ass for breakfast. "Gives us more time to get to know one another a little better. Don't ya think?" he taunts.

Doing my best, I lean back as far as I can and breath through my one good nostril to avoid the stench. "Jesus, your breath could gag a maggot. Never in my life have I smelt ass-mouth that bad before."

He sneers.

Oh yeah. He's pissed.

Reaching into his cut, he pulls out a cigar and bites the fuckin' end off. *Who does that?* This guy has watched way too many movies.

"You're a funny guy, aren't ya?" Striking the lighter he sets fire to the torn tip and takes a few tokes to get the tobacco leaves burnin'. "You like the movies, pretty boy?" he asks.

His use of the word *boy* rubs me the wrong way. I can handle a lot of insults, but callin' me a boy—. "Boy?" I glare at him. "You're dealin' with a man, motherfucker." I spit in his face, which in return earns me a bitch-slap across my cheek.

"You'll be cryin' like one by the time I'm through with you." With the cigar dangling between his lips, he crosses his arms over his chest. "We're gonna film ourselves a little video." He puffs on his cheap smellin' cigar, then blows the thick smoke in my face. Twiggy sticks both hands into his front pockets and steps aside, revealing a cell phone mounted on a tripod.

He's been recording this whole time. Dammit.

I can do this.

Whatever he has planned for me today—I'll make it out on the other side. I tell myself a few times as I cut my eyes to the phone, hoping the guys take notice.

I try telling them with a look. *Don't give in to these motherfuckers.*

He thumps the built-up ashes from the end of his cigar, letting them fall to the floor, then studies the hot end for a moment. The chair he's sitting on creaks from his weight when he stands. Helpless, I keep my eyes trained on him while trying to watch out for the dickhead on the other side of me.

Not gonna lie, it's pissing me off that the fucker is wearing a satisfied smirk, knowing they got me by the balls.

"Let's see if your brothers value your life more than their club or this town." He pauses and grabs me by my hair. Lurching my head to the side, he takes the hot end of the cigar and burns my neck with it. Instinctively I recoil from the pain. But even through the agony and fire ripping through my neck, and the smell of my skin being singed, I refuse to show these assholes weakness.

Releasing me, he picks the bag off the floor and pulls out a hammer. Twiggy slides the chair out of the way as his President stands in front of me with the hammer swinging at his side. I know the blow is comin'. Doesn't mean I'm prepared for it as he raises the hammer bringing it down across my left kneecap. Not as hard as I anticipated, but hard enough.

Clenching my teeth, I ride through the pain.

The hammer switches hands, and while I'm still trying to ignore the pain from the first blow, he almost shatters my other knee with the second.

I hold in my curses. 'Motherfuckers' and a 'son of a bitch' are on the tip of my tongue. It's not easy, but I won't give them the satisfaction.

Dickhead laughs.

It fuels my anger. Rage starts to dull the pain, and I focus all my energy on that feeling alone.

"Impressive," the Reaper prick says, lookin' down his nose at me. "Seems you have a high tolerance for pain." He turns his back toward me and rummages through his bag of tricks. When he turns around, he's clamping a small pair of vice grips onto a long thin sewing needle. Reaching over his shoulder, Boulder grabs a small torch from the shelf behind him. Lighting it, he heats the tip of the needle until the metal glows as red as the flame.

The President kneels in front of me and grabs hold of my right pinky and shoves the searing hot needle under my nail bed.

Every muscle in my body tightens, and I growl in pain as he pushes it in further and leaves it there. He repeats the process nine more times. Each time I lose the ability to keep silent. Each time I scream because the pain becomes too much.

I die a little inside, knowing I've shown weakness.

One last needle comes into view. One, I am more than eager to feel the prick of. Another sign of defeat, but the thought quickly leaves my mind only to be replaced with hunger. I don't want to be here. I know I'll feel better than I do right now.

I won't feel at all.

I know if I close my eyes, I'll see her.

TIME DOESN'T EXIST for me. The drug they continue to inject into my veins has fucked with my senses. Everything has become distorted, but I'm okay with that.

The line between needing to keep my wits about me and wanting to escape has become a war I would have never in a million years thought I would have to deal with.

I'm supposed to be the opposite of the man sitting here strapped to this chair, smelling of piss and hangin' on by a thin thread of hope. The positive 'take life by the balls and make it your bitch' kind of guy has walked out on me.

21

THE KINGS

JAKE

It's two o'clock in the morning, and I am sittin' here in mine and Grace's room at the clubhouse holding my baby girl as she sleeps on my chest. Logan, Gabriel, Reid, and I rolled in about an hour ago from yet another dead-end search for Quinn. The club has been working in shifts. Once my boys and I returned Austin, Blake, Grey and the rest of the men hit the road. There is not a minute that goes by when one of my men is not out looking for Quinn. When I said we wouldn't sleep until he is found, I meant it. The atmosphere at the clubhouse has become somber over the past few days. Emerson walks around in a daze. I'm thankful for her brother being here. If not for him, she wouldn't be holding up as well as she has been. I talked to him briefly yesterday, and he informed me that he spoke to his manager and bandmates and was able to get his tour pushed back another couple of weeks.

Standing, I walk over to the crib and lay my daughter down.

When I'm satisfied she's not going to stir, I turn and make my way over to the bed where Grace is sleeping. Leaning down, I place a kiss on her lips. Since I know sleep will not be possible, I decided to get myself some coffee. Walking out of the room, I shut the door quietly behind me, careful not to disturb my girls. When I come upon Remi's door, I open it and peek in on her. Lying in bed next to her is Katalina. When Quinn's sister is not with her mom, she clings to Remi. The two are best friends and practically inseparable. I'm glad Kat has a friend like Remi during a time like this. We haven't told the children a whole lot of what's happening, but they're not stupid. They know something has happened to Quinn, and with his presence missing for so long, they know it's bad.

When I walk into the kitchen, I'm met with Quinten sittin' at the table with a cup of coffee. He was released from the hospital the other day and is on the mend. He acknowledges me with a nod.

"How ya holding up, man?" I ask, taking a seat across from him at the table.

"I'm hanging in there. I have to keep it together for Vicky and Kat."

"How's Vicky doing?"

"Not good, Jake. This situation with Quinn is killing her. My wife is strong, but this—I don't think she will be able to handle it if he doesn't come home."

"That's not going to happen, brother," I say with certainty. "We're going to bring your boy home. You have my word."

"I know the club doesn't like to divulge too much information, but I have to ask since we're talking about my son. What's the plan? What are you all doing to bring him home?"

"I put in a call a few days ago to the Louisiana chapter. Riggs and his men should be rolling in sometime this morning. The last time I spoke with him, he said to expect him around eight o'clock. I also talked with Bennett and asked him to get in touch with Ian. He's the best damn tracker we know. He's also not the easiest person to get a hold of, but Bennett said he'd run him down."

"Thanks, Jake. I appreciate everything the club is doing for Quinn."

"No thanks necessary. Quinn is family. We love him. My guys and I are prepared to go to hell and back if it means bringing him back. You're Quinn's father, but I love him as if he were my son too. I would dance with the devil and trade my life for his without a second thought."

"I know you would, Jake. Vicky and I both want you to know we don't blame you or the club for what has happened. We have and will continue to support Quinn's decision to be a part of The Kings. His mom and I are not naïve. We know the club has done some bad shit, and even Quinn has not always followed the law, but at the end of the day, he is our son. He's happy, and he's healthy. We couldn't ask for more."

Once Quinten is finished speaking, he stands from his seat and tips his head before walking past me and out of the kitchen. I didn't realize how much I needed to hear those words until this moment. There was a small part of me that feared Quinn's parents would hold some sort of hatred toward the club for his kidnapping. In a way, I would understand if they did. Hell, I've been blaming myself for days. I keep replaying the shit in my head, wondering what I could have done differently to better handle the situation with Satan's Reapers. The one thing I regret was not killin' every one of those motherfuckers when I had the chance. As the President of The Kings, it's my responsibility to steer the club in the right direction. The choices I make as their President can sometimes mean the difference between life or death. Now I have to face the consequences of my decisions, but it's Quinn who is paying the price.

Peering down at my watch, I see it's nearly eight o'clock already. I can't believe I've been sittin' here lost in my thoughts for the past two hours. After finishing my coffee, I make my way out to the main room of the clubhouse and find Glory sittin' on the sofa, chatting with Ember with her dog Bo lying at her feet.

"Hey, Jake. Grace up yet?" Glory asks.

"I'm sure she is. Our baby girl usually wakes up around seven every mornin'. Grace is probably in the room changing and feeding her now."

"Good," she says, standing from the sofa and heads up the stairs. "I need my Ellie Kate loving this morning."

A second later, Ember abandons her perch and makes her way past me. "I'm going to get breakfast started. Lisa was up late last night, waiting for Bennett to come home. I'm sure she's exhausted and doesn't need to be worried about tending to everyone this morning."

Reaching out, I halt her movements by placing my hand on her shoulder. "Appreciate ya, sweetheart. You and Raine have stepped up to the plate this week and done so without complaint. The club is grateful."

Just then, the clubhouse door opens, and Ian comes strolling in with Sean trailing behind him.

"Look who I found, Prez."

It looks like Bennett came through after all and was able to track him down. I don't know a whole hell of a lot about what Ian does, but I do know people contract him for his services. I suspect he works for the government but can't say for sure, and he's tight-lipped about his business. I also don't make it a point to meddle. The man's business is his own. "Ian, I'm glad to see ya, brother," I greet, offering my hand.

"When I received word you and Bennett needed me, I came as quick as I could," Ian returns. "Now, I'm going to cut to the chase and get down to business. Bennett gave me a rundown on the situation. All I need from you is a place to set up."

This here is why I like Ian so much. He is all business. "Yeah, man. Follow me," I lead Ian to the room we hold church. I also had Reid set up all his computer shit in here too. With us being on lockdown and having a full house, this was the only room available. When I open the door to church, I am not at all surprised to see Reid still awake and working. "Reid, this is Ian. He's going to be settin' his equipment alongside you."

"No problem, Prez." Standing from his chair, Reid holds his hand out to Ian. "Nice meetin' ya. How about I help you bring your stuff in and set up."

I follow Ian and Reid out to the parking lot to Ian's truck. I'm alerted to a rumbling sound in the distance. When I look behind me, I notice Logan, Bennett, and Gabriel, step out of the clubhouse. "The cavalry has arrived," I announce.

Pulling his phone from his cut, Reid uses it to punch in the code to the gate opening it. A couple of seconds later, five Harleys and a cage roll onto the compound. Leading the way is our Louisiana President Riggs, followed by Kiwi, his Road Captain, Fender the SGT. AT ARMS, and two prospects bringing up the rear.

Once Riggs has dismounted his bike, I pull him in for a hug and clap him on the back. "Glad to see ya, brother. I hate it's under these circumstances."

"I always got your back, brother."

"So, what's in the van?" I ask.

"Oh, you know me, Jake. I always bring my toys to the party," Riggs grins.

"Well, in that case, let's get the motherfuckin' party started."

SLAMMING THE GAVEL DOWN, it echoes off the walls and brings church to order. "Alright, everybody settle down. For those of you who don't already know him," I say, pointing to Ian, "this is Ian. I brought him in on this because he's an expert tracker, so I'm turning the floor over to him." Once I have taken my seat, Ian stands and wastes no time dishing out his plan of action.

"We have approximately ten hours until nightfall. That's when I want every one of you to be ready to fall out. Also, whatever supplies you're going to require will have to be able to fit in these packs," Ian informs, holding up a standard military tactical backpack. "So, I suggest you pack smart."

"Why do we need packs?" this coming from Fender.

"Because I believe those motherfuckers have Quinn underground in the mountains. You'll be searching on foot."

"What makes you think they're holding Quinn underground?" Kiwi cuts in.

"Because I know," Ian replies. "Look," he continues, "this club has torn Polson and every surrounding town apart, and you haven't come up with shit. I've done my research on Polson dating back to the early 1940s. Did you know that during the Cold War, some Americans feared the worst and built underground bunkers? They would use them to stockpile supplies."

"Like Doomsday Preppers?" Kiwi asks.

"Yes, exactly like that. The mountains are the perfect place to build these sorts of bunkers. They are nearly impossible to spot among the trees. Hell, you don't even know one may be right under your feet until you come upon the ventilation pipes sticking out of the ground."

"Damn. You do know your shit," Kiwi remarks.

With a brow lift, Ian levels Kiwi with a look that says, 'no shit.' "Now, as I was saying, because bunkers like this may be in the mountains, the only way you will be able to access is by foot. All you need to be worried about is getting your shit together and be ready to move once I have a location," Ian finishes.

"Okay, brothers. You all know what to do." Standing, I'm about to slam the gavel and dismiss the guys when Blake burst through the door.

"Prez! I have something for you," he says, handing over a manila envelope. "I was riding by the garage, and something on the entrance door caught my attention. This envelope was tapped to it."

Dread settles in my gut. Something tells me this has to do with Quinn. Opening the package, I pull out a cell phone. When I power it on, the welcome screen has the message, 'watch me.' Tapping on the video icon, I see a single video. I pass the phone to Reid. "Hook this up and play it for everyone."

Taking the cell from my hand, Reid goes about plugging a cord into the phone and then to his computer. A couple of seconds later, the video begins to play on the screen mounted on the wall.

"Fuck," Reid mutters when the image of Quinn strapped to a chair as he chokes on water being poured over his face comes into focus. Next comes the taunts of the Satan's Reapers President followed by him snubbing his cigar out on Quinn's neck. The whole time my brother staying strong and grits his teeth through the pain. Even through the torture, Quinn does a little taunting of his own with his smart-ass mouth. But he soon loses the battle of wills as the motherfucker who will quickly die at my hands picks up a pair of pliers, uses them to grip a needle, then torches it until it's lit with a fiery red glow. By this point in the video Logan, Gabriel, and Reid are on their feet. The tension radiating off their bodies, barely holding on by a thread. Seconds later, the room erupts with the sound of Quinn's blood-curdling roar of pain as the President of the Satan's Reapers drives hot needles under the tips of his fingernails.

"The next time you see your boy, it will be in a body bag unless you give us what we want," the son of a bitch on camera says right before he injects something into Quinn's arm with a syringe followed by the screen going black. Now the only sound filling the room is heavy breathing. With my hands braced on the edge of the table, I look to my right and stare each one of my men in the eyes. "Get your shit packed and ready. It's time to go huntin'."

22

EMERSON

An hour ago, I watched as ten men walked into the room where church is held. Forty minutes later, I watched as Blake tore through the clubhouse carrying an envelope as he made his way behind the same door my eyes have been glued to. Now I'm watching as those same eleven men storm out with the kind of looks on their faces that have me fearing the worst. I want to know what was in that envelope. I want to know what happened.

"Hey, Sweetheart," Vicky greets with a sad tone as she takes a seat next to me on the sofa. Turning my body slightly toward her, I hang my head and shake it back and forth. I'm afraid if I open my mouth, words will fail me, and I'll break out in sobs. I don't want to do that. I want to show the people around me; I am stronger than that.

"Emerson," Vicky whispers, cupping my left cheek. When I gain the courage to look up at her, I'm met with the warmest brown eyes and a look of understanding. It's her look which has me losing it all over again. When I do, she pulls me in and hugs me while making a shushing sound in my ear. "Everything is going

174

to be alright, Sweetheart. It's going to be alright," Vicky says comforting me.

No matter how old you get, there is nothing that will ever compare to a mother's comforting embrace. The fact that it's not my mother holding me breaks my heart. But at the moment, I welcome the love Quinn's mom is giving. The more time I spend with Quinn's parents, the more I realize they are the kind of parents I strive to be. They love unconditionally and without judgment. They support their children in whatever path life leads them on while cheering from the sidelines. I hope that one day, my parents will come to terms with the life I have chosen to lead, accept the man I love, and his club. But at least I know if that day never comes, I have the love of Quinn's parents, and the love of his club; the men he calls his family because they are my family too.

23

THE KINGS

JAKE

"Hold up," Ian's voice commands, and the room falls silent. "Before we go traipsin' in the woods in the middle of the damn night, I have to get my drone in the air." Looking toward Kiwi, who happens to be standing closest to the door, Ian pulls a set of keys from his pocket and tosses them in his direction. "The van out there, grab the padlocked trunk for me but don't touch any of my other shit," he orders as he fires up his laptop and sits down.

Kiwi looks to Riggs, who nods his approval. "Take Fender with you," Riggs orders.

Ian knows his shit, so I let him take the reins for the time being. The rest of us wait until Kiwi walks back in and plunks the trunk down on the table. "Careful," Ian says, unlocking the trunk, lifting back the lid, and proceeds to pull out a drone. "I need one of you to get this to a remote area close to—" pulling out a map of the town he points to a location thirty minutes north of the clubhouse. "—here." His finger taps the map's surface. "This is where I want to deploy this baby."

Before I can speak and give the job to someone, Logan steps forward. "I'll take it."

"These men are most likely keeping tabs on you. All of you," Ian's glance spans the room. "You have to find a way to get this out there, undetected," Ian slips the drone into a pack and hands it to Logan.

"Got it," he answers and leaves without looking back.

Hours pass while we all mill around waiting for something—anything to help lead us in the right direction. The women and children have been told to keep to the upstairs rooms for now amid all the chaos taking place in preparation to rescue Quinn. I'm sitting at the bar with Austin when the church door swings open, and a tired Reid announces, "We found something."

In a flash, I'm off my stool, sprinting toward the door straight past Reid stopping when I reach Ian. "Talk to me, brother."

"As you're aware, we've been flying our drone equipped with thermal technology for the past few hours. We've only detected bears, deer—normal activity you would find in the woods around here. But, this—" he taps the computer monitor. Leaning a bit closer, I try to analyze the white dots on the screen. "These three dots are a heat source. Fixed heat sources. It's a possibility these are air vents. Vents that may lead down to a bunker below," Ian informs me as he writes location coordinates on a piece of paper.

"Reid, go round up the men," I order and turn my attention back to Ian. "How far?"

Getting up from his seat, Ian strides across the room and flips the switch turning the overhead light on and walks over to the grid map of Polson hanging on the wall. Taking the cap off a red Sharpie, he starts marking. "Your club is here," he circles the area. Looking back at his coordinates, he studies the map and pinpoints the exact location of interest with an x. "If my calculation is correct, that's where we want to be."

I study the map. "How soon do you think we can be there?" I

ask, eager to bring my family home and hoping like hell, I can bring him home alive.

Ian shakes his head. "Looks to be at least a two-hour trek if we enter here," he says, checking the map.

"That's old river bend pass," I inform him.

"Good. You know where we need to go then. There's—" Ian checks the watch on his wrist. "We have eight hours until the sun comes up. We want the cover of night on our side, so I say we head out at midnight."

Goddammit. "We don't have a lot of time, Ian. You saw the video. My instincts tell me this sinister motherfucker won't let him live much longer before killin' him and moving on. It's a game to them. One they don't mind losing as long as they take one of my men to the grave along the way." The church door flies open. Every one of my boys, along with the rest of the calvary pile into the room. Most of them dressed and ready to go to war for one of their own.

"Ready, Prez." Gabriel shrugs his cut on over his shoulders. Pulling his pant leg up, he places his sheathed blade inside of his boot.

"Hold up," I put my hand in the air halting the movements of every man in the room. "We have a couple of hours to prepare for this mission."

"So, we have to sit around here on our asses when we finally have a lead on where our brother is?" Logan runs a hand through his hair. Frustration etched across his face as he continues. "Don't get me wrong. We all understand the reasoning behind it, but it doesn't change the fact our brother is out there dying or dead."

The room goes silent. I can't be mad at him. Logan is only saying what the rest of us are thinking and feeling.

"Then let that be your motivation, men," Ian addresses the room.

I look at Ian. "Fill them in." Taking the lead, Ian explains to my brothers what the drone discovered and the reasons for waiting. Huddling around the table, we all keep our eyes trained either on the computer screen or the map and pay close attention to Ian's plan of execution.

"We'll enter here," he points to the bridge pass, "it's going to be a two-hour hike north. This is our target location. There will be eight of us on this mission, so no matter what, stay in pairs. We know five assholes have your man. They may or may not have one or two of them posted somewhere around the perimeter of the bunker.

"Logan—" I turn to my right and look at him. "Fill your dad's men in on what's going on tonight. I need them to make sure no one comes downstairs. If someone in the family needs something, they need to get it for them. Gabriel—"

He steps forward with his hands clenched at his sides, ready for a fight.

Out of all his brothers, Quinn annoys him the worst, but the big Cuban would lay his life down for him any day of the week. We all would. "Double check with Ian on everything we need before loading up and make sure it's accounted for."

Reid is doing what he needs to do, which is assisting Ian with the technical aspects, so I let him stay right where he's at, staring at the computer monitors. After Gabriel and Logan leave the room, I walk over to Doc, who's standing at the table in the corner, fixing himself a cup of coffee.

Grabbing my attention, Riggs asks, "What do you need from us, Jake?"

"We need a makeshift triage room constructed downstairs. You should find a few rollaway beds down there along with some unopened boxes of medical supplies we may need later. If you and your men can throw that together before we head out—" I leave my words hanging.

Riggs nods. "We take care of our own."

I hate the waiting game as much as the next man, but we have no choice in the matter. I turn back to get some coffee. "Bennett." I grab a paper cup, and he fills it with coffee. "I'm gonna need you to make sure your medic bag is fully stocked. Going by what we saw —" I have to pause a moment and fight the lump forming in my throat.

Bennett stirs in the sugar and creamer he poured into his coffee, turning it from black to beige. "Not gonna lie, Jake. He looked bad. I'm not saying just his injuries. They've been injecting him with something for days now. We have no idea until we get to him what that may be."

The same thought has played through my head more than once. Bennett and I know the tactics these sons of bitches are using. They want him to want the escape the drug gives him after inflicting the amount of pain they make him endure. Break the spirit; you break the man. "I still can't wrap my head around the reasoning behind all this." I down some coffee.

"Bad seeds like the Reapers," Doc shrugs. "I don't think they have a clear motive other than they want to prove they can. They thrive off fear. To them, fear and respect go hand in hand."

True. We've seen some shit. Watched people die. Innocent people. All to invoke fear. They used fear to bend people to their will. "I'd rather deal with that scenario than bury one of my family members," I admit.

Doc clasps his hand on my shoulder. "Me too, brother—me too."

For the next hour, we wait. Needing to keep busy, I join some of the other men in preparing for what we all hope will be tonight's mission to bring Quinn home, so I take the time to go upstairs and check on the women. I find them huddled in the room where Victoria and Quinten have been sleeping.

Victoria and Emerson immediately jump from where they are

seated. Quinten stays resting with his back against the headboard of the bed.

"Jake, tell me you found him," Vicky pleads.

I take in her red-rimmed eyes. "We have a possible location. In another hour, me and the rest of the men will be heading out," I inform her.

"So, you don't know for sure that he's in this location. What if he's not there. What if—" Vicky chokes on her words.

Pulling her into my chest, I try my best to comfort her. "Sweetheart, Ian is very good at what he does. I need you to trust him as much as I do." Pulling back, I lift her chin, so she is looking at me. "I'm gonna bring him home. I promise."

She blows out a shaky breath. "I believe you."

I look around the room. "Demetri's men have the place secured. I also have Blake, Austin, and Grey staying behind. I need all of you to remain upstairs even after we've gone. We have too much going on downstairs, and I don't need the kids to see anything that might scare them."

Grace, who has been quietly sitting in a chair by the window, holding our sleeping little girl in her arms stands. "Most of the children are settled in for the night. Them seeing anything shouldn't be a problem." She smiles, and my heart melts. "Remi and Kat are still awake. As to be expected, Kat is worried about her brother and can't sleep. We all are," Grace comments. Bending forward, I kiss my daughter on her forehead.

"Prez," Grey grabs my attention. Turning, I see him standing in the hallway. "Everyone's ready to go."

I kiss my wife, but before exiting the room, Quinten stands. "Jake," and pulls his wife into his side, "stay safe."

Giving him a curt nod, I exit the room. When I get downstairs, all seven men are dressed and ready to go. I waste no time shucking on my gear and joining them. One van is the only vehicle we take. It's a tight fit, but necessary. It was also needed having Austin drive us to our drop off point then double back and wait for my call. We don't want someone spotting us or our transportation which is also why we stopped about a mile or more back and walked the rest of the way to the drop off point.

"Cloudy skies tonight, men. I'll need you to put on the night vision gear. Those trees already block out much of the natural light from above. You won't be able to see four feet in front of you," Ian whispers before we enter the tree lines. "From here on, its silence." He makes eye contact with me before sliding his goggles over his eyes.

Ian was right. It's pitch black as we navigate our way through the trees. So far, the terrain hasn't been terrible. The eerie stillness as we follow Ian is more noticeable than anything. We haven't heard a sound. Not even the wind is blowing through the trees. Even the sounds of our feet walking across the forest floor are barely audible.

Ian comes to a stop and lifts his hand, signaling for us to halt our movement. After making our way for almost two hours, we've come upon the image displayed on the monitor earlier where the heat sources were detected. Pivoting my head from left to right, I scan the clearing and sure as shit there they are. Three small tube-shaped hotspots are protruding from the forest floor. Still hidden in the tree line, I motion for Gabriel and Logan to make their way toward my left while signaling for Riggs and his men to circle the opposite side of the location so we can surround the area. Our objective is to find Quinn, but I'll be damned if we let one motherfucker slip through our fingers. Holding our positions, we watch for any signs of activity, and so far, we've seen none. This means all five Satans Reapers have to be underground.

Ian speaks low. "There," he says, and points across the field. I watch as a door begins to rise from the ground and four men emerge. Two stand watch while the other two walk off toward the tree lines where Logan and Gabriel have positioned themselves. Ian's voice whispers through our earpieces. "Alright, men. On my word, I want Logan and Gabriel to handle the targets heading in your direction. Reid—Bennett, drop the two by the entrance. That leaves two of their men unaccounted for down below. Jake and I are going in. Riggs, you and your men, cover our six." Ian directs his attention toward me and gives a final nod. "Go-Go," he announces. Simultaneously four rifle shots echo through the trees. My focus is on getting to that door. We have no way of knowing what they can hear down below, so we have no way of knowing what we are walking into. Squatting, I grab the cut of one fallen Reaper's body that's blocking our way in and drag him to the side. Logan, Gabriel, Reid, and Bennett jog their way toward us as I pull open the heavy wood door letting it land with a loud thud on the ground and peer down in the hole illuminated with dim amber light.

"I know you're up there, motherfucker. Come on down and join the party."

I recognize the voice. It's the President himself. My trigger finger twitches. "I'm going in first," I tell the men. "No matter what happens, Quinn comes first. You got me?" I order.

The sounds of approaching footsteps cause us to raise our weapons in the direction it's coming from only to watch Riggs and his men make their way over with an extra man in tow.

"Look who we found. Dumb fuck was slumped against a tree over there with a damn needle hanging from his arm." Fender pushes the high as a kite Reaper Twiggy forward, causing him to stumble.

"We take him with us," I tell him then step down onto the steps lowering myself into the ground. Nothing to protect me from a bullet, I step forward after I take the last step down into the long rectangular bunker. The strong smell of urine is the first thing that hits me before my eyes adjust to the low lighting and take in the sight before me. He has the barrel of a sawed-off shotgun pressed against Quinn's head.

Jesus. My gut clenches, seeing my brother this way. His head rolls from side to side. He's pale— no color to him whatsoever. Quinn is in bad shape.

"Put the gun down." Boulder jams the tip of the gun barrel against Quinn's head. "Or I'll shoot the poor bastard and put him out of his misery while you watch," he sneers.

Keeping my rifle raised, I stare down my scope. "He dies; You die," I warn him.

The Reaper bastard grins, sealing his fate.

I pull the trigger.

24

QUINN

Thirty Minutes Prior

I feel like shit. I've been in and out of it for a while now. I can't make out if anything going on around me is real or a hallucination brought on by fever and the effects of the drug. Images continue to come in waves like someone is turning the screen on and off, and I keep missing pieces of what's happening.

My eyes burn. My entire body feels heavy, and I'm drenched in sweat. The last thing I remember is screaming in pain before it all faded away to black. I take a shuddered shallow breath, trying to clear my senses. Jesus, how much did they give me this time? Waking up from it feels different than before.

"Where the fuck is Twiggy?" I hear the loud voice of my captor, the President of Satans Reapers.

"He stepped out over an hour ago. Probably passed out somewhere high on that shit you've been giving this piece of shit." I feel a boot kick my shin.

"You guys get out there and find his ass. I swear if he weren't useful in making us money with his drug and gang connections, I'd kill him myself," he says with disdain.

It's not long after I hear the sounds of them climbing the steps and closing the door that everything fades away again.

Voices wake me up, but they sound distorted. Managing to lift my head, I open my eyes. *Prez?* I see him standing several feet in front of me with the end of a rifle aimed in my direction.

Is this real?

I keep my eyes open a second longer, staring at the image of Jake trying to make out if he's real or not. That's when I hear a voice. Emerson is calling my name. It's so crisp I believe any moment I'll feel her lips press against mine, so I close my eyes—and wait. In the middle of all of this— at this moment, I make peace with whatever has happened, and whatever is about to happen. A strong sense of calm washes over me. *It's going to be okay. I'm going to be okay.*

Present

What the hell is up with the constant bursts of bright lights? "Calm down, Quinn. Gabriel, get over here and hold him still. Watch his hands. Those fuckers left the needles in his fingers. I can't remove them until we get him to the clubhouse."

Doc?

I feel my body vibrate and sway from side to side, almost as if I'm in a moving vehicle again. The Satan's Reapers must have decided to either move location or find a place to get rid of me once and for all. Sharp, massive pain in my chest causes me to fight my way out of darkness, and I blink a few times before I'm able to focus on a face looming over me. "Fuck." I go to reach for my chest but can't lift my arm. My eyes feel heavy, and keeping them open becomes a challenge.

"Quinn, wake up."

I feel the pain in my chest again.

"Just kill me, motherfuckers!" I roar. My body aches. I'm tired. I'm done. I have no more strength to fight off whatever else they have planned for me.

Suddenly, background noise fills with the sound of tires skidding along the gravel. "Estás seguro, hermano. *You're safe, brother*; Estás en casa. *You're home,*" I hear Gabriel's voice though it sounds muffled and far away.

Home? Straining to gather every ounce of energy my body has left, I lift my eyelids once more and take in Gabriel's face staring down at me. "You gonna kiss me already, Prince Charming?"

His head shakes from side to side, but a rare grin accompanies his reaction.

"Let's move. Get him downstairs," Logan orders. Once they lift me, my defeated body becomes weightless as my brothers carry me toward the clubhouse door.

"Let me pass. Is that my son?" The desperate sound of my mom's voice pleading with someone upstairs rings out, followed by Emerson crying out my name and piercing my soul. "Quinn?"

I can't handle it. I won't let them see me this way. As much as I need to feel them beside me, I won't do that to them. "I don't want to see them!" I roar as the pain from all the abuse my body had taken starts to take over.

Prez's voice booms above the chaos. "Has anyone heard from Riggs and his men since we left them to wait for his prospects to pick them up?" he questions no one in particular.

"Still waiting on his men, Prez," Reid calls out.

"Keep me informed. I want to know the minute him and his men arrive," Prez orders.

"Get him on the bed. I need to start getting fluids in him." Doc starts barking orders. Logan and Gabriel set me down, and Logan immediately picks up a foot and begins removing my boot.

"Quinn, I have to remove your clothes and clean you up before

I can assess your injuries," Doc informs me as he starts cutting clothes away with a pair of scissors. "I'm gonna give you something to relax you before taking care of everything else."

Thank fuck. I don't say the words out loud, but I won't fight him on it.

"Do you have any idea what they were giving you?" Doc examines the inflamed sores on my arms where they injected me.

I grit my teeth the moment he picks my hands up. Looking down at them, I realize the needles are still embedded under my nail beds.

"I need to sanitize them and sedate you before removing them, Quinn. I'm sorry, brother." He wraps a blood pressure cuff around my arm before placing an oxygen tube up my nose.

Damn. Does he think all this is necessary? He must have read my thoughts because he answers them.

"You have possible cracked ribs along with a broken nose. You've been like this for a few days, Quinn. Which means you haven't been able to get enough oxygen in your system. I also need to keep tabs on your blood pressure because judging by the leg wound there," he darts his eyes down toward my thigh, "you have an infection. Sepsis is something we need to be concerned with as well. I need to keep a close eye on all your vitals for a few days," Doc clarifies as he cleans my stab wound.

"Do what you gotta do, brother," I say to him, eager to feel no pain. Giving an understanding look, he finishes hooking me to the IV and administers a couple of syringes of medicine.

I happen to glance over at Jake. His body is tense, and his face was etched with a mixture of anger and relief.

"Prez." My voice cracks because my throat is so dry.

Coming to stand beside the bed, he peers down at me. Damn, he looks exhausted. Logan stands at the foot of the bed, looking on. Gabriel has pulled a chair up beside the bed, his anger evident as he watches Doc do his thing.

Gratitude is what I'm feeling more than anything right now. From the weary looks on their faces, I know they have been going nonstop, night and day trying to bring me home. I'm so fuckin' proud to call them my brothers. Looking back at Prez, I stress, "Don't let them see me like this."

He gives me a look respecting my decision and gives me a firm nod. "I'll go talk with them," he says, then leaves the room.

It's not long before the medicine Doc gives me takes effect, and I begin to feel a little drowsy. Doc starts swabbing my fingertips with the feel of something wet. I don't look. I just lay there and stare at the ceiling. By the time he pulls the first needle out of my finger, I feel nothing but a slight sting. Eventually, the sounds of each needle pinging one by one as he drops them into a metal bowl slowly fade into the background.

25

EMERSON

Blinking my eyes open, my gaze lands on the green glowing numbers of the alarm clock on the table beside the bed that reads 4:37 a.m. For a moment, I forget where I am and what kind of hell my life has been the past seven days. But in a blink of an eye, it all comes rushing back. Working at the hospital, the kid who was assaulted being brought in, finding out Quinn was taken, the club being on lockdown, my brother showing up, and then the members of the Louisiana chapter arriving. My head is spinning, and I'm angry. Angry because nobody has given me any answers.

Rolling out of bed, I go to make my way across the room to the bathroom when I hear a commotion in the hall. It sounds like people arguing. When I open the bedroom door, Vicky's voice is the first I hear. "I want to know what the hell is going on. Have they found my son?" With my heart feeling like it's about to beat out of my chest, I rush down the hallway toward Vicky who is in a standoff with one of Demetri's men. The man who is currently blocking the stairs exit. "I'm sorry, ma'am. I don't have the details. I'm just doing what I was told," he says in a heavy Russian accent.

"What's going on here?" I ask, coming up behind Quinn's mom.

"Something is going on downstairs, and this brute won't let me pass."

Turning my attention to the man, I ask, "What's your name?"

"My name is Alexei ma'am."

"Well, Alexei, is there a reason why we are not allowed to go downstairs?"

"I was told by my boss to come upstairs and make sure nobody came down."

"Your boss is an overbearing, controlling asshole," Glory remarks dryly. When I look over my shoulder, I see that she is not alone. Our little spat has woken not only Glory but Bella, Alba, Grace, and a very pregnant Mila.

"Is there a problem, Krasivaya *Beautiful*?" Demetri says, appearing from behind Alexei with his heated gaze aimed directly at Glory.

"Speak of the devil," Glory sasses back. "Hello, asshole. Mind clueing us in on what's going on and why we're being held hostage?"

With predatory movements, Demetri strides up to Glory and leans in close to her face. "Careful, Krasivaya," he warns, "you keep opening that smart mouth of yours, and I'll be inclined to fill it with something and show you the true meaning of hostage," Demetri's smooth Russian accent rumbles in a low tone, but not low enough I couldn't hear what he said.

What's even more shocking is Glory doesn't say a word back. I don't know her well, but one thing I do know is she is fierce and very opinionated. She has no qualms telling anyone exactly what's on her mind. Glory has no brain to mouth filter. However, it appears the promise in Demetri's tone has her keeping her words on lockdown. Steering his attention away from Glory, Demetri continues, "As you can hear, Jake and the men have made it back, and before leaving, he informed you to stay upstairs. I ask that you, please heed his request."

"We want some answers. Have they found Quinn? Are the rest of our men okay?" This is coming from a worried-looking Mila.

When I glance at all my friends standing in the hall looking scared, I realize that I haven't given much thought to how they must be feeling. It may not be their husbands who are missing, but it is their men who have been working day and night, placing their own lives on the line to bring Quinn home. At any moment, while they are out hunting down the enemy, something can go wrong, and Jake, Logan, Gabriel, and Reid all have wives and children that count on them to make it home safe every night.

When Demetri is about to open his mouth again, the sound of the clubhouse door slamming open, and a slew of male voices coming from downstairs vibrates off the walls. "Move—move!" we hear Jake yell.

Next, we hear Bennett. "Let's get him downstairs!"

With my breath getting caught in my throat, I rush up to Demetri and fist his shirt. "Is it him? Do they have Quinn?" I choke out. "Quinn!" both Vicky and I holler out. A second later, we hear Quinn's agonizing roar, "I don't want to see them!" Demetri gives us a look of sympathy. That, along with Quinn's outburst, has all the air leaving my body and my knees buckle. It's my brother who catches me before I hit the floor. I don't even remember seeing him come out of the room.

Moments later, Jake appears before us. "I'm sure you all have heard by now that we have Quinn."

I shrug out of my brother's arms and step up to Jake. "Let me see him." Thinning his lips, Jake shakes his head. "I'm sorry, sweetheart, but Quinn was adamant you and his parents are not to be allowed to see him in his current state."

"I'm a doctor, Jake. I've seen it all. Plus, I can help," I plead.

"Look, I don't agree with Quinn's orders, but he is my brother, and I respect his decision. He doesn't want you to see him."

I'm about to protest once again when Jake gently grabs me by my shoulders. "Emerson, I get it. I do, but Quinn's head is a hell of a mess right now. Give it some time. Doc is with him now, and I'll come back with another update soon."

Kissing the top of my head, Jake turns on his heel to leave when Quinten calls out. "Jake."

Turning Jake regards Quinn's father.

"You know I respect you and your club, and I have always done as you asked without question, but this I will not do. That is my son downstairs, so I'm telling you, man to man; father to father, nothing is keeping me from seeing my son," he declares.

Tipping his head, Jake motions for Quinten to follow him. Quinten turns to his wife and mutters something into her ear, before kissing her and following Jake back downstairs.

A couple of hours later, I still can't get the devastated look Quinten wore on his face when he came back from seeing his son. After nearly wearing a hole in the floor from pacing, I decide I've had enough of this waiting around bullshit. "Fuck it." Walking over to the door, I open it and peek out into the hall. Noticing our guard is no longer standing at his perch, I totter across the hallway to Vicky's door and give it a couple of taps. It only takes her a second to answer. When she does, I ask. "You coming?" Without a word Vicky, closes the door behind her and the two of us march downstairs. When we come upon the room we know Quinn is in Vicky is the first to burst through the door with me trailing behind her. We don't bother with knocking, and our sudden appearance has the guy known as Kiwi jumping to his feet. Both of us want to run to Quinn's side, but we stand firm and square off with the man standing between my man and us. Kiwi stands there stunned. He's looking at us as if he hasn't a clue how to handle the two very pissed off women standing in front of him.

Placing her hands on her hips, Vicky says in her best mom voice, "Are we going to have a problem here, young man?"

"Uh—no, ma'am. I'm not one to stand in the way of a mum and

her boy," he says, and steps aside and strides out the door. "I give it two minutes before he snitches on us," Vicky huffs.

A second later, we both turn, and I'm not at all prepared for what I see. Quinn is lying on a bed hooked up to an IV. His skin is pale, and his cheeks are flushed. He's unconscious, with visible jerking movements. Quinn's entire body is dripping in sweat, and he looks like he's lost a few pounds as well.

The doctor in me is making a mental checklist of all the things that could be wrong with him and what course of action needs to be taken, while the girlfriend in me wants to climb into his bed and hold him. Knowing Quinn needs immediate help, the doctor in me overrules. Spotting Bennett's bag beside the bed, I grab it and begin rummaging through it until I find what I am looking for. Just then, the door opens, and Jake, along with Bennett, enters the room.

"Whatever you're about to say, you can save it," I tell them while continuing the task at hand. Using an alcohol swab, I sterilize the inside of Quinn's arm. I don't miss the visible track marks either. My stomach clenches knowing what that means. I take a 21-gauge needle along with a blood specimen vile and collect a blood sample. "I need to find out if he has any drugs in his system." Without missing a beat, I place the vile in the front pocket of my shirt. I pull the blanket from his body. Quinn has been stripped down to his boxers, and it only takes me two seconds to find a bandage. Peeling it back, I see that he has an infected stab wound, and the area is extremely swollen and inflamed.

"I was on my way to get ya, Sweetheart," Jake confesses. "But when I got to your room, I saw that you had already given us the slip."

Shocked, I turn to face Jake to see he has a slightly amused look on his face. I was fully expecting him to be angry. I disobeyed his order to stay upstairs and away from Quinn. Though, his amused expression quickly replaced with one of concern. "Doc checked Quinn over and came to the same conclusion as I'm sure you have. We can confirm he has been injected with drugs repeatedly over the last seven days, though we don't know what kind. Doc cleaned and examined the wound to his thigh and concluded it is infected. We felt we needed to bring you in to help."

"So that's what these marks on Quinn's arm are?" Vicky asks, pointing to the apparent track marks on the inside of both arms.

"Yes," I answer. "The withdrawal from the drugs is most likely what's causing involuntary twitching. The cold sweats are from both the withdrawals and infection." I turn toward Jake. "I need to get to the hospital. I'm going to have a toxicology test done, and I'll bring back the proper antibiotics as well. If we can't get a handle on his infection over the next twenty-four hours, he's going to need to be admitted to the hospital."

"I agree with Emerson," Bennett adds.

"Alright then," Jake pokes his head out the door and hollers for Kiwi. "Kiwi will take you to the hospital." Without wasting any more time, I lean over Quinn's bed, palm his cheek, and place a gentle kiss on his lips. The moment my mouth touches his, his twitching body relaxes, and his eyelids flutter open. "Sunshine?" he rasps.

"Yeah, baby, it's me," I choke out. "I want you to hold on for me, okay. I'm going to take care of you."

"I didn't want you to see me like this."

"Well, tough shit, because nothing and no one can keep me from you." I place my hand on Quinn's chest over his beating heart, "It beats for us, right?" I whisper into his ear. "Now you be good and don't give your momma any trouble. I'll be back soon."

Rolling his head to the right, Quinn regards his mom. "I know better than to sass my mom. She'll whoop my ass."

I can't help but shake my head at his remark. Only Quinn

would be laid up after going through hell, suffering from withdrawals and severe infection, and still give us lip.

On the ride to the hospital, I lean my head back on the headrest, close my eyes, and let my mind wander. When I was looking over Quinn, I didn't miss the other numerous injuries to his body. Not only was he drugged repeatedly and stabbed in the thigh, but I also saw significant burn marks on his neck. One that is too big to be a cigarette, so I'm going to guess it was a cigar. His nose was broken but looked as though it had already been reset. His entire torso is covered in bruises as is his face. The tips of all ten of his fingers are swollen and bloody too.

"You okay over there, doll?" Kiwi asks, bringing me out of my thoughts.

I'm just about to answer him when nausea hits, and bile rises in my throat. "Stop the car!" I shout covering my mouth with my hand. Suddenly jerking the car to the side of the road, Kiwi barely comes to a full stop before I throw the passenger door open and I stumble out. With my palms braced over my knees, I vomit onto the grass on the side of the road.

Kiwi comes up beside me and offers a bottle of water. "Here ya go, doll."

After chugging half the contents, I wipe my mouth with the sleeve of my shirt. "Thanks." Tilting his chin, Kiwi leans against the side of the car and patiently waits as I compose myself. A couple of minutes later, we're back on the road.

"Quinn's a lucky man to have an old lady like you. I don't know ya, but I know enough, and I can see you're tough as hell. I admire the way you and his mum came into his room and decided nobody was going to keep ya from him. That's the makings of one hell of an old lady."

"Thanks, Kiwi," I say, giving him a weak smile. After his brief compliment, we ride the rest of the way to the hospital in silence.

After we make it to the hospital, it only takes about forty-five minutes for a friend of mine that works in the lab to run the toxicology for me. I go about gathering a few supplies and some IV antibiotics and place them in my bag. On my way out, I pause when I hear someone calling my name. Turning, I see my boss and attending physician, Dr. Brewer.

"Dr. Evans, I have been trying to get in touch with you for a week. My phone calls and messages have gone unanswered."

"Yeah, I'm sorry about that, Dr. Brewer. I've been dealing with a family emergency."

"I can understand that, Dr. Evans, but you have a responsibility to this hospital. The least you could do is notify me in such an event."

Blowing out a breath, I try to compose myself before I go off on the woman in front of me. "I understand, Dr. Brewer, but work was the last thing on my mind this week. Sometimes there are more important things."

"If that is the way you feel, Dr. Evans then perhaps we need to rethink your position at this hospital."

"You go on and do that," I say through gritted teeth. "I have someplace more important to be than standing here with you." Without a second thought, I turn and walk out of the hospital.

26

QUINN

It's been a little over forty-eight hours since my brothers found my ass and brought me home. I'd like to say my recovery process has been easy for me, but that would be a lie. The physical injuries I can handle. My fingertips hurt like hell. Each nail bed has formed a blood blister underneath them from the trauma caused by the needles. Thanks to Doc, I can breathe out both sides of my nose again. My ribs feel a hell of a lot better with the compression wraps giving them much needed support. Taking a deep breath still hurts like hell, but it's much more manageable. My knees let's just say they have swollen to the size of a grapefruit with the amount of fluid buildup in them.

Currently, I'm sitting on the edge of the bed. Prez still has me in one of the rooms located downstairs. At least until I've improved a little more.

With a shaky hand, I reach for the bottle of water sitting on the bedside table. This—the shaking and overall feeling like roadkill is the worst part of my recovery. My body continually shivers, accompanied by waves of nausea and lightheadedness. Both Emerson and Doc say they are mild side effects from the drugs that were injected into me. Heroin, to be exact. Emerson had a toxicology report done the same night the men rescued me. Let's just say by the high levels found in my system everyone was surprised I didn't suffer a fatal overdose.

I wholeheartedly believe it was my woman's voice that helped pull me through. Knowing my future was back home waiting for me gave me the extra strength I needed to hold on. Emerson and my unborn child were my guiding light when I felt like I couldn't possibly handle any more.

The Satan's Reapers put my body through hell. They tried to break my spirit. They almost succeeded, but every time I closed my eyes, she was there. Every time my heart kept beating it was for her and my child.

Clenching my fists in frustration, I try to stop my muscles from twitching after spilling water on my lap. "Fuck. All I want is to have a drink without sloshing it all over myself."

Emerson comes to sit beside me. "Your symptoms should subside in another twenty-four hours. You're already doing much better than you were twelve hours ago."

"I'm sorry, Sunshine. I know I'm a massive pain in the ass right now. I'm not one to bitch as much as I have lately, but I'm not feeling like myself, and it's pissing me off." Placing my trembling palm against her cheek, I lean in pressing my lips to her mouth, then rest my forehead against hers. "I love you so fuckin' much, Sunshine."

Her hand threads through my messy hair. "I love you too." After we have our moment, she leans back. "Would you like to shower today?"

I do smell. Doc and Logan cleaned me up a bit the other night, but a hot shower would be nice. "How about we play doctor, and you give me a sponge bath?" I grin.

Emerson smiles and laughs. It's good to see her face light up like that again. "Nice try," she says, bursting my bubble. "Besides, Doc will be here any moment to drain the fluid off your knees."

Before I can protest or convince her otherwise, the door swings open. Doc strides in, followed by my mom and dad.

"Son, you're looking better this afternoon," my dad observes.

"You're not lookin' too bad yourself, Dad."

Pulling Mom into his side, he places a kiss on the top of her head. "Your mom has been taking excellent care of me," his hand runs over her hip. The apples of my mom's cheeks begin to blush. Emerson takes notice of the body language the two share and casts her eyes down to her lap for a moment, hiding her amusement. I'm used to it. My parents have been affectionate with one another my whole life. They've never hidden the attraction they have for each other. I find it endearing. Why hide it?

"Quinn, Kat wants to see you. Do you feel up to her coming down today?" my mom asks.

Kat must be a mess. She's always had access to me when she's wanted to see me. "Let me grab a hot shower first, Mom. It's bad enough she has to see me all banged up like this. The least I can do is wash the stink off."

Her head nods in understanding, and she walks toward me. Before she bends to hug me, I stand. Every inch of my body aches with the movement. Emerson tucks her body carefully into my side offering the support I need to finish getting myself in an upright position.

"Honey, you shouldn't be trying to get up—" my mom softly scolds me for my action. I shake my head and cut her off. "I'm going to give my parents a proper damn hug."

My mother's eyes begin to water as she carefully embraces me. Dammit, the women in my life always find my soft spot. Doing my best, I choke back my emotions. Without hesitating, my dad wraps his arms around me after mom steps aside and wipes a few fallen tears from her lovely face.

"Your mom and I are damn proud of you, Quinn—Damn proud. It's so good to have you home." My dad's strong voice cracks with his confession.

"Well, Dad and I will let Bennett and Emerson take care of you. It will put a smile on your sister's face when she learns she will get to see her brother today." My mom hugs herself and smiles.

After my parents have left, Emerson slowly helps me to sit down on the edge of the bed. I watch Doc retrieve a syringe from his bag and remove it from the sterile packaging. "The last time I did this, you didn't feel much because of the pain medicine you were on. Since you've asked us to dial back the dosage, you'll feel me drain your knees this time," he explains. I didn't like my senses dulled. I understand the medication helps but I prefer taking just enough to take the edge off. I'm okay with feeling some pain. It lets me know I'm here; I'm alive, and I have complete control of myself and what's going on around me.

Emerson continues to sit at my side while Doc disinfects both knees. I would have thought my woman would want complete control of my recovery process, but she has stepped back and given most of the responsibilities—medically anyway to Doc. I love her so much more for doing so. She recognizes and respects the way the club and the brotherhood works. We all have a job to do. Doc's is taking care of us when needed. I've watched them both find the perfect balance as they take care of me.

Rubbing my knees down with iodine, Doc turns to Emerson. "Will you get the lidocaine from my bag and numb him up for me?"

"I can do that." She walks past him, digs in the bag, and steps back. "This will be easier if you lie back. I'll place a pillow under your knees for a little support to make you more comfortable," she says, then helps me adjust myself. Once the area has dried a bit, Emerson uses a topical solution to numb the area Doc will be inserting the needle.

Pulling a chair alongside the bed, Doc asks, "Are you ready? Not gonna lie, it will be uncomfortable, but afterward, the pressure you're feeling will start to lessen."

I let out a heavy sigh. "Go for it."

Almost four syringes later, he has pulled most of the fluid from both knees, and they do feel a little better. While Doc properly disposes of the used needles by placing them in a hazardous waste container, then placing the container into a thick red hazard bag, he turns toward Emerson as she cleans the iodine from my skin. "Sweetheart, can you wrap his ribs once he's taken a shower?"

"Sure," she responds.

My face lights up. I may be busted up, but other parts of me aren't broken. Seeing the look on my face, Emerson shakes her head and waits until Doc has left the room to say something. "Not happening."

"Come on, Sunshine. Can't I at least feel your soft lips slide down my cock? Caress your tongue across the tip? Hell, I can't even give myself a handy right now, but you could," I plead with her.

Leaning over, she hovers her lips over mine. I see it in her eyes. I know she wants me. Lifting my hand, I run the back of my knuckles along the side of her breast, then across her taut nipple. "See? Your mouth says one thing, but your body says another."

"Quinn," she whispers. Her tone leads me to believe she's about to give in and help her man out. "Give me a minute. I'll be right back." She kisses me. Like a teenage schoolboy lost for words at the thought of filling her mouth full of my cock, all I can do is nod my head and watch her leave the room.

The good thing is, there's a small bathroom in here. It's nothing fancy: just a toilet, a small sink, and the smallest fuckin' shower stall known to man. Hell, you can stretch your arms out wide and touch both walls on each side of you. This is the room our prospects usually occupy. I remember staying down here with

Logan, Gabriel, and Reid when we prospected together. It didn't matter that Logan and Reid grew up in the club, they were treated like any other prospect, and like me, all of us had to pay our dues to the club.

Coming to my senses, I decided to slowly shuck off the only article of clothing I have on, which is a pair of gym shorts, rest myself against the wall behind my back, and wait for her to return. Hearing footsteps outside the door, I eagerly wait for the doorknob to turn and Emerson to walk back in.

"Put that motherfucker away." Logan breaks out in laughter as he abruptly enters the room.

I know he's referring to my dick, which is standing at full mass because he thought he was about to get a lip massage. "Don't be a cockblocker, brother. Whatever you need can wait." I notice Emerson behind him, but she lingers by the door as she tries to hide a smile by biting her bottom lip.

Logan moves further into the room. "I'm here to help your skinny ass across the room so you can take a shower." Logan tries to look serious though he's finding it hard. It might have to do with the fact that my woman over there called in reinforcements to avoid giving me what I want—what I need. I don't care that I'm in pain. My hard as fuck cock doesn't care either. Looking past Logan, I fix my eyes on Emerson. "Sneaky woman. You did me dirty, Sunshine," I tell her, trying to hide a playful smile of my own. It's hard to be serious laying here stark naked, with a hard on, and in pain, while she stands there smiling at me like she is.

She giggles. "You shouldn't exert yourself, Quinn. I'm not giving you the chance to talk me into any sexy time. Logan agreed to stay in the room to make sure you make it in and out of the shower without falling." Blowing me a kiss, she steps out the door, closing it behind her.

Now, I'm left staring at my brother's amused face. He chuckles once more. "Come on, man. Let's get your naked ass to the bathroom. Just make sure you keep your dick to yourself."

I glance down and quietly apologize to my dick—*sorry, dude.* I look at Logan. "I can't help that he hasn't gotten the no-go for launch memo. He has a mind of his own. My disappointment hasn't caught up to him yet."

Sliding my legs over the side of the bed, I use the bedside table for support to help me stand. I'm determined. If getting some head or some pussy means I need to get better, then I'm going to speed up the process somehow.

Logan reaches to put his hand under my arm.

"Unless I look like I'm about to pass out, let me do this on my own," I tell him, steadying myself.

"You got it." He nods, knowing I need to do this myself.

With every step, my knees burn and feel like they are about to buckle from the piercing pain, but I grit my teeth and bear through it. I make it to the bathroom before using the wall to lean on while the water warms up. Logan stands just outside the open bathroom door as I step into the shower. The instant the hot water hits my skin, I close my eyes, and my shoulders sag. The warmth feels good.

I grab the bottle of shampoo. Finding it painful to apply pressure to my fingertips to open it, I cave and ask for assistance. "Logan?"

"Yeah?"

"Dammit," I mumble to myself, "I can't open the shampoo."

He doesn't say a word. That's one thing about Logan—about all my brothers; they won't make a big fuss out of what has happened. Not that what happened wasn't a big deal, but we won't dwell on it. It happened. I survived. Most importantly, our family is safe.

His hand reaches in and grabs the bottle. With his thumb, he flicks the top open and squeezes some shampoo in the palm of my hand.

As best as I can, I scrub the soap through my hair, using mostly my palms. Standing under the spray of water, I let the soap wash down the rest of my body. It's not the best of showers, but I'm feeling invigorated just by being clean. I'm finally able to remove the stench of the Reapers I've been smellin' for days. As soon as I turn the water off, Logan hands me a towel. I feel good, but I'm exhausted, and my stomach growls telling me I'm hungry.

I dry myself then wrap a towel around my waist before stepping out. I wouldn't mind getting a look at my face, but there isn't a mirror in the bathroom, so I shuffle out back toward the bed and find some clothes folded in a pile near the foot.

"I had Bella grab you some clothes. Emerson is in the kitchen. She wanted to help your mom make lunch." Logan takes a seat in the chair on the other side of the room.

"I hope I can keep some food down because my stomach feels like it's about to eat itself. What are my ladies cookin' up today?" I ask. Grunting, I lift my foot and try to figure out how to pull up my pants without my sore fingers catching on the fabric.

Logan stands. "Your mom is showing her how to make your favorite." Without asking, he kneels and pulls my pants up to my knees. "Stand up, brother." Placing my hand on his shoulder, I push myself to stand. Because I'm going commando Logan turns his head to avoid being dick-slapped and pulls them up the rest of the way. He doesn't miss a beat and moves the conversation along. "She's showing her how to make BBQ meatloaf. The other women are seeing after all the kids since they finally get to play outside."

Emerson couldn't be more perfect. "Perfect."

"What do ya say we wrap those ribs and go upstairs?" Logan reaches over and snatches a clean elastic bandage from a shelf beside the nightstand. After he finishes, I carefully pull a white shirt over my head, and we make our way up the stairs leading to the common room.

It finally dawns on me as we pass the room we sometimes have to handle unethical business in that I haven't inquired about what became of the Reapers, or anything to do with the club finding me. "When do I get the deets on what went down the other night?" I ask as we climb the stairs. By the time we've reached the top, my knees are on fire again.

"Soon, brother." He doesn't elaborate any further.

As soon as I clear the last step and move further into the room, the sound of my sister squealing my name catches my attention. Peering across the room, I watch her run toward me, and I brace for impact. She slams into my stomach and throws her arms around my waist. I have to catch my breath. "Hey, KitKat," I say through a grunt.

Realizing I'm in pain, she quickly releases her hold on me. "Oh my gosh, I'm sorry." Her eyes fill with tears.

"Come here." I hug her. "Don't apologize, and don't you dare cry."

"I was—" she hiccups through sobs. "I'm so glad you're okay," she sniffles.

"Me too kiddo." I don't sugar coat it by telling her otherwise.

I'm happy I'm here too.

"Hey, Quinn," Remi says, walking over. She's been my sister's rock and from what mom and dad have said she's helped my sister a lot over the past few days.

"Come here, kid." I open my arm for her to join Kat and I hug them both.

One thing I don't notice is the rest of the men. "Logan, where are the rest of the guys?"

"On the backside of the property. They should be showing up in a minute." He reaches into the cooler back behind the bar and pulls out a cold beer, then takes a seat on a barstool. *Okay?* The only thing on the backside of the property is the old barn with a rusted-out tin roof. It's original to the place. The property behind the clubhouse was once farmland. However, we don't use it for anything, and it leaves me curious.

Kissing the girls on top of their heads, I release them and wait for them to skip back across the room to where they were before. Just as I'm about to ask Logan why the guys were out there, the front door swings open, letting in the afternoon sun.

"Damn, brother. It's good to see you movin' around." Prez strides over and clasps his hand on my shoulder.

"That goes for us as well," Reid echoes the same sentiments as he gestures to the rest of the men behind him, which includes our brothers from the Louisiana chapter.

"Quinn." Prez waves a hand toward the back of the crowd and a face I don't recognize steps forward. "I want to introduce you to Ian. If it wasn't for this man, we might not have found you." He says the last part with a crack in his voice.

Ignoring the fact that my hands are throbbing from all the activity today, I stick my hand out. "Thanks, I owe ya."

"You don't owe me anything, friend." He shakes my hand.

Logan passes beers around. I don't join them. Not because I don't want to share a drink with my brothers, but I can't have one due to the medication I'm taking.

"I hate that we can't stick around, brother." Riggs walks up and greets me with a handshake. "But we need to get on the road."

The magnitude of the past few days hits me like a punch to the gut as I look at every face of every brother standing in the room with me. All of them rallied together for me. I stand here with no words to adequately thank them, but I know no words are needed.

A few minutes later, lunch is announced and served outside. I welcome the warmth of the sun as we sit and eat. As I'm biting into my meal, I feel a tug on my shirt. Looking down, I take in Ava holding a box in her tiny hands. I'm close with all the kids in the family, but Ava here thinks her Uncle Quinn put the stars in the sky just for her. Not that I told her so or anything.

"Hey, princess."

With a serious look on her face, Ava doesn't wait for me to scoop her up. She places the box next to my plate and, without a word, climbs onto my lap. "Uncle Quinn, I have a present for you."

Mila and Reid happen to be sitting across from Emerson and me. Mila smiles at her daughter then explains, "She heard you were sick and trying to get better, so she used some of her bad word money—" Ava interrupts her mom. "I have a LOT of bad word money too," she confirms, bobbing her head, which causes everyone to laugh including myself.

"She used some of it to buy you something," Mila finishes.

Ava's hands clasp together with excitement as I push my plate to the side and lift the lid off the box. Inside underneath mounds of pink tissue paper lays a teddy bear—a teddy bear that looks almost identical to hers except he's wearing a tiny leather cut. I pick it up. All the women gasp at the same time, followed by the sounds of "Aww."

Turning the bear over, I take in The Kings Logo on the back of the tiny vest. I blow out a breath to ward off the emotions trying to break free.

"My Mr. Pickles always helps me feel better, and he helped daddy. Now you can have your own Mr. Pickles," Ava assures me. I have to swallow several times past the knot in my throat.

"I love it," I tell her and hug her close. "I feel better already."

WITH LUNCH OVER, Riggs and his men head out. Ian didn't stick around long either and left shortly after. It's been a long day, and my body is feeling it. Emerson notices me rubbing my head.

"You are ready to lay down. You've pushed yourself a lot today." She looks at me with concern.

I tug on the belt loop of her jeans and bring her to stand between my legs. "I'm okay, Sunshine."

"You sure?"

Peering around her, I notice Prez, Logan, Gabriel, and Reid, walking toward us. In Jake's hand—my cut. Emerson turns her head to see what I'm looking at, then turns back around. "I'm going to go inside and help the women get all these kids bathed and ready for bed." Kissing me, she takes her leave.

"I have somethin' that belongs to you," Jake announces.

He waits for me to stand, then helps me slide it on. It smells freshly cleaned. I smooth it out. The weight of it feels good on my back and shoulders. Then I remember the bullet. The one I never got the chance to use. Reaching into the inside pocket, I dig around shocked to find it still there and pull it out. Holding it between my fingers, I study it.

"We got somethin' to show you. Walk around to the front and hop in Reid's truck, and hold onto that bullet," Logan says.

I trust my brothers. Not asking any questions, I make my way to the truck and climb in. The others pile in the back, and we take off toward the backside of the property straight toward the old barn. Grey and Blake are standing outside of it.

"Before we go in. I'll tell you now, that the other fuckin' Reapers are dead," Prez informs me.

I look at him. "All of them?"

"All but one."

"Twiggy?" I question and hope he says yes.

He nods.

"We may have had a little fun with him," Logan confesses with a grin.

"But he's still alive," Gabriel grunts.

"You want us to come in with you?" Prez asks.

I don't hesitate, "I do." My brothers are what it means to be family, and we have each other's back. Always a united front.

Grey swings the rickety door open, and the hinges make an ominous sound as if the old place knows what is about to happen. Tied to a chair in the middle of the barn is Twiggy himself. Blood and bruises mar his face. Surprised to see me, his eyes widen.

"Who killed their President?" I ask.

"I did," Prez speaks.

The thing is, I don't remember a hell of a lot. None of it matters anymore, because I'm here and the Satan's Reapers aren't, and the last one is about to fall.

Gabriel reaches inside his cut and pulls my revolver out, placing the handle in my hand. I grip it. My fingertips pulsate with every beat of my heart, but I push the pain to the back of my mind.

I don't take my eyes off Twiggy. I don't say a word.

He doesn't speak. He doesn't plead for his life.

Wouldn't make a difference if he did.

I've done some bad things in my life, and I'm about to do another.

With the men standing behind me, I don't have to justify my reasons. They let me choose for myself. With a flick of my wrist, the cylinder pops out. I slide the bullet I'm holding between my fingers into the chamber. Closing the cylinder, I raise my arm and take aim.

Staring down the barrel of my .44 Magnum, I pull the fuckin' trigger.

27

EMERSON

It's been nearly a week since Quinn was rescued. Once his fever broke, and he was through the worst of the withdrawal effects the heroin had on him, we haven't been able to keep him down. I, for one, am surprised. Those assholes had been pumping his veins full of heroin for seven days. That for Quinn has been the toughest part about the whole ordeal to deal with. Quinn will be the first to tell you he's no saint when it comes to his health. He has on occasion, smoked weed, and he smokes cigarettes, but he has not once delved into the heavy stuff. Quinn said he could handle a lot of shit, but not being able to have control over his own body is not one of them. I am so proud of the way he has been walking through his recovery. In true Quinn fashion, he has taken the situation by the balls.

Feeling strong arms snake around my middle, I look over my shoulder and smile at the handsome man lying next to me in bed. "Mornin', Sunshine."

"Good morning." Rolling over to face Quinn, I ask, "How did you sleep? Are you in any pain?"

"Yes, I'm in a lot of pain."

Sitting up in bed, I pull back the blanket and begin to look over his body from head to toe. "What—where? Tell me where it hurts." Taking my hand Quinn places my palm over his very hard and very noticeable erection.

"I hurt right here, Dr. Pretty. My cock is in desperate need of your expertise." Glaring at him, I pinch his side. "No! You are in no condition to even be thinking about sex. You need to heal."

"Come on, Sunshine. I promise to lay very still and not exert myself while you rub one out for me."

I shake my head. "You're too much. What am I going to do with you?" Just as Quinn is about to answer my question, I cut him off before something smart comes out of his mouth. "Don't answer that."

"Come on, babe," he whines. "It's been too long."

"I said no. Now come on, let's go downstairs for some breakfast. You know Bella has something good waiting for your spoiled ass."

With the mention of food, Quinn's face lights up, and his quest for sex is forgotten. "Hell, yeah. It's waffles and bacon today. I put my request in last night," he says, climbing out of bed. I swear sometimes I don't know what Quinn likes more, sex or food. "It's sex, babe. Although food is a very close second. It's neck and neck," he answers me.

I didn't realize I had mumbled that out loud. I narrow my eyes at him and go to say something back but stop when I see he has a spaced-out, faraway look on his face. "What's that goofy look for?"

"I was thinking about you naked, on my bed on all fours, wearing a chef's hat while I eat cake off your luscious ass. Then, I want to smear icing all over you and lick it off before I fill your tight pussy with my cock."

"Sometimes, Quinn—I have no words."

"Well, you asked, babe."

"Yeah, I should know better by now," I say, walking out of the bedroom with Quinn laughing behind me.

When Quinn and I make it downstairs and into the kitchen, he announces his presence. "Well, I'm here. What are your next two wishes?"

Bella turns from where she's frying bacon at the stove and gives him a megawatt smile. "Good morning, you two."

Striding toward Bella, Quinn places his hand on her shoulder and kisses the top of her head. "Mornin', darlin'."

I don't miss the tears in Bella's eyes as she pats his hand. Bella and Quinn have a close relationship. Bella often refers to Quinn and the other men in the club as the brothers she never had. "Food is almost done. You guys get some coffee and have a seat."

"I'll get it," Ember jumps in. "You two can go on out and sit with the rest of the family, and I'll bring the coffee. I believe everyone is already out there." After giving Ember a warm smile and thanks, we make our way out to the main room where everyone is seated, and conversation is flowing. The entire extended family is still here. Even though the threat of the other club is gone, the families wanted to stick around and see Quinn through his healing process. But with Quinn on the mend, the families will be returning home today.

Except for my brother. Easton left a couple of days ago. His manager was up his ass, so I told him to quit worrying about me and go. He'd put his life on hold for me long enough, and his band was counting on him. We all decided on a family breakfast before they do.

Before Quinn and I take our seats, there is a round of greetings from all the brothers. Vicky stands and hugs her son, followed by Kat. A few minutes later, Bella along with Raine and Ember, emerge from the kitchen with the food. As breakfast is placed on the table and everyone has taken their seat, Jake, who is seated at the head of the table, stands.

"I'd like to say a few words." He waits a beat, gathering everyone's attention. "I started this club years ago because my life was missin' somethin'. Some people might look in from the outside and wonder how I could feel that way. I had my parents who loved me. I had friends, I had a job, and a place to lay my head at night. What could I be missin'? For anyone who's not been in my shoes or the shoes of any one of my brothers sittin' at this table, then you would never understand. All I know is I no longer feel incomplete. It's because of this club and the men I call my brothers." The men at the table nod their heads at Jake's declaration. "Quinn," Jake turns his attention to the man sitting next to me. "The Kings would not be The Kings without ya, brother. I knew you were somethin' special the first day you walked your skinny ass into my club. I knew by the gleam in your eyes you had found that something you were missin', just like the rest of us. It's the same look I once witnessed in Logan, Gabriel, Reid, and all the other men sittin' at this table. I'm glad you're home, brother."

Quinn squeezes my hand under the table and gives Jake a nod. "Thanks, Prez."

A moment later, Jake continues, "So for our families, I want to say thank you for standing by our sides without protest and judgment. Lastly, I want to thank our old ladies. Our women are the backbones of our relationships. They stand by our sides and support us in everything we do. Every king needs a queen, and we have been blessed to have found ours."

Jake has just finished his speech when Grey interrupts us.

"Prez?" Every eye at the table looks toward the entrance of the clubhouse to see Grey, and standing next to him are my parents. The sight of them has me choking on the bite of waffle I just shoved in my mouth. It's my mother who speaks first. "We're sorry to drop by your...uh clubhouse unannounced, but Emerson wasn't at her apartment, and her supervisor said she no longer worked at the hospital. I tried calling multiple times, but there was no answer," she finishes.

She and my father both look nervous. Standing, I look at Jake. "I'm so sorry they showed up like this."

Jake waves me off with a look of understanding. I'm sure Quinn has informed him of what went down with my parents a couple of months ago. "No apologies needed, sweetheart. Go talk to your folks."

With Quinn at my side, we make our way over to my mom and dad. I'm shocked when my father reaches his hand out to Quinn. "Good to see you again, Quinn." With bated breath, I wait to see what Quinn's reaction will be. The last time we were in the same room together, my parents were very disrespectful to not only me but to him. But my man shows us just how wonderful and forgiving he is by accepting my dad's offered hand, and they shake. "You too, Mr. Evans."

"Please call me Martin."

A beat later, Quinn ushers us over to the sofa. "Why don't we sit?"

My parents take their offered seat then look around the room awkwardly while everyone sitting at the table behind us watches. A giggle bubbles up in my throat because they are so blatant about it. God, I love them. "So, uh...what are you guys doing here?" I ask.

"Easton called us," my father replies.

"What!"

"He called us two days ago," my mom says, fidgeting with the purse on her lap. "He said it was time your father and I removed our heads from our asses. Excuse my language." I hear a bark of laughter from behind me but don't know whose. "Anyway," my mother continues, "we haven't heard from Easton in over a year, so we figured if he was reaching out on your behalf, then we owed it to him and you to come to Polson and see you. To tell you the truth, we are ashamed at the way we left things the last time we were here. We had no right passing judgment on Quinn. I've also come to realize that our past behavior toward you was wrong. All we ever wanted was for you to be happy, but we now realize that you can't choose someone's dreams for them. That's exactly what we were doing to you. We're sorry if at any time you ever felt we weren't proud of you, Emerson. Your father and I couldn't be prouder of the talented, caring, and beautiful woman you have become. You are NOT a disappointment. To walk in here and witness the speech that was just given made me realize why you chose the man sitting next to you, and why you chose this family. I am grateful that you had them when your own family wasn't there for you like they should have been. Can you ever forgive us?"

By the time my mother finishes, I'm a sobbing mess. And by the sounds of the sniffles coming from the table behind me, I'd say my girlfriends are just as affected. Throwing myself into my mother's arms, I murmur, "I forgive you."

My father then joins in on our hug and wraps his arms around both my mom and me. "We love you, Emerson."

"I love you guys too."

"Damn," Quinn pipes up. "There's a whole lot of love in this room today. Now that we both have our parents in the room together, I think it's a good time to discuss titles." Quinn turns to my parents, "What would you like to be called? Grandma and grandpa, nana, and papa, or mawmaw and pawpaw? You guys have roughly seven months to figure that shit out."

My mom and dad look at Quinn for a minute like he's lost his mind before my mom snaps her head in my direction. "Are you pregnant?"

With a big smile, I nod. Then my mother shocks me again when she jumps from the sofa, her purse spilling to the floor as she screams and claps her hands. Vicky comes over and whisks my mom away, and I hear the two of them rattling on about a baby shower as Quinn wears a cheeky grin, wraps his arms around me, and pulls me into his chest. Closing my eyes, I breathe in his scent and place my palm over his heart, and he puts his hand over the top of mine. "It beats for us, Sunshine."

Later that night, Quinn and I are lying in bed, and I begin to reflect on today's events. I called my brother and thanked him for sticking his nose into my business and convincing our parents to come to Polson. I hope the next relationship they repair is the one they have with Easton.

Mom and Dad left two hours ago with a promise to visit again in a few weeks. My mother even exchanged numbers with Vicky. The two of them are in full grandmother mode.

"What are ya smiling about, babe?"

"Nothing, I'm just happy." Quinn is about to reply when someone begins banging on our door. Without waiting for an answer, Logan burst through. "Mila's water broke. Let's move!"

Without wasting time, Quinn and I jump out of bed and throw on our clothes. By the time we make it downstairs, Reid is carrying Mila out the door bridal style while she gives him sass. "I can walk."

Six hours and forty-seven minutes later, Reid walks into the waiting room of the maternity floor where the whole club is waiting on pins and needles. The chatter in the room comes to an abrupt halt at his presence. With a massive smile, Reid delivers the news. "We have a son. Noah Quinn Carter weighed in at 8lbs 5oz. Mom and baby are doing well."

The room erupts into cheers as Reid makes his rounds with his brothers, and they congratulate him on the birth of his son. When he gets to Quinn, Reid says something into his ear right before he takes Quinn's head in his hands. They stare silently at each other for a moment before they pull one another in for a hug and clap each other on the back.

It's after sunrise the next morning when we leave the hospital. Quinn and me, along with Logan and Bella, Gabriel, and Alba, are standing in the parking lot about to load up when Jake speaks.

"Ma just called. She said breakfast would be ready in about an hour."

"Fuck yeah, Prez. You don't have to ask me twice," Quinn says. Mounting his bike, Quinn holds out his hand. "Come on, Sunshine. My stomach waits for no one."

Rolling my eyes, I take his offered hand, climb on behind him, and wrap my arms around his waist. As we cruise down the road, through the countryside and we pass the lake on the way to Jake's parents' place, I look around at my beautiful surroundings. The sun rising over the mountains is lighting the lake up with colors of orange and yellow, and with the cool, crisp breeze beating down on my face, I can't imagine a moment more perfect than this one.

28

QUINN

I wake to the sun creeping through the slates in the window blinds, and Emerson tucked into my side. It's been several weeks since shit with the Reapers took place, and I'm feeling great. So, my life and the club's have finally started to get back to normal.

My woman and I had a long talk about all the things we plan to do, and she likes the way things are right now. She has become very comfortable staying here at the clubhouse, so Emerson decided not to renew the lease on her apartment last week.

Laying in bed, I watch my woman sleep while I think about our future. I haven't asked her to marry me yet, and Emerson hasn't brought it up. Not that I don't want to make her mine legally, I only want to give her a moment she will remember for the rest of her life. Plans have already been set in place long before now to make sure that happens.

As much as living here at the clubhouse has been great, we've also talked about finding a house before the baby arrives. What she doesn't know is that we won't need to find a home because I had one picked out and paid for several months ago. The only thing I'm waiting for is the final phase of remodeling to be completed in the master bedroom before I surprise her. Reid should have that wrapped up by the end of the week.

Emerson stirs, and her eyes flutter open. "Good morning." She smiles. "What time is it?" She blinks, letting her eyes adjust to the sunlight.

"Good-mornin' to you too, beautiful. Time for us to start the day. We have to be at my mom's and dad's place in an hour." I rub her thigh.

"Sorry I crashed on you last night. I've been tired more than usual these days." Emerson stretches her arms above her head, causing her tank to rise and expose her baby bump. I love that she's finally starting to show. The fact she is carrying another life inside her leaves me awestruck.

"Sunshine?"

"Hmm?" she moans through her stretch.

"You're beautiful," I confess, watching the sunbeams dance across her skin. "I love you."

Giggling, she teases as she rubs her tummy. "I'm gonna gain more than I should if I continue to eat my weight in waffles every day. Will you still love me then?" Her bottom lip pokes out, and she looks down at her body.

A body I see nothing wrong with.

Whether she's serious or not—I don't like her asking that sort of question. Gently grabbing her, I bring her to straddle my hips, and I let my eyes roam her body. She is absolute perfection in my eyes. "Don't joke about somethin' like that." My eyes stay fixed on hers. "I could never unlove you."

Her face softens. Grabbing my hand, she places it on her chest. Her heart thumps against my palm. Then she puts my other hand on her growing belly, and my little girl kicks. "They beat for you." She smiles down at me.

I smile. *Fuckin' Perfect.*

Feeling my cock harden, Emerson rotates her hips. My hands

fall to her ass, helping her grind down harder. Tilting her head back, she moans. Clasping the hem of her shirt, Emerson pulls it off over her head and discards it to the floor. Bringing my hand up, I cup her breasts. When I pull on her sensitive nipple, she grinds down on my aching cock and I can feel the heat of her pussy through the thin material that's separating us. Needing to taste her breast, I swipe my tongue over her sensitive rosy tip before pulling it into my mouth. Her hands go to the back of my head and she fists my hair. Using my teeth, I tug on her piercing.

"Oh god," she moans. My mouth on her nipple causes some a switch to flip, and Emerson's movements become frantic. Scooting back slightly, she grabs the waistband of my boxers and slides them down just far enough to release my raging hard on. In lightning speed, Emerson tugs her panties to the side and I barely get a glimpse of her glistening pussy before she grabs a hold of my shaft and impales herself down on it all the way to the hilt causing me to curse. "Goddamnit, fuck!" I've heard that women who are pregnant become extra horny. I'd say by the way Emerson is bouncing up and down on my dick right now, it's true. Her pussy is eating every inch of my cock up. I have to say it's a huge fuckin' turn on seeing my woman use my body for her pleasure. Digging my fingers into Emerson's ass, I stare up at her bouncing tits and watch her face as she rides me. "That's right babe, take what you need."

"Oh god, Quinn. I'm going to come," she says, digging her nails into my shoulders nearly drawing blood. "Come now, Sunshine." Before the last word leaves my mouth her pussy clamps down on my cock triggering my release, Emerson's limp body falls against my chest as we both take a moment to catch our breath. "I swear I don't know what just came over me," she confesses.

"Babe, that was hot as fuck. You'll get no complaints from me."

MY DAD HAD my car parked in the driveway waiting for us when Emerson and I finally arrived an hour late this morning. I wasn't even aware he knew someone had vandalized it until he informed me Jake talked to him about it the week he was camped out at the clubhouse while I recovered. Dad made some calls, had it towed to Bozeman, and a few weeks later, here it is.

I run my hand across the hood of the car, then walk around and open the door. "It looks fuckin' amazing, Dad. How much did this set you back?"

"Don't you worry about all that, Son," he says, waving his hand. "A friend of mine owed me a favor."

I glance back at the house. Kat ran out and kidnapped my woman the moment we parked and got out of the car. With Emerson being inside, it gives me the perfect opportunity to talk to my dad. "I'm gonna ask Emerson to marry me."

His face lights up. "I'm happy to hear that. When do you plan on popping the question?"

Closing the car door, I prop my arms on the hood. My dad does the same on the opposite side of the car. "You planning on asking her dad for her hand?" he questions.

I've thought about this question many times. Each time I always come back around and ask myself the very same question. Would I expect a man to ask my permission to marry my little girl? The answer is always the same—he damn well better. "Her parents are coming for a visit this week. I plan on talking with him then," I tell him.

He nods, "You plan on marrying her before the baby arrives?"

If everything goes according to plan—"That's what I'm aimin' for."

"Breakfast is ready!" Kat yells from the front porch then skips back into the house.

Dad steps back and rubs his stomach. "It's a good thing I've started back to work. I've put on twelve pounds eating the leftovers your mom keeps in the fridge."

The two of us walk toward the house. "That's why Mom hasn't dropped food off by the garage in forever? You've been hoardin' it all for yourself?"

My exaggerated reaction causes him to chuckle. "Quinn, don't ever change." He pats me oen the back.

THE MORNING FLEW BY, and before we knew it, Emerson and I had spent more than half the day hanging out with my family. Mom even dug out the family photo albums. Emerson's favorite was one of me when I was around four years old. My mom had snapped a picture of me from behind while I stood out in the snow-covered yard with my pants around my ankles takin' a piss.

"He went through a phase where he only wanted to tinkle outside. Once, after coming home from the grocery store, he started to pee right there in front of the house on the hedges. His pants around his ankles and his little toosh visible for every neighbor to see." My mom's laughter fills the room, and Emerson breaks out in a fit of giggles herself.

"This is good to know. It prepares me for what I could expect if we have a boy." Emerson rubs circles on her belly.

"It's going to be a girl," Kat joins in on the conversation.

I point in her direction. "See, what did I tell ya. Even my sister knows," I boast. I keep telling her and everyone else my woman is going to give me a daughter.

"What makes you think the baby is going to be a girl, honey?" my dad asks, smiling down at her as my sister continues thumbing through photos scattered across the living room floor.

"I keep having the same dream at least once a week. Emerson is wearing a yellow summer dress, sitting on a white blanket at the edge of a lake, while holding a little girl on her lap." She looks up to see us all staring at her. "What?" Kat shrugs, "I mean, I guess I could be wrong. It is only a dream."

But my heart believes every word my baby sister says.

We stay a while longer before we decide to leave. "We have to get going." I stand and help Emerson off the couch. With the sun starting to set, we make our way to the front door and say our goodbyes.

"It's been such a wonderful day," my mom hugs Emerson then embraces me. I give her a quick kiss on the cheek before KitKat wraps her arms around my waist, giving me the tightest squeeze she can.

"You kids be careful, and Quinn," my dad clasps my shoulder, "you need any help with anything let us know." He smiles.

He's referring to the plans I've made and have already begun to put into motion after shooting off a few texts earlier. I have big ideas, and it's going to take the entire family coming together to make it all happen. "Thanks, Dad." I return a smile.

"Emerson, Sweetie. Isn't your mother supposed to be in town soon? I'd love to have lunch with her," my mom asks.

"Oh, yes, I forgot." She looks at me, then back to my mom. "My dad texted earlier. They decided to see us a couple of days ahead of schedule, so you'll have plenty of time for a visit," she tells her.

Finally making it out the door, Emerson stops.

"You okay, Sunshine?" I ask.

"I'm just happy." She smiles, and I smile back.

Pulling the car door open, I grin. "Hop in, beautiful."

We're cruising down the road with the windows down. I look over at Emerson with her hand out the window, dipping it high and low through the breeze. The weather is starting to change. Personally, this is my favorite time of the year. The leaves are beginning to turn from green to bright hues of orange and red, and the air carries the smells of delicious food from the county fair that rolled into town two days ago. I still can't believe my woman has never been to a fair. Mom and Dad took me every year to both the county and state fair. We would get up early in the morning and make a three-hour drive to enjoy the rides and stuff our faces with fried food.

All that is about to change, because I'm going to surprise her by takin' her there tonight. It's not as big as the one in Great Falls, but big enough she can experience the sights, smells, and bright lights of the Ferris wheel after dark.

"Oh my god. Do you smell that?" She inhales and closes her eyes. When she opens them, the Ferris wheel comes into view, and her eyes light up. "You're taking me to the fair?"

"If you're not too tired." I reach across the seat and grab her hand. Her eyes water a bit, and she vigorously shakes her head no.

After parking, we start walking down the short midway. "So, what do you want to do first, Sunshine?"

"I want one of those foot-long corn dogs coated with hot mustard sauce."

"You read my mind, sweetheart."

Later, after the sun has set, we walk hand in hand. "Well, beautiful. I think we have played every game on the strip," I announce, holding a giant unicorn, a sizeable inflatable hammer that makes a squeaky noise whenever you bop someone with it—I know this because she has used it a few times on my head, and a goldfish—a living goldfish.

Grabbing the bag containing the fish from my hand, Emerson examines it. "What are you going to name it?"

"Name it? It's your fish, Sunshine."

Her eyes lift to mine. "I won this for you. You have to give it a name."

I pull her close. "We can name it later. You ready to take a ride with me on the Ferris Wheel?" I kiss the tip of her nose. She smiles.

Leaving our loot next to the ride operator, I help her onto the seat, then sit down beside her and pull the lap bar down. I wrap my arm around her shoulders as she snuggles into my side as the wheel begins to move. I watch her face light up like a kid at Christmas as she takes it all in.

"This is amazing. It's so beautiful," she says.

I haven't been able to take my eyes off her. Her happiness has me grinnin' so hard my cheeks hurt. The words almost spill out of my mouth at that moment, but I stop myself. *Soon.*

"WHAT THE HELL is that doing here?" Gabriel grumps after taking his seat at the bar. He's referring to the goldfish swimming around in the bowl that's sitting on top of the counter.

"What? James Pond?" I sip my beer, and Logan chuckles beside me.

Raine steps behind the bar and hands Gabriel a cold beer. "You named the fish James Pond?" She laughs.

I shrug. *What's the big deal? It is a great name.* Setting my empty bottle down, I look at the time. "Gotta run and meet a man about a woman." Standing, I face Logan. "Have you heard from your woman?"

"Everything is good, brother. All the women are out for lunch and a little shopping. Go do your thing," Logan responds.

Shortly after leaving the clubhouse, I made it to the hotel where Emerson's parents are staying downtown. When I walk into the lobby, Mr. Evans is waiting for me. I can't tell you how happy my woman has been since her parents made up with her and finally accepted her for who she is and what she strives to become. The difference in their relationship is like night and day. The only thing she worries about anymore is the fact things are still strained between them and her brother. "Mr. Evans." I extend my hand.

"Quinn, it's good to see you this afternoon. I hope everything is alright?" He says with a look of concern.

"Everything's fine. I needed to ask you somethin' and needed to do it in person." The worry disappears from his face, and the corner of his mouth lifts in a grin.

"Alright." He casually sticks his hands in his front pockets and relaxes his posture and waits for me to say what I want to say.

I clear my throat before speaking. "Mr. Evans, I love your daughter. My happiness feeds off of hers." He nods as I continue, "I want you to know I'll always take care of her and our family—I'll always do whatever it takes to keep them safe."

"I believe you," he says with confidence.

"Martin, I want nothing more than to make Emerson my wife."

He studies me for a moment. "Son." The word comes from his mouth for the first time. I wasn't expecting it to feel as good as it did to hear him say it. "She's always been yours. I'll be damn proud to have you marry her." Stepping forward, he puts out his hand, which I happily accept.

After the thirty-minute conversation that followed has wrapped up, I head toward my bike. My phone rings. Digging it from the inside pocket of my cut, I swipe the screen, answering a call coming in from Easton. "Hey, brother. What's the word?"

"It's a go, my man. Fuck bro, this is gonna be epic." His voice sings with excitement. "Shit, gotta run—see ya soon."

Sticking the phone back in my pocket, I swing my leg over my bike. There are several more things to take care of, and a few more people to see before the sun sets.

"ONE THING I've noticed since being around the club is you guys like to throw parties. What is this one for?" Emerson asks as she shimmies on a pair of jeans, then slips her boots on.

I've been awake since before sunrise helping the guys set things up out back. Easton's road crew showed up roughly three hours ago and started to set up a small venue stage. Emerson has no idea any of this is going on since I didn't wake her. She has no idea her brother will be here today, either. All my woman knows is Jake decided we needed to celebrate the club and family. Emerson is right though; we never need a reason to have a good time. Walking up to her, I snake my arm around her waist. "Life is good, Sunshine. That's what we wanna celebrate." I kiss her.

There's a light knock on the door, followed by Lisa's voice. "Quinn? The guys need you outside."

"I'll be down in a minute," I call out. "Come on, beautiful." Dropping my arm, I grab her hand in mine, and we head downstairs together and walk into the kitchen. "Our moms have been cookin' up a storm this morning." Pulling a chair from the table, Emerson sits.

"My mom?" she says, stunned.

"Yeah, babe. Right alongside all the other women." I set a plate of scrambled eggs and jellied toast on the table in front of her.

"There's a lot of food here, Quinn. How many people are you guys expecting to show up? The whole town?"

"Everyone—the whole family."

"You should have woken me up sooner. I could have been down here helping. I'm surprised I slept through all the hustle and bustle. It's nearly noon." She bites into her toast.

"I wore that ass out last night, Sunshine. You snored all night, too." I grin.

"I don't snore."

"You do, and it's cute." I chuckle when she rolls her eyes.

Finished with her meal, Emerson stands at the sliding glass door that leads to the back and peers out. "Holy shit. There's a stage back here."

"Yeah, we put some money together and hired live music for tonight." Grabbing her sweater hanging on a hook beside the door, I slip it over her shoulders because the air is a little chilly today, and we walk outside. Tables are spread out across the yard. We have a few outside heaters and a large fire pit with wood ready to burn to keep people warm as the afternoon turns into night. Off to the far side of the yard, we even have a bouncy house set up for the kids.

When I say the entire family has come out today, that's no lie. I spot Gabriel toward the end of the building quietly talking to his sister Leyna and I wonder if Lex came with her. I scan the yard locating them all one by one. Sam, Sofia, Leah—and there's Nikolai along with his and Logan's dad Demetri talkin' with Jake and Reid. All The Kings' women are standing around laughing at the little kids' actin' like goofballs inside the bounce house.

"I'm gonna go say hi to the girls." Leaning on her tiptoes, Emerson's lips press against mine. I watch her cross the yard and hug all her friends.

"Big day today, brother." Logan appears from out of nowhere and slaps my back. "You ready?"

My eyes connect with Emerson's when she looks my way. "Been ready."

The family begins to cluster around the stage. I stride over to Emerson, who has her hand over her mouth, shocked to see her brother. "How did you get my brother here?"

"It's about family today, babe. He's part of the family."

"Alright," Easton's mellow laidback voice comes through the large speakers at each end of the stage. "I'm here to perform for an extraordinary person—my twin sister Em." He points in our direction. All heads turn our way. "But I'm gonna need a little help. Quinn, my man, get your pretty ass up here." He ushers me with a wave. The women gather around us. Emerson looks at me, confused.

"What's going on?"

"Surprise." I grin. "All this—everyone you see is here for you, Sunshine. This whole day is yours." Leaning down, I kiss her, then jog off toward the stage, leaving her speechless.

Grabbing my guitar, I stroll onto the stage. I've played my guitar a few times for Emerson but have yet to sing for her. It's not something I often do in front of people, but for her, I'll do anything.

Making her way to the front of the stage, I look down on Emerson's beautiful face, and everyone around us disappears. It's only Emerson and me. Her lovely smile encourages me to sing. *Hanging by A Moment* by Lifehouse.

I lose myself in her eyes as I sing her the rest of the song. Tears stream down her face, and all I want to do is kiss them away.

When I finish, my eyes stay fixed on hers. "Emerson Evans, will you marry me?"

"Yes!" she yells then wipes her tears with the backs of her hand.

"Today," I say for everyone to hear. Her eyes widen, and for a split second, I start to worry my best-laid plans will have to wait, then she runs up on the stage and throws her arms around my neck and kisses me.

"Okay."

I look at her and grin. "Okay?"

"Mmhmm," Emerson hums.

Picking her up, I swing her in a circle before announcing, "Let's have a wedding!"

"I have nothing to wear." She suddenly frowns.

"Got it covered, Sunshine." I jerk my head to the side of the stage where all the women are standing. "Go with the girls."

I give her one more kiss. Yeah, we kiss—a lot, but who the fuck cares. I get to spend the rest of my life kissing this woman, and I'm not wastin' any of them. She pauses long enough to hug her brother, then is ushered inside.

Easton and his band sing a couple of songs to pass the time while the women help Emerson get ready, which pleases the younger crowd.

The little shopping trip the other day was a perfect way for her mom to get a little insight into what kind of wedding dress her daughter would like to wear one day, and her mom paid for the dress and bouquet. Grace baked the cake, which we hid in church. Every detail was planned out. Every family member was somehow involved with helping me pull off my proposal and a surprise wedding.

I couldn't choose the best man because all my brothers mean too much to me, so here they are—all of them—standing at my side. Except for our President, Jake. He's going to marry us today. And all of our women will stand with Emerson as she becomes my old lady.

An hour later, Lisa appears, signaling us that it's go time.

Perfect by Ed Sheeran starts to play low in the background. The glass doors slide open, and Emerson steps out.

Breathe.

Harleys line both sides of the white cloth rolled out for my woman. With her father by her side, she takes her first steps toward her husband to be.

"Finally, we are all here to celebrate Quinn and Emerson's union," Jake announces with a grin, causing my brothers to cheer. "All, kidding aside, I couldn't ask for a better match for Quinn than Emerson. She's proven her love and loyalty to not only our brother but to this club. I speak for all of us here today when I say we are damn proud to call you family. Quinn." Jake takes a small step back givin' me the stage.

"Sunshine, my words are straightforward—I love you. Loving you is like breathing for me. Forever doesn't even seem like enough time for me to cherish you. We could live a thousand more lives after this, and my soul would always find you, beautiful." I hold her hand in mine.

"Quinn, I love your outlook on life. I love how kind-hearted you are toward everyone you meet. You have a way of making people around you feel important and special. You're unapologetically who you are—who you were born to be, and you showed me—you gave me the courage to spread my wings and do the same. You taught me that we write the chapters of our own stories, and I want nothing more than to spend the rest of my life filling those pages with you."

Jake extends his hand. The rings I bought the other day are lying side by side in his palm. "Repeat after me."

Sliding her ring on her finger, I recite, "From this day forward, you will never walk alone. I promise to love, honor and cherish you for the rest of my life." Gently, I wipe a tear from her cheek.

Emerson slides my ring on my finger and stares into my eyes as she tells me, "From this day forward, you will never walk alone. I promise to love, honor and cherish you for the rest of my life."

"Well, what are you waiting for? Kiss your old lady!" Jake announces. I waste no time placing my lips on hers.

AFTER CUTTING the cake and sharing our first dance as husband and wife, I can tell Emerson is starting to tire out from the long day, but I have one more thing to show her. Standing behind her, I brush her hair to the side. "I have one more surprise to show you, Sunshine," I whisper in her ear.

"How could you possibly have another surprise? I was proposed to and married all in one day. Nothing could top that," she sips on her glass of ginger ale.

Grabbing her by the hand, I lead her toward the clubhouse. Passing the guys, I wave my hand in the air, letting them know I'm cuttin' out for the night.

"Wait, we're not going to say goodbye to everyone?" Her hand tightens on mine.

"They know where I'm going. Don't worry, babe. You'll see them all again tomorrow," I promise. *We'll have a houseful come tomorrow afternoon. I have no doubts about it.*

Trusting me, and still wearing her dress, she slides into my car. The house I bought is a couple of miles from Logan's home. As soon as I pull onto the long driveway leading to our home, the two-story house comes into view. The sun hasn't completely set yet, so she gets to see what it looks like from the outside.

The moment I saw this house, I knew it was the one. Cedar shingles, wooden shutters, and a large front and back porch. "You want to go look at it?" I ask.

"Can we do that?"

"Come on." I rush around to the other side of the car and open her door.

"Every window has a flower box, and look." She points as we step onto the porch. "I've never seen a porch swing the size of a twin bed. Quinn, wait—we can't walk through someone else's home."

I pause in front of the door and pull the key from the front pocket of my jeans. "I have the key, babe." Unlocking the door, I push it open, then turn and pick up my bride.

"This is my surprise—a house?" Her face lights up.

"You ready to add another chapter to our story?" I step over the threshold. "Welcome home, Mrs. Emerson Beckett."

29

EMERSON

Ten months later

"CAN you tell me where it hurts?" I ask Grayson, the six-year-old little boy sitting on the exam table in front of me.

He points to his ear. "Right here."

Using my otoscope, I gently examine the inside of Grayson's ear, and as expected, he has an infection. Grayson's mom, Kinsley, brought him in today. She said he's been running a fever for two days and has been complaining about his ear. Turning my attention to a worried-looking Kinsley, I tell her, "Grayson has an ear infection. I'm going to prescribe him some antibiotics. I also want you to give him some Tylenol for his fever."

"Umm—are the antibiotics costly?" she asks in a nervous tone.

"I'm not sure, but your insurance should cover most of the cost."

"I uh—I don't have insurance."

I don't know much of Kinsley's story, only that she is a single mother and has been living in Polson for a couple of years. I also know she works at Charley's. Quinn told me once that Charley has always run the bar himself since he doesn't get too busy on any given day living in a small town and all. Charley had a feeling about Kinsley the day she walked into his bar looking for a job, and he didn't have the heart to tell her no. Other than that, I don't know anything else about her. She keeps to herself.

Giving her a warm smile, I excuse myself. "Wait here. I'll be right back."

Walking into my office, I unlock the supply case that holds all our samples. We get pharmaceutical reps who come in from time to time and leave some with us. I gather the ten-day supply of the antibiotic Grayson will need, place them in a bag, and make my way back into the exam room. "Here you go," I say, handing Kinsley the bag. "This ten-day supply should cover him. Also, I'm going to make a note on his chart for my receptionist telling her to set you up on a payment plan to cover today's visit."

Swiping a tear from her cheek, Kinsley nods. "Thank you so much."

"You're very welcome." This right here is how I know I made the right choice opening my practice. After Quinn and I married, he told me it was time to fulfill my dream. So, with his love and support, I wasted no time going after what I wanted. I put a call into a realtor, and two weeks later, I was signing a lease on the building my office is now housed in.

It was a little overwhelming at first with being pregnant and newly married while setting up my practice, but I've enjoyed every minute of the journey. It also helped to have the club behind me. Everyone pitched in. Reid and Nikolai handled the few minor remodeling aspects of the office, while the girls jumped in and helped me order furniture and decorate the waiting area. My waiting room is sectioned into three areas. I have a space for well check-ups, one for those who are sick, and I have an area for children to play. Alba even set up a reading corner and stocked it full of books. Then there is the front counter where my receptionist Zara sits, and in the back, I have three exam rooms.

In my opinion, the place is perfect and turned out just as I envisioned it. My office is open Monday through Friday and my hours are from eight o'clock am to five o'clock pm. I love being able to set my own pace. My evenings and weekends are for my family. When I'm at work, I'm wholly dedicated to my patients. Unlike the hospital, I get to spend more than five minutes with them. I take my time to get to know every person that walks through my clinic doors. I treat patients of all ages. They range from newborn to my oldest patient Mrs. Porter who is 97 years old.

Besides my work life, another thing that has come full circle is my relationship with my parents. They have done a complete one-eighty. My practice had only been open a few weeks when I went into labor and had to go on maternity leave. Imagine my surprise when I found out my mom took a leave of absence from her job to come to Polson and help out at my office. She took on my entire workload for six weeks. I have now been back at work for two.

Before my mother left and returned home to Washington, she told me once again how proud she is of me, and I did the right thing by opening my clinic. She even expressed that with her and dad getting older, they have considered opening their practice much like mine. Something where they could still do what they love but be able to slow down. I think my mom got spoiled with the nine to five hours and free weekends.

I told her life is too short to spend every minute of it working. You have to take the time to enjoy your family and the people you love. Almost losing the love of my life taught me that.

Thinking of my man, I look down at my watch and see its already lunchtime. I told Quinn this morning I'd come by the garage and eat lunch with him. Walking out of my office and down the hall, I stop at Zara's desk. "I'm going to lunch. Be back in an hour."

"Okay. Have a good lunch, Dr. Beckett."

I still get butterflies every time I hear someone call me Dr. Beckett.

Walking into the garage, I spot Quinn with his back to me, talking to Logan. I'm just about to open my mouth to say hi when Logan alerts him to my presence. When my husband turns to face me, my smile fades when I see who he has with him. Strapped to Quinn's chest in a baby carrier is our eleven-week-old daughter Lydia.

Lydia Faith Beckett came into this world almost three months ago. She has Quinn's dirty blonde hair, but the rest of our daughter is all me, right down to my fair skin complexion and grey eyes. "Quinn, why is Lydia here? This is Alba's day."

Yes, we all have our kids on rotation. Some days Alba has them, then two days out of the week they are with Grace at her bakery. She even had a playroom built and hired two ladies who look after our kids. The parents who come in for coffee and donuts can keep their kids in the playroom as well.

Then on Fridays, Bella has the kids at the shop. Fridays are the shop's slowest days, plus Jake's mom has been coming in to help. She spends as much time with her granddaughter Ellie Kate as possible.

The problem here is my husband has a bad case of separation anxiety. Typically, it's the mom who has a hard time going back to work after maternity leave, but not me. I was more than ready. It helped me to know my daughter was in good hands when she wasn't with me. When I was home on leave, Quinn would stop by the house every day for lunch. It got to where he started sneaking back throughout the day. Finally, one day Jake had enough and showed up at mine and Quinn's house. He threatened to put a bullet in my husband's ass if he didn't get back to work.

"Come on, Sunshine," Quinn grumbles. "I needed my Lydi loves."

"Quinn, it's only noon. You loved her just four hours ago."

"Babe," he says, letting out an exasperated sigh.

"What?"

"Get your ass over here and kiss your husband."

Shaking my head, I do as he says. Stepping up to Quinn, I stroke my daughter's silky blonde hair with my finger then kiss her chubby cheek. Quinn steals my attention by swooping down and taking my mouth.

Breaking our kiss, I lay my head on his chest next to our baby girl's face and breathe in Quinn's smell mixed with Lydia's sweet scent. Reaching up, I place my hand on my daughters where it's resting over her daddy's heart. Kissing the top of my head and then Lydia's, Quinn murmurs.

"It beats for us."